The SILENT HOURS

C.D. MAJOR

ABOUT THE AUTHOR

C. D. Major writes books inspired by events in the recent past. Cesca worked in television and teaching before writing full time. Alongside her thrillers she writes feel-good reads under the pseudonym Rosie Blake. She teaches creative writing and vlogs writing tips over on her website www.cdmajor.com. Cesca lives in Berkshire with her husband, son and twin daughters. She can be found on Twitter, Facebook and Instagram and enjoys connecting with readers.

ALSO BY C.D.MAJOR:

The Last Night

The Other Girl

Writing as Rosie Blake:

How to Get a (Love) Life

How to Stuff Up Christmas

How to Find Your (First) Husband

The Hygge Holiday

The Gin O'Clock Club

Silently the shades of evening
Gather round my lowly door;
Silently they bring before me
Faces I shall see no more.

Hymn by Christopher C. Cox

'I am a mother who has lost everything.' Madame Rouffanche at the 1953 Bordeaux trial

I am standing outside again, looking up at that window.
Through the glass I can see hands reaching up, grasping at nothing. I can make out their wails in amongst the barrage of bullets, the foreign shouts and my ears buzzing so noisily that I want to clap my hands to the side of my head and scream for it to stop.
But I can't reach, so I just watch their movements, knowing I can do nothing but stand outside.
I am always looking up at that window.

PART I

ADELINE

1952, St Cecilia Nunnery, south-west France

They are talking in hushed voices through the grille in the door. Sister Marguerite has a distinctive southern accent and, even when she is trying to speak quietly, her words seem to echo off the thick stone of the corridor walls with an energy for which she is often chastised.

'She said something,' she insists, pleading with her listener.

'Marguerite, we've discussed this before…' The voice sighs.

From my bed I tilt my head to catch a glimpse of its owner: Sister Constance. Although her voice is firm, it doesn't fit her face. The woman seems to have aged twenty years in a fraction of that time. Her watery eyes are practically hidden in the folds of her face; her lips are thin and cracked. Even from this distance I can see the veins in her hands, the large blue lines protruding from her skin look like great rivers on a map of France.

'She was muttering something. I'm sure I heard some distinct words, I'm sure I heard her speak…'

'Don't excite yourself, child,' says Sister Constance. 'If the Lord has made this woman mute then it is not for us to question why or try to change her predicament. We can only wait and…'

'But don't you think there's been progress? If we could encourage and…' The younger nun trails off as she catches sight of Sister Constance's expression. 'Forgive me for interrupting,' she says quietly, dropping her head.

'Get along, Sister Marguerite,' Sister Constance says, not unkindly. 'No more of this. You know what has to happen.'

'I… I… Yes, Sister Constance,' comes the defeated reply, and with one last look back at me I watch her turn and walk away.

Sister Constance stays there watching her go before peering through the grille at me lying still. Then, making the sign of the cross at my door, she turns away, her steady steps echoing rhythmically down the stone corridor, to Vespers.

A mute: a mute woman in a nunnery. I've been that woman for years. I draw a finger along my bottom lip and pray the same prayer to whoever is listening: 'God, forgive me.'

A crucifix hangs on the wall opposite my bed. Jesus is staring at me. He is always staring at me.

Sister Marguerite has spent weeks, months, now years, sitting at my bedside, on the bench in the garden, at meals. In the early days, as a young postulant, she took my silence in her stride, chattering on about the everyday – the men planting in the neighbouring fields, the dreadful food served up, the bone-seeping cold… but she mustn't complain – others have so much less.

Recently she has grown quieter, watchful.

Others take my silence as a personal slight, readily giving

into Marguerite's pleas for her to attend to me. I notice every shadow, every new line as each year passes. She has the dancing eyes of another and sometimes, when something has tickled her, the past tugs at my heart and the other face skips across my mind in a whisper... and it's gone, as quickly as Marguerite muffles the little laugh in her hand.

Some mornings, at the edge of sleep, I see that face in the shadows of the room; moments before I am awake, I am convinced she is there, her long hair tousled, her straight neat nose, long neck, her tiny waist.

I get up and trace an outline on the wall opposite. Sister Marguerite finds me, palm resting on the stone, staring into a past I can't reach, guiding me back to the chair by the fire, searching my eyes with hers as I return to the room.

She says a prayer for me, hand resting on mine in my lap; her words are quick, tripping into each other as she mutters an 'Amen.'

The automatic way that I mouth it. Empty.

How would she find me now? How would she learn where I've ended up? I remember being discovered after I'd left her. Men found me submerged in the mud. There were three of them. I didn't recognize their faces. The tallest one lifted me out. Pain shot through my lower body as he placed me in a wheelbarrow. That was how they got me out, with my legs over the side, him trying to manoeuvre it as gently as he could over the cobbles, to a waiting motorcar.

I'd never been in a motorcar before. They folded me into the seat; there was earth and red on my clothes, skin, smears on the leather. They drove me out; I couldn't look out of the window, didn't want to see. There was a younger man with kind eyes looking back at me over the front seat, asking me questions. I didn't know the answers, couldn't hear him properly. Felt the soil in every crevice, blocking my throat, nose, ears, dulling everything. Then images came lapping over his words: the green, the people, her face, the snatch of Vicente's hand as he left me – a reassuring squeeze, then gone. The relentless shuffle behind the person in front of me and then losing him, wishing I had a second more. Not realising that at the time.

I can't pinpoint the day I appeared here: those days, or was it weeks? A patchy phase of blacks and greys, a numb coldness that settled and has never left. I know I travelled, I remember vaguely the rattle of a train: a mail carriage, perhaps? I remember the scratch of the hessian sack beneath me… or perhaps I am adding details, frustrated always by the gaping holes in my memory. Large chunks of my life are removed; other parts return to me quietly, subtly; others in a sweeping, sudden, roaring rush that leaves me spinning and breathless, as if I'm back there, witnessing it all anew. And then there is the blank. A huge expanse of nothingness. Whispers sometimes, sounds that I don't want to dwell on. The edges get cloudy, as if someone has blown smoke straight into my brain. A smell, familiar, sickly, and I want to sleep, to nestle down, wait for the noises to subside until it is just me, on the edge of darkness, trying to feel my way back into the light.

What do I remember really? Where it started. I always return to that day: seeing Paul burst into the shop, his sandy hair wild, waving his hat; as if he were here, bursting into my room in the nunnery.

'Maman, have you heard?' He starts to speak with the energy of a younger boy, only just missing tripping on a stack of newspapers. 'They've confirmed it,' he rattles on. 'I heard it on the wireless myself. Old Man Renard kept us there for an age talking, otherwise I would have come sooner.'

And so it is confirmed. I feel something leaden in my stomach, reach my hand up as if I can dull the sudden ache, shore up the hole. Frozen behind the counter, I know he is waiting for me. I try to smile at his enthusiasm, to play out the reaction he wants. He takes a step towards me, an eager look in his eye. I notice a patch on his chin that he missed shaving and feel a rush of love for him. 'Come on, Maman,' he says, enveloping me in a hug. Normally I might wiggle away, embarrassed, but this time I let him hold me. I breathe in deeply, trying to ensure his familiar smell fills my nostrils. Leather and grass and the pages of a favourite novel. A tear threatens and I stiffen in his arms. Paul draws away, his hands on my shoulders, looking at me seriously, already playing the role of heroic young man. Paper-thin lines around his dark green eyes deepen as he assures me, 'Maman, don't be like that, it's going to be fine. I'm going to be fine.'

'It's like the last time,' I whisper, pushing him away lightly with one hand. I turn and walk over to lug the last box of apples from the door, leaving a smeared path on the lino as I drag it over to the wooden counter.

'Here, let me,' Paul says, taking over. 'It's not, you know. We're better prepared, Maman. We're...'

Paul's words are drowned out as the door is pushed open once more and Isabelle stands on the threshold of the scene. Strands of blonde hair have broken free from her plaits and she is panting slightly. 'Is it true? Are we? Is it really happening?' she asks, looking to both of us for answers.

Paul straightens up and nods at her. 'I heard it on the wireless myself.'

At this Isabelle launches herself across the shop and throws herself into his arms. 'My big brother, the soldier!' She laughs and then takes his hand. 'I can't believe it.'

I retreat behind the counter again, wipe pointlessly at the surface of the wood, sit down on the stool, flick the last pages of the ledger, stand up again.

'Can you watch the shop?' I ask, moving through to the door at the back, the stairs to our apartment. They don't hear. They're swapping their pieces of news, as they have done since they were children.

I go straight up to our bedroom and close the door behind me, lean back against it. On the bureau, amongst the clutter of Vicente's small change, is a photograph of my father back home in the garden on his first leave. The portraits were usually sombre affairs: the patient wait, the held pose as the photographer worked his magic, but my father always seemed to be on the edge of a great joke, his mouth twitching with quiet amusement in the picture. This was my father before it all.

He would return a few times the following year a different man, somewhere else, in amongst the constant rattle of machine-gun fire and barrages of artillery shells, his mouth turned down, his eyes dulled. And then in 1916 he would return no more. Bits of him, maybe interspersed with parts of another man, were buried there.

He looked so like Paul.

I can hear them both laughing through the floorboards of our room. I close my eyes and pray with all my might that this time things will be different, this time they will all return.

The walls of the nunnery are dark, lamplight softening the stone as we file into the great hall for dinner, a long snake of women winding around the passage. Waddling forwards, heads bowed, nothing but the scuff of our feet, an occasional cough or the rumble of a stomach. The relentless march so that we can eat as a community.

I am standing behind Sister Marguerite's delicate frame, looking determinedly forward at the black cloth of her habit so that I do not have to look at the door on my right, think of what is behind it. They took me there when I first arrived; it smelt of cinnamon and damp. I had trembled as I stepped into it, felt the walls shifting closer as the room became a tunnel, narrower; the wood, the stone, the light, all pressed in on me, so that I had to back out quickly before the whole room collapsed, before the ceiling came down.

I shuffle forwards once more, attempt to focus again on her back and think of the food that awaits, the comforting sound of a hundred women spooning soup out of bowls. I can't stop a glance as I pass the door, think again of the room beyond it.

Sister Marguerite turns: I flinch, but then feel the warmth of her look.

The door is behind us now. They don't make me go there anymore.

ISABELLE

Dear Paul,

It is so dull now you've left. The house is as silent as the grave, which is wholly appropriate as Maman seems to be already in mourning for the loss of you. Don't be absurd and do anything silly like die on me, darling brother – I would be very annoyed.

Father has been visiting the Hotel Avril a little more than usual but hides his feelings – and the whisky fumes – well… It is strangely quiet here all of a sudden, I'm often bored. My only entertainment is seeing Claudette Dubois pining for you when she moons about in the shop, doe-eyes staring out of that sad little face of hers. Honestly, it's rather repulsive – you must promise me never to marry her, even if you do become old and desperate to settle. As for me, I will definitely be dying an old maid as it seems all the men have left France. And I know it sounds selfish but I wish it would all be over so we could all enjoy a good dance and forget all this gloom.

Do you remember last summer when we snuck out to the little copse by the river and I lit my hair on fire with the gas lamp after you told me that terrifying ghost story and I was only saved when you had the sense to throw me in the river? I can't remember ever laughing so hard. Oh, you see, you HAVE to come home soon as it is simply no fun without you.

Tell me news – is it terrible? Are you very scared? I know you probably wouldn't admit it if you were, but I do hope you would be honest with me. Father says Hitler is heading east so maybe he will stay over there and won't trouble us. I am terribly proud of you, brother dear, and I'm sending you a hundred kisses from here – let me know if we can send anything useful out to you – socks? (I could even try and darn some!) Bon bons? Caramels? Whatever you want, I'll make it my personal mission to acquire it.

Your loving sister,

Isabelle

ADELINE

1952, St Cecilia nunnery, south-west France

I lean over and push my fingers into the earth, widening the hole I've made. The soil spills down the edges, filling up the bottom again. Nestling the small seed in the hole I close the earth back over the space, pressing down with a hand, feeling the ground give a little, spongy; then sprinkle water over it, watch the dark patch leak outwards, spread; press down on it again, leave marks in the surface. Pausing briefly, a flicker of a moment lost, I move across to start the process again.

The soil sticks to my damp fingers as I burrow down, pushing out. Another flicker, jarring, and I snatch my hand away, watching the soil trickle back into place once again. Breathing out slowly, I close my eyes. On opening them I can make out Sister Bernadette beyond, head bent over her task, planting in the row in front of me. I can hear her quietly humming.

I try to stay with her, stare at the soles of her shoes, feel my head get cloudy, a familiar lurch in my stomach as unbidden memories start to thrust and jostle their way out.

Sister Bernadette… the soles of her shoes are muddy, worn in the middle.

The sun is burning my neck, the top of my head exposed so that I can feel the heat in my hair, close. Feeling the hot, remembering heat filling me up, I wobble. The hand I thrust out to balance myself pushes into the mud. The garden of the nunnery fades away and the light shifts. It is late afternoon and I am reliving it once again.

There are shouts in the distance and I know I have to get away, have to hide. I crouch down, low to the ground, the past few minutes and hours making my head fill up. My lungs constrict, I gasp for air. I have to hide. I stumble over a fence post, crushing the grass as I get to a garden. My leg screams as I drop to my knees and tear at the ground. My fingers plough into the dirt and I look down at my hand, now five tiny strips of flesh, the rest submerged in the earth. Clawing with two hands as quickly as I can, I feel the dry grains and tiny stones scratch at my fingers as I push them aside.

The trench deepens and I drag myself around a curtain of green stalks – pea pods dangle in the semi-darkness, dripping down, their bobbled exteriors still. The colours merge with the shoots; the stalks are like thin tendrils winding, suffocating, around the canes, around me. Clutching my useless leg, I heave it across and push through the pods; they brush against my face and body like ghostly fingers as I lie in the soil, try to bury myself. Scooping great clumps over my body, shuffling into the dip I've created, pressing down so that I can't be seen, delicate stalks snapping. More soil as I push into the earth, the grains spilling over my legs, trying to hide my torso with every scoop. Then, lying still, surrounded; the smell, the sweet fragrance of the pods as they tickle my face, whisper above me.

I look out from my shallow grave through a curtain of green.

I hear voices. Footsteps on the stones beyond. Words passed between them. Soil over soil, I wriggle, sink deeper, push my head into the earth. My ears are covered and the world becomes muted. Voices gone. Some of the soil brushes over my lips, my nostrils, breathing it in. The ground swallows me into its cool. The heat has gone, the raging heat has been extinguished and now there is a dampness seeping into my clothes as I try to be still.

The peas hang above me, no sky beyond. A cloying smell, sickly. Maybe I will die like this.

Sister Marguerite finds me bent over the ground and whispers to me to follow her. Some of the nuns are looking at me from across the lawn – a rake scraping, a bucket slopped. Sister Constance is frowning, mouth clamped into a line, as we walk past her.

Pushing open the enormous door, we are back in the cool of the corridor, a smell of stone, history and dust, the air forcing me to wrap my cardigan around myself. My room is at the end, the square grille showing a brief, barred glimpse into my world.

Sister Marguerite stops before we are there, outside the other door, the one I will not enter. Panels of wood are set into the wall: the doorway is a mere hole cut out of the stone; you have to duck to get inside the room. Enormous iron hinges wrap themselves across the planks.

Through it is the small chapel: dark wooden pews, stained-glass windows above them, blinding glints in the little space of reds, oranges, and gilt. Candles dance in brackets. I will not go in again. I pull back sharply.

'The others, they want…' She pauses to take a breath, turns to me. 'If you don't start to attend services she will send you away. There is talk. Sister Constance feels you will be better served elsewhere.' She looks over her shoulder, behind her. It is a touching gesture: she has pitted herself against them. 'We could go in now, just you and I, and kneel at the altar.'

I step backwards, shaking my head, like a horse refusing a jump. My chest rises and falls faster now and I can feel my eyes roll backwards as I resist.

Sister Marguerite's shoulders drop, her face falls; she soothes again. 'Tomorrow perhaps,' she lies, drawing me to my room.

SEBASTIAN

I have lost her in the crowd. She was right there, just for a moment. I nearly walk straight into the man in front of me. My eyes scan the strangers moving around the street. Limoges at its busiest. Tipping my hat to the man, I apologize to him. The early morning commuters are swarming to their offices, men in suits and hats all flowing along, with a purpose, peeling away into side streets, stepping onto the cobbles, the occasional tinkle of a shop door, a greeting, the smell of an automobile idling, engine running as a man steps out.

My heart leaps as I see it: a flash of olive-green coat.

The girl from the tram crosses to the other side of the road. I am late for my meeting but I don't want to lose her again; I want to run after her, spin her round, ask her name. She is walking with purpose, her heels click-clacking on the pavement as she skirts other people in her path. I take half a step forward. Her long blonde hair bounces in time to her steps as she rounds a corner.

Briefly looking back over my shoulder at the direction in which I should be going I falter, then I return to the blank space the girl occupied seconds previously. With a last look at the corner, I turn and break into a jog to our offices two blocks away, pushing through the revolving door, panting a little.

Mademoiselle Fourie greets me at reception with a raised eyebrow and points at the stairs. 'They'll be waiting for you, monsieur.'

'*Merci*.'

She rolls her eyes, smiling.

Pausing briefly at the top of the stairs to straighten my tie and smooth down my jacket, I take a breath and walk into the conference room.

Father and Monsieur Phane are standing at the end of the long, oval table hunched over a semi-circle of documents. The morning sun is bouncing off the table's smooth mahogany surface, its rays showing the tiny dust particles that hang suspended in the air. A tray of cups, saucers and a cafetière lies at the other end and I busy myself with it, grateful to be able to do something useful. I pour the coffee into the cups, the distinctive smell tempting the men to look up and acknowledge my presence formally.

Monsieur Phane, a portly gentleman, comes over to pump my hand warmly. An antique watch hangs off the pocket of his waistcoat, which is starting to show signs of strain around the midriff. 'Good to see you, Sebastian. You're looking older, always older,' he says, shaking his head ruefully.

'Monsieur Phane.' I shake his hand and then pass him a coffee.

'I've told you a dozen times before, call me Jean-Paul! We've been going over the plans for this new branch in Couzeix, and Pierre here tells me he is sizing you up to take on the management,' he says, sipping from his cup.

'That seems to be the plan.'

'Well, excellent, excellent! Good to know we have someone on the shop floor, so to speak, who can let us know what is going on and how the employees are working…' He guffaws, almost spilling the boiling liquid down his front.

'We're not planning on spying on them, Jean-Paul,' Father says.

'Well, not *all* the time…' Jean-Paul winks at me.

Father joins us and there is a brief silence as we all enjoy the taste of the coffee. As I place my cup down, in the circular window beyond I can see the tops of the trees in the park: a mix of oranges and reds, the grass almost olive. I blink, returning to the room.

Father is planning to open a new bank in a nearby town and he has hired an architect to come up with a modern design for the building, which is currently a disused garage.

'Are the plans what you'd hoped?' I ask.

Jean-Paul's whole face lifts, his brown eyes filling with reflections of the tiny lights from the chandelier above. 'Incredible to think we'll have another branch up and running within a year,' he says.

'This impending war, though…' comments Father, shaking his head. 'What they've been doing to the Jews in Germany. And we run a bank, Jean-Pa—'

'Don't start up again, Pierre,' says Jean-Paul, cutting Father off with a tap of his cigarette case on the table. He raises his eyebrows at me. 'It's all doom and gloom around here, boy.' He nods his head in the direction of Father. 'Anyway,' he continues, draining his coffee in one go, 'I've got to get off. I'm sure Pierre will fill you in on our evil schemes. Until next time,' he says, holding out his hand.

I move across to scan my eyes down the pages on the table as Father shows him out of the room and closes the double doors behind him. He places his hand flat on the wood, pausing. He seems strained.

'So, tell me about the plans for the new branch,' I say, deliberately trying to distract him from gloomy thoughts.

Father allows himself to be diverted, eyes creasing as he states: 'It is going to be the most wonderfully modern building.' He moves across the room in quick steps, a bounce back in his step. 'The architect has come up with some ingenious designs.'

The next couple of hours are spent sifting through the early plans, discussing the precise profile of the people we need to employ. Not for the first time I feel a warmth flood through me as we work on these plans, as we see his vision coming together.

'What made you late this morning?' he asks when I'm about to leave the room. 'You're normally very prompt for these things.'

'Just a beautiful day,' I mumble, not turning around. 'Just soaking up the sights, I suppose.'

I can hear the smile in his voice. 'Was she very pretty?'

My mouth twitches as I turn the handle of the door. 'Very,' I reply, looking at him over my shoulder.

He nods and returns to the business; he hunches over the documents once more, dwarfed by the enormous room, the mahogany table, the large oil paintings that hang on the walls. My father has made it, and no war can take that away.

This is France, things are different here.

When Armistice Day comes it seems all the more poignant this year. Ticker tape has been tied to the lampposts: the red, white and blue triangles flutter in the breeze; *tricolor* flags are draped out of many first- and second-floor apartment windows. The vendors sell hot chocolate, candy floss on wooden sticks, croissants, nougat. A nearby boy is focused on devouring a fresh *pain au chocolat*, the insides of it smeared around his mouth. The cold November air makes my breath visible as I stamp my feet in an effort to try and warm them. My knee twinges, but I'm used to the sporadic pains and I'm distracted by the mood: it seems the whole of Limoges has come out to have a good time. With the Germans on the doorstep, it seems we will not forget who we are, that no one can dull the love a man has for his country.

The celebrations are louder this year. People are singing 'The Marseillaise' and proclaiming victory to France. Bands play, people dance in the street, swapping stories, talking about their sons, fathers, sweethearts who are all away, ready to fight for the honour of France. The voices and the familiar melody blends, swirling about me as I stand for a moment longer on the street before returning home.

An old man perched on a stool nearby, cigarette dangling from his mouth, taps one foot, bangs his walking stick on the cobbles in time. There is a girl, no more than twelve, leg in a brace, sitting and watching her friends as they dance an eight-some with boys in the village. One of their fathers has been forced to join in and he grimaces at me from over a shoulder as I smile at the group.

The girl on the seat looks downcast, scuffing the toe of one shoe backwards and forwards on the ground as another tune starts up and she is left out once more. A couple of boys nearby point at her, one of them smirks and the girl grows redder as she tries to ignore their gestures. Toe back, forward, back, forward.

I walk over to her, holding out my hand. 'We'll go slowly.'

She looks up, shy and uncertain, and then grins at me, a face full of freckles and now two rows of white teeth. She takes my hand and we move to join the group. The steps are simple; even so we get it all hopelessly wrong but the girl seems happy; she shows me how her mother taught her to move in a triangle, one foot back, to the side and then the front, and we start to get the hang of things. A friend calls to her and she waves, jutting her chin out proudly. Another boy cuts in, asks her to join him, and I bow out. She looks at me, mouthing a thank-you.

Returning to the safety of the pavement, I feel the familiar throb just above my knee. I rub at it absently – nearly missing her. A head of thick blonde hair, an olive-green coat…

My arm reaches out and I find myself tapping her on the shoulder. 'Excuse me.'

The girl looks startled and then, when she recovers, an inquisitive expression replaces the surprise.

'I…'

'Can I help?' she asks.

'I, well, I saw you once before and I…' My voice trails away into a whisper of jumbled words as my eyes explore her face. She has the smoothest skin: glowing. I've seen a photograph of Greta Garbo in a picture magazine and she has skin like this. Her wide eyes are an unusual shade of green, like a forest lake, flecked with brown; the left iris has a muddy dot, like a leaf disturbing the surface.

Her smile falters a little as I struggle to say something, anything, coherently. The mood of the day has given me the confidence to approach her; now I've done it, I'm suddenly at a loss.

'I thought…' What did I think, oh God, what did I think? 'I thought you might like to dance,' I say, pointing at the couples nearby who are dancing on the cobbled street as a man plays an accordion and sings in a wobbly tenor.

The girl's face lights up again as she glances across at them, then she crosses her arms and looks back at me. 'I thought you only danced with little girls.' I can feel my cheeks burning and she laughs. 'It was sweet of you, and I'd love to,' she continues, in a voice like melted caramel. 'I'm Isabelle.' She offers her hand.

I take it. 'Sebastian, and I have to warn you, I am a terrible dancer. She was just too polite to reject me.'

'Sebastian the bad dancer,' she repeats. 'Enchantée.'

'And you.'

We step off the pavement into the street. My palms are beginning to sweat and my feet are clumsy. Isabelle appears not to notice, chatting happily to me as we dance. I nod at a nearby acquaintance, a friend of Mother's. She waves, raises an eyebrow.

I am a head taller than the girl in the olive-green coat and momentarily relieved that I can focus on the top of her hair as we move in time to the music. Who is this woman in my arms, who seems full of restless energy? Her movements are fluid: they match my own, as if we have danced together before, her light steps in low-heeled shoes so soft she could slink away without a sound. I had better say something or she might disappear again.

I ask her where she lives, mentally congratulating myself on getting the words out in the right order. She lives in a village not far from Limoges, a little place called Oradour that I know by reputation because many of my colleagues have fished in the river there at weekends.

'Excellent pike,' I comment.

'Quite,' she says, looking up and meeting my eyes.

I want to roll my eyes at myself. *Fish, Sebastian?*

The accordion stops for a moment and our dance comes to an abrupt halt. Isabelle doesn't move away. I feel my chest rise and fall. I'm aware of my knee protesting, sending sharp signals to stop and sit. I can't bring myself to move away, to ruin this moment.

'I've never seen the town like this,' she says, doing a quick spin about her and breathing out. 'It's fantastic, don't you think?'

I picture Father that morning saying something similar, qualifying the statement with bleak predictions. I don't want to dampen her mood; I want to agree, see the street through her eyes, vibrant with colour and life and people whipped into a fever of patriotism.

I nod. 'This is what we do. We dance.'

'It's the right thing to do,' she says. 'I think we owe it to them to live in the present, to carry on as they left us. Isn't this what today's all about?'

The passion in her voice surprises me, her eyes fiercely lit from within. She has thrown her arms out wide, and I focus on her upturned wrist, the sliver of flesh, thoughts crammed into my brain, the noises outside fading. I hear her voice repeating the word 'them' again and again.

'Sebastian?' Her head is tilted to one side, the sun on her hair making each strand glow.

'I wish I was fighting with them,' I begin, 'it's my leg, I can't,' I gesture at it before taking a breath, 'but sometimes' – I look beyond her now, admit these words to the space above her head – 'there are moments when I'm... relieved.'

I stop short, astounded that I have shared this, my deepest, ugliest thought with her. I look down at her, wait for the green eyes to grow dull, narrow, for her to make her excuses, to leave me in the street with the dancing crowds.

But she stays there, reaches out a hand and encloses my hand in it.

I look down, blink once, feel her fingers encircling, pressing on my skin.

'Everyone has their own story,' she states. So simple.

She removes her hand almost immediately, tucks it protectively under her arm as if stopping herself repeating the action. I miss her touch, that instinctive gesture that made me feel for the first time in weeks that someone understood.

She laughs twice, quickly, eyes dart quickly back to the crowd of people, a line forms on her forehead, the atmosphere shifts, becomes thicker. The music has slowed, couples have stepped closer, cheeks pressed against each other's.

'I'm sorry,' she says, without explaining what for.

'When can I see you again?' I hear my voice, cutting across hers and feel heat in my stomach as her eyes open, her smile widens and her whole face lifts. A forest lake, deep pools focused on me.

'I, well…'

For the first time in our meeting she seems on the back foot, younger, pulling at a sleeve of her cardigan. The action makes me feel braver.

'I'm sorry. I don't want to make you awkward.'

'You haven't. I'm just not used to…'

A young boy in shorts jostles past, momentarily disturbing us, and I lose the rest of her sentence, replaced by a muttered apology.

I offer her an arm and steer her back from the street to stand under the striped awning of a shop. The window is piled high with dusty antiques, rolled-up rugs, a tea set Mother would love. A large mirror shows our cloudy image; Isabelle's profile a blurred picture of blondes and green. I turn back to her. The speckled shade makes it harder to read her expression. It seems the sounds of the day have receded, are streaking past as we stand there.

'I've noticed you before,' I state, relishing her reaction, the flush of colour in her cheeks. 'Do you work in Limoges?' I ask.

She shakes her head. 'Trying.'

'No luck yet?'

'There are just so many girls with the same idea.'

'Well, you mustn't give up hope.'

'That's what Paul said.' She laughs. 'God, I miss him.'

Paul?

'He volunteered,' she explains, mistaking my confusion.

I nod, my hand involuntarily forming a fist as a monster within me stamps around my head, the name 'Paul' thundering in his ears. *Who is this Paul?* I hate him instantly.

'He's wonderful,' she gushes. 'Just marvellous, so brave. He's north somewhere, I'm not sure exactly where,' she explains. 'He already seems so much older.'

The music starts up again from the street, the beat fast, but I barely register the lightening mood. I look hopelessly over her head at other couples, bereft of all words now. This Paul has thrown me into a brooding silence. I see one woman nearby reaching up to place a light hand on the chest of her companion, a young man with a smattering of a beard, her hand hovering over his heart. Their faces are lit in the stark light of the day and I feel like I am watching from the depths. Their laughter jars, it's mocking.

'It doesn't feel quite like war should, does it?' Isabelle muses. 'I do miss him.'

I step back as if someone has pushed me and, I know this is bad, but I wish for all kinds of horrible things to happen to this Paul. I see a quick flash, hear the sound – a long, low whistle, a groan, a punctured noise as a bullet lodges, a gasp from the man. Or a short, sharp burst, the ground exploding into dust, a body blown backwards. Something that might delay his return. Indefinitely.

I'm convinced I'm going to hell but when I look back at Isabelle's expectant face, I wonder if it might be worth it.

'The house is gloomy without him. I don't have any other siblings,' she goes on.

Siblings: my ears prick up. He's a *brother*. The wonderful, brave, ridiculously dashing and fabulous Paul is a brother. I can almost feel the blood flooding back into my limbs, the ice melting. I can't wait to pump his hand and hear all his glorious tales from the frontline. My heart swells with hope. The relief I feel is so palpable I find myself exhaling loudly.

As Isabelle turns her head to look back at the dancers in the street I trace her profile: the gentle slope of her neck, tiny strands of hair tickling the collar of her coat, the curve of her eyelashes.

This war is turning out better than I could have hoped.

ISABELLE

Darling Paul,

I met a man today. I saw a young girl looking so forlorn on the side of the pavement as all her friends danced and the boys nearby, all leers and spittle, pointed at her, forced her to feel different. And then I saw him walking to her, his left leg a little stiff, his gait affected. He'd noticed too, Paul, and there he was, a knight in shining armour, holding out his hand to the girl, her face so downcast and then the most enormous grin as she took it and they stepped into the street together. I felt jealous of her.

He steered her over to the group, careful not to go too quickly, getting all the steps wrong so that she could laugh at him and my heart just bloomed for this man. His brown eyes kind, his thick hair curling at the neck as if it couldn't lie still, his arms assured as he gently helped her feel dainty, his wide frame obscuring my view of her so that I just got flashes of her chatter and smiles as she turned. I wanted to know him. Felt so curious, excited, when I wandered past, felt a genuine bolt of surprise when he stopped me (hoped he would, of course).

That first look, Paul – I can't tell you. He looked familiar, like we'd known each other in another time. It was strange. It was like nothing I'd ever felt before, like something had guided me there. I feel like he is important. I felt so bold, a brighter version of me as we spoke. There was something, an understanding of each other, a gentle calm in amongst the frantic mood of the day.

Oh, listen, I'm not going to post this letter, am I? I was never going to.

Anyway, it's hopeless to tell you these absurd things when you can't tease me about them…

ADELINE

1952, St Cecilia nunnery, south-west France

I have been given the basket to carry as Sister Marguerite sips from the flask she had the foresight to bring. It has turned into a scorching day: the sun, now full in the sky, briefly disappears behind another great puff of cloud that provides only seconds of relief from the blaze. The nunnery is a silhouette behind us, the grey walls dull against the brilliant yellows and greens of the fields, the thick stone now insignificant from this distance.

We are visiting a family on the outskirts of the village, eight of them in two bedrooms; the father, a farmer, recently lost a hand in an agricultural accident, and has been bed-bound for the past few months. We have brought them rich, orange carrots, courgettes and a whole load of muddied potatoes heaved up this morning by Sister Bernadette.

A child is playing in the garden as we approach the house, a small, dark-haired girl no more than five, who catches sight of us and instantly runs inside, her words lost to the wind. Sister Marguerite smiles at me, rattling off her name, as she can with every member of the village. She greets the mother – who has a tanned face and a dirty apron – at the door, and hushes her thanks for the generous offerings with a small smile, bending to talk directly to the little girl who has peeked out from behind her mother's skirts.

The replies come in quiet monosyllables. She answers Marguerite but is staring at me, her gaze taking me in, a stranger. I avoid her eyes.

We step into the cottage, heads bent as we move through the doorway, the smell of damp earth and the cool darkness an instant refuge from the heat outside. Above the stove is a plucked, scraggy, trussed-up chicken; a couple of flies are picking at it. Our muddied carrots are put on the table, awaiting the knife. The girl is foraging in the basket as she stands on a small stool by the scrubbed wooden table. I feel the sides of my mouth turning upwards involuntarily. She notices and hops off the stool, diving behind her mother's skirts once more.

A memory tugs at my mind and I feel the small kitchen fade away, snatches of a vision crowding in.

The girl clutches at her mother's skirts in bewildered desperation, tugging at her as if she can provide answers, comfort, reassurance. Her mother is distracted, looking towards the door, trying to catch a glimpse over the heads of other people. The soldiers are carrying something inside: she can see it. At my side someone whispers: fast, furious babble to soothe, the words lost in the noise that is everywhere, swirling about the room, rising in panic, punctuated only by short, sharp shots from outside the walls.

I know that I, too, am crying out that they mustn't hurt them. They mustn't hurt my boy.

I am ushered to a chair by the table, my eyes are unfocused – the carrots a blur of colour. I am made to sit down and drink water.

Recently it feels that all my memories are shuffling inwards, rattling at the door, refusing to stay hidden in the corners. Maybe it is the talk of moving me, the numbness lifting; or simply time marching on with no empathy, no pause to mark anything, just the steady *tick tock* of the seconds: the sun rising, a new day; its middle, no matter; its end.

And that day, played out in parts: a few moments repeated, or a minute new and clear.

The mother of the house is looking at me as if I have offended her – she wants us out of her home, everything about her posture shouts it. She tucks the hand of her youngest in hers, enveloping it. Sister Marguerite is making hasty goodbyes.

As we step back through the door the full midday sun dazzles me. The past is obliterated in the glare; the crowd, the shots, the soldiers – gone in a burst. It is as if I have stepped into another place, a heaven: objects and landscape are nothing but bright yellow, white shades, and, before my eyes adjust, before I can make out the fields, the fences, the cottage, I allow myself to think that I have arrived and it is over.

TRISTAN

'We should have left earlier,' Papa says for the millionth time. 'Why didn't we leave earlier? This is hopeless.' He drums his fingers on the steering wheel. He looks enormous, all folded over in the driving seat.

'How were we to know, Davide? We couldn't really have known,' Maman says.

We have hardly moved anywhere all day and I am all bunched up. Elèonore is staring out of the car window at the thousands of people on the streets of Paris all carrying bags, boxes, children. Every now and again her ponytail twitches. We are in a jam, a never-ending queue of people.

Dimitri is watching too, then he turns to me. 'How long till we leave Paris?' he asks in a quiet voice, his eyes enormous behind his glasses.

I shrug. He's ten, one year older than me, but he is always asking me questions.

Papa honks his horn and Maman snaps at us to be quiet so they can think.

Luc fell asleep in the first minute of being in the car. He

can sleep anywhere. My legs are scrunched in and the leather of the seats makes my clothes slip around. Luc's head is angled funny and his blonde fringe lifts every time he breathes out. His mouth is slightly open, just wide enough that I can see his missing front tooth. Maybe I could stick my finger in there to wake him – anything to give us something to do.

I've only ever been out of Paris two times and once I was only a baby so I don't remember it. Last time we went to the seaside to stay with an aunt. Now we are going to people called the Villiers. I'm not sure where they live and Papa doesn't like lots of questions. I hope they live near the sea too, and that we are going to eat ice pops and build enormous sandcastles that you can throw yourselves on to before the tide comes in and washes them all away. This time I might dig a big hole as Arnette in my class told me that if you dug a hole deep enough, you'd be able to get to Australia. Arnette is quite clever and her father is a professor at the university so you can't just dismiss her, even if she is a girl.

I would probably have to dig a long way; I imagine I'd have to get other people to help me. Elèonore would probably refuse because she hates getting sand in her hair or on her clothes, but Luc and Dimitri would be keen. It would be so exciting to be digging down into the wet, cold sand that smells of the sea, and see a pinprick of light below my feet. I would dig harder and faster until the pinprick of light was about the size of my yo-yo and the rays of the sun would beam through the gap and we'd see all sorts of animals and strange-looking plants and trees below us. I imagine myself arriving in Australia through my hole and being made King of the People with all of them prancing about me, giving me their gifts from the wilderness and making me overlord of the land. Maybe King Kong lived there. Years ago, I saw a poster of King Kong, outside a cinema in Montmartre, and he looked fearsome, just the kind of animal you would imagine living in Australia. We'd go hunting for him and—

There is a tap on the car window just where my head is resting. I sit straight up and stare. It's a witch at the window: her wrinkled face presses into the glass, mouthing words at me. Papa is staring ahead and Maman is hissing at me to ignore the woman, but I feel odd trying to do that when she is so close that I can see lines of powder in the wrinkles around her mouth. She taps again. I turn my head and talk to Dimitri but can't think of anything to say, am just aware of her there on the other side of the glass. She stays there for what seems like for ever as I pretend-talk and will the car to move forward.

Eventually the woman gives up and we finally get moving, breaking off into various side streets. All the shutters of the buildings are closed. It seems to me the whole of the city is on the road, not in their houses. My back is aching and Luc's woken up and wants another game but we are all bored of playing I Spy. He is useless at it. He keeps spying everyone in the car so, after the first round of 'M' ('Is it Maman?' – a nod from Luc), we soon worked it out.

We eat onion tartlets balanced on newspaper in our laps and have grenadine with water from a flask Maman passes back. The tartlets are freshly baked and satisfactory, but I prefer our normal hot meal. Maman says it's impossible and Elèonore has told me to stop talking about it. I know Clarisse, our maid, packed up the silver earlier anyway, so we don't have any cutlery even if we had been given something hot.

Packing up our house seemed to take for ever. I imagined we'd still be doing it when I was ten. Clarisse went back and forwards, back and forwards, cleaning every room for a week, with Maman pointing at the things she wanted put in newspaper. Papa was never home: when we were brought down in the evening to say goodnight, only Maman was there to kiss us.

We were only allowed one bag and one box of things so I had to choose carefully. Elèonore spent a whole day crying because Maman said she couldn't bring Madame Delancy because she was too big and the china would break. I filled my box up full so Elèonore wouldn't make me take her. She has enough dolls, anyway.

When we were finally ready we stood in the hallway in our hats and coats, even though it was much too warm outside. The doorway to the sitting room was open and it looked peculiar, like it was already lonely without us. The furniture, a lot of it very old (Papa once told me that his desk had once belonged to a cousin of Louis XVI) was covered in great big white sheets. You couldn't make out where the sofa ended and the leather armchair that Papa sat on in front of the fire began. The chandelier still twinkled in the half-empty room from the sunlight that poured through the windows. It will have stopped winking now we have left and the shutters are closed.

This thought makes me sad and I pinch Dimitri quickly so that his bottom lip wobbles. He doesn't say anything as he knows Papa will get cross, so I grin at him. I can feel onion in my front teeth. He pushes his glasses up his nose and leans away from me. Luc is trying to stick a marble up his nose and Elèonore is talking to him in that gooey way she does, telling him not to. He rolls his eyes at me and I laugh. Papa catches my eye in the driving mirror and I stop.

I wonder how long we will be in the car. I wonder if the answer is the same as last week.

We'd been in the kitchen when I'd asked.

'We'll be back soon,' Maman had said, in a voice that didn't sound certain to me.

'When?' I'd asked, turning my head. Clarisse had started crying at the oven.

'Soon.'

'We'll be coming home in time for school, won't we?' checked Elèonore.

'Yes, we will. After a summer in the countryside.' Maman looked at Clarisse as if she'd dropped the gravy dish again.

Clarisse kept crying. 'Poor Paris,' she muttered.

School hadn't seemed that far away. Not that I much liked it. I pictured the face of Monsieur Hébert, the headmaster – all lines and wrinkles and bags. I'd visited his office one too many times in the past few months and my backside was still marked with the proof. A holiday in the countryside hadn't seemed quite so bad then. I'd wanted Clarisse to stop crying.

I wonder now where Clarisse is staying as it seems the whole world is leaving Paris. She waved goodbye to us this morning from the top of our front steps, handkerchief in hand as the car turned out of sight at the end of the cobbled street.

I forgot to say goodbye.

'How long will we be gone?' I blurt from the back seat.

'Tristan,' Papa warns, his eye back in the driving mirror.

I can feel the others all waiting for the answer.

'Not long, my darlings.' Maman sighs, her head tilted to the right. She is wearing very big earrings that catch the light and make tiny white spots dance on the car ceiling. 'It will be just like a holiday,' she sing-songs.

I lean back in the leather and try to get comfortable. The air smells of petrol and onion. I feel my stomach turn. Maman and Papa sit in the front of the car in silence for a moment looking at each other.

This doesn't feel like the start of a holiday.

SEBASTIAN

She emerges from the bakery, stepping out onto the pavement, her skirt briefly swirling up around her, showing off shapely legs. Her feet are encased in scarlet suede shoes. She is wearing a shirt that seems to nip in her tiny waist and her hair is pinned back into a low chignon. She looks like a movie star in this small town. She glances in my direction, her eyes widening a little in surprise when she sees me. Her face breaks into an easy smile and she crosses the street to join me. I raise my hat as she approaches, already unsure whether to kiss her on both cheeks or shake her hand, and feel both relief and a hint of disappointment when, instead of a cheek, she proffers a bag at me, to peer into.

'Papa hates it when I eat in the street, but I'm starving,' she explains, removing a latticed apple strudel entirely from the bag, tearing it in half and holding out half for me.

It is like no time has passed since we stopped our conversation under the awning on Armistice Day; no olive coat, and the tip of her nose a little red, but otherwise she is unchanged.

'I wouldn't want to deprive you.'

'I can always get another one. Go on, they're delicious.'

I thank her, a huff of air as I breathe out. I stamp my feet but I haven't felt cold since seeing her.

Isabelle settles into a steady pace beside me, although I have no idea where I am going and know I should return to the office.

'How did the job hunt go?' I venture, trying not to spit pastry her way.

Isabelle flaps a hand in front of her mouth, mid-mouthful.

'Oh, dear, how unladylike!' She swallows. 'Well enough, thank you for remembering. I've been filing for a local solicitor these last few weeks, but I'm starting work as a teacher at the boys' school in the village soon.'

We have reached the black iron gates of the park at the north end of town. As I follow Isabelle through them a woman nearby looks at me, a frown on her face. I try to place her: her crinkled brow, set curls, simple string of pearls. Isabelle is waiting for an answer to a question she must have asked as I turn to face her. I try to pick up the thread. 'I'm sorry, I was somewhere else,' I bluster.

'Oh, don't apologize. It was me being typically curious and rude. I was asking what stopped you, well…' A blush touches the edges of her cheeks, the colour instantly making her eyes seem even brighter, her teeth even whiter.

I know what she wants to ask and point to my leg. 'I had polio as a child. It seems silly of course, but then the pain, and my knee joints… well they won't...'

She touches my arm, cutting me off. 'As I said, it was rude to ask.'

Our eyes meet. I shrug. 'Understandable.'

We settle ourselves on a bench in a patch of green dotted

with clumps of clover. I feel over-dressed in my woollen coat and polished office shoes. On the other side of the park, an old man on a bicycle clatters down the pathway, causing startled pigeons to make way, his shopping jigging up and down in the basket on the front. A couple, lost in conversation, look behind them as he passes.

'Any news of Paul?'

She shakes her head; a blonde ringlet comes loose. 'Nothing new. Poor Maman.'

I nod, picturing my own mother in our apartment, a light hand squeezing my shoulder in passing.

A woman nearby is handing out lavender posies from a basket, their faint aroma mingling with the smell of sweet chestnuts. Passers-by are shuffling past either avoiding her eyes or seeing her off with a few centimes, promises of luck in their ears as she thanks them. Her ageing eyes light up as the money changes hands and she bids them good day.

Isabelle gets up from the bench and walks towards her. 'Don't go anywhere,' she calls behind her.

I watch her as she greets the woman, both of them glance over at me. The woman reaches into her basket for another posy. The little purple bunches are tied with thin, coloured ribbons, and Isabelle selects one, handing over some coins in return. The woman says something that makes Isabelle's light laugh ring across the park as she pockets the coins. Isabelle returns, even brighter now against the background of the park, the trees stripped of their leaves, the sky a threatening grey. She sits by my side on the bench and presents the posy with a flourish.

'She said it will bring the young gentleman some good luck.'

'Thank you.' I accept it. 'How nice of her.'

'It's not nice, it's fact. You can't question magic,' she says, watching the woman accost someone else a little further off.

I clutch the posy in my hand, looking sideways at her, and hope that she's right.

PAUL

Dear Isabelle,

I know you will probably think my letters flat and too brief. I don't claim to have your talent for writing and how I love getting your letters. You give me a glimpse into the village, the shop with its dusty floorboards, no matter how much Maman sweeps, all the customers clucking about. Madame Garande lecturing Maman about the stock. I feel I am back there with you all hearing the little bell greeting an arrival. How I suddenly miss the moments of quiet, those long walks beyond the river and into the woods with no route planned, drinking cider on the picnic rug as I fish. It seems I can never be alone here. The lads are in good heart, it is not what we'd thought at all, there seem to be so many men from so many villages. I've never known the hum and buzz of so many bodies together and yet everyone has his own history.

We have travelled some distance since I last wrote and my feet seem permanently blistered. I am glad to have had some experience of work in the fields because carrying this back-pack around can be hard-going for some. The ground is like iron. I have struck up a friendship with Rémi, a lad the same age from Saint-Junien who spends a large part of the day telling me about his old job in a paper mill. I had never known there is so much to know about paper. Fortunately, when he is not talking about paper, we have a great deal in common. Whenever there is a free moment we manage to rope the others in to some kind of ball game. You would roll your eyes at so many men getting excited about a football, although I have told them my sister could be quite a force at the back. I am not sure Maman has ever forgiven you for ruining that dreadful candy-pink dress in aid of such a heroic save. What a shame you don't still play.

As for Claudette you can rest at ease my sister dear, for she hasn't captured this soldier's heart just yet. I am not sure I will ever be ready to relinquish the memory I had of her when she snapped at Mother for dropping the flour and messing up her suede shoes and you called her an idiot and threw her out of the shop. I did not know a girl's mouth could open that wide. You never were destined to be best friends. Still at least now I know the easiest way to annoy you when I return. Although I'm not sure even I could marry a girl just to have the last laugh.

Much of our daily life is training but I think we will soon be ready. Obviously I'm not allowed to share a great deal in these letters but be reassured that I fight alongside the best and bravest men of France. They are pretty formidable as a bunch – when we sleep under the same roof the whole place vibrates with snoring. I never had a brother, although you were always keen to play the part, but I imagine this is what a whole family of brothers is like, or a great boys' school (although none of us is any good at spelling or mathematics – boxing perhaps).

Promise to look after Mother and keep Father from

becoming too glum. You could always make him smile when nothing else could. As for me I shall continue to daydream of Mother's rillettes de boeuf and the lemon soufflé like air that melts the moment it is in the mouth. I'm practically slobbering over this letter now. I think we've all become quite obsessed, continually talking about food and drink. It seems everyone's mother makes the best meat course in France.

Don't be too bored – someone needs to act as caretaker for the lives we will return to soon.

Paul

ADELINE

1952, St Cecilia nunnery, south-west France

She reads to me from the Bible. She has a sweet voice, a quiet lilting accent, and the familiar words wash over me, words that were such a comfort in another life. The extract today is from Exodus; she is retelling the story of Moses, adding little thoughts and prayers of her own as she reads the passages aloud. She knows this chapter so well she could read it fluently without looking at the text, but Sister Marguerite carefully ensures every word is spoken with due reverence.

'Every son that is born to the Hebrews, you shall cast into the Nile, but you shall let every daughter live.'

I used to find it hard to believe anyone could ever rule in such a way, that a human being could expect people to follow such an absurd order. I don't think that way anymore. I simply wonder why the daughters were allowed to survive. Some men would have wanted to be more thorough.

'... and she put the child in it and placed it among the reeds at the river's brink.'

I picture the scene on the muddy bank, the little basket made of bulrushes, a distressed young girl so desperate for her son to survive that she is willing to cast him out into the currents of the river rather than hand him over to the authorities. Surely this desperate act is one only a mother can understand? I never truly loved anything completely and wholly until the day they handed me Paul, wrapped tightly in blankets, his face a violent shade of pink, wailing.

The labour was long and the birth complicated. They used forceps so silvery and alien I felt faint when I looked at them. I was wrenched open, could smell blood, could feel my pulse throbbing in my neck, head, through my limbs, could hear myself screaming as if I was someone else. But all was forgotten once I realized what I had brought into the world. A release, every muscle relaxed, I could feel the mattress beneath me, see my baby swaddled, knew it was over. The doctor later told Vicente that I almost died.

In the days that followed his birth I remember seeing Paul from a distance, too weak to raise my head or hold him for a long time. I strayed from certain bliss to blind panic when I woke, imagining that the birth had never taken place.

After a week I was strong enough to sit up in bed. Paul was placed in my arms and I looked down at him and realized utter perfection. This tiny being, created by me and my husband, was beautifully formed, a life in my arms, the opportunity to become anything, unspoilt. He looked at me with his wide eyes and all I could see was my own happiness reflected back in them.

His skin was so smooth I spent hours stroking his arms, his chubby legs, tickling his stomach. Neighbours bought us blankets and clothes and I scrubbed the fabrics to ensure they were clean and welcoming. Vicente bought a rocking chair in which I could nurse him and I would quietly hum lullabies from my own childhood as we watched the sun rise in the early mornings. He would sleep with a little screwed-up expression, breathing softly and evenly, and then he would wake fully and look at me, his gaze resting solely on me, his mother. He had wisps of sandy hair, grass-green eyes, and he fitted so neatly into the crook of my arm.

'... when she opened it she saw the child and lo, the babe was crying.'

So Moses was found but his poor mother, on a distant bank somewhere, would never be sure of his fate. She would simply be praying to someone that her baby would be discovered, saved, taken out of danger. All she would know was uncertainty.

I smile, look down at my son, but something is wrong. He is breathing but his breaths are different, quicker, shallower. He is thinner, his arms and legs longer, no longer the chubby little boy I know. His wisps of sandy hair are darker, cover more of his head. The blanket he is wrapped in isn't mine. My breathing comes faster, great panicked gasps as my hand reaches out to pull back the blanket from his face. The eyes that look at me are black, the lashes are dark. This is not my baby. What have they done to my baby? What have they done?

Arms shake me awake. Sister Marguerite is by my side, her eyes frantic. 'What is it?' she asks. 'Are you in pain? What is it? How can I help?'

A silent scream.

SEBASTIAN

'I'll go over the plans for the opening of the new branch with you today. We must start to arrange...'

Father stands and smacks the table with flat hands, making us both jump. My mother drops the spoon for the jam. I am left hanging mid-sentence, my train of thought entirely forgotten. He clutches the edges of the table and breathes out slowly. 'It's this waiting that's so awful.' He scrapes his hands through his hair and sits back down. He looks at Mother, taking her hand in his, an apology in the gentle stroking of her wrist.

She calmly picks up the spoon and squeezes his hand back.

We both know what he means.

I have attempted to convince myself that France won't see any fighting and, though doubts edge in, I like it this way. I am not helped by Father insisting I am foolish to think so.

These days, I seem to be finding any excuse to leave the house. The weather is warmer and, as I shut the door to the apartment, head down the stairs to the high street, I feel my muscles loosen, the downturned mouth of my father fading from my mind as I open the front door and look around Limoges in the daylight. Rubbing my aching leg, I shouldn't have rushed the stairs, I turn left, always surprised by the everyday buzz of the high street.

Thick coils of *saucisson* hang in nets in the window of the butchers opposite; peaches sitting plump and appealing under an awning in the greengrocers next door. In a small road off the high street, men on stools sit outside their houses half in shadow, smoking stubs and swapping news. One woman, a scarf knotted at the front of her hair, is beating a rug from a window on the second floor, clouds of dust spiralling to the ground. The men don't break their talk. A soggy newspaper lies forgotten in the gutter. Someone has stepped on Petain's face.

Up ahead I can see the library, imagine the figure waiting for me; then wonder briefly if she will be wearing her olive-green coat. She is always wearing it in my head. Perhaps it is too warm.

By chance I saw her at the tram stop last week. She looked at me like she had been waiting for me, that same look, familiar, as if we have known each other for years. Her face lifted up to mine as we swapped news; I felt awkward, aware of the other people waiting listening to my inane remarks. The tram trundled up the high street, quicker, I felt, than normal. I rushed the next sentence, felt lost in the sudden din of its noise. Beneath the rumble, the call of the conductor, someone ringing the bell, she asked me to meet her again.

As I approach the stairs leading up to the library entrance she emerges from another side street. A motorcar passes in front of her and she waits to cross the road. She is wearing a pale blue dress, her hair hanging in loose curls, held up by a single clip. She turns her head to check the street and then crosses, her mouth widening into a smile that warms my whole body.

'You came,' she says.

TRISTAN

Our car is now at a complete stop and Maman tells us all to get out. Papa goes over and talks to one of the other drivers, whose car seems full to bursting with belongings: lampshades, bed sheets, books and clothes are all piled high. If he had a wife and children no one would know, as they'd be buried under all the items. He waves his arms around a lot and shakes his head at Papa. He offers to light a cigarette for Papa, who never normally smokes. Papa cups his hands around it; the light shows up his moustache, a thin angry line.

Maman gives us all a macaroon and tells us to be patient. Elèonore is stretching her arms up like a ballerina, leaning one way and the next to 'loosen her muscles'. People are looking at her. Luc is asleep again in the back seat. Dimitri is cleaning his glasses quietly next door to him, pinned by a leg. He shrugs at me helplessly. I wouldn't let Luc sprawl all over me like that.

We climb back into the car and continue on as the sun sets in front of us, leaving great streaks of pink and orange that give the people outside an unnaturally rosy glow and make the whole day even more dream-like. There is a girl, a little younger than me, about eight, dabbing at her mother's face as they rest under a tree. There is another family all huddled onto a rug underneath an enormous umbrella, bags scattered about them, too tired to go on. An elderly man and woman are slowly pushing a trolley of books in front of them, one hand on the bar of the trolley and one hand in each other's.

It seems to me the whole of the city is on the road, not in their houses. One man is carrying a saucepan and a guitar. A woman is dragging her child on a sledge; another goes by with a wheelbarrow full of bags. An older boy walks quickly as the younger brother holds his hand, doing little, quick steps to keep up. The older boy looks over at our car as we pass. He's about my age, I think. His reddish hair is combed into a neat side parting like he's walking to church. He glares back at me. I look away, pretending to be looking at the sky. My face burns. Why can't we be there yet?

The minutes crawl by and our car is no quicker than anyone outside. I think we will never get there. It is getting dark now and Papa is talking to Maman about the needle that shows the petrol. Everybody on the road seems quieter in the night, or maybe I have just got used to the sound of boots and belongings dragging, the sighs of those walking. You can't see them clearly anymore but you know they are all out there, like a sea of ghouls walking alongside our car.

If I really try to listen I can make out the artillery fire in the distance, a sort of echo. Papa told me to stop talking about it. I have slept a little but my legs are so cramped now and stupid Elèonore has stretched right out so that she has practically shoved Dimitri into me. Luc woke up a while ago, his blond hair all sticking up so I laughed at him, but then he started to cry so Maman had to shush him and ended up telling us all a story that we used to love to listen to about a merman and his adventures in an underwater kingdom. But she started crying in the middle of it and Papa stopped the car and they hugged. She sniffed and apologized and said she was being silly, but the whole thing made me angry and I wanted to kick the stupid car and run outside and go home back to Paris.

It is past dawn now and Papa says we are going to stop soon and eat a sort of dinner and look for somewhere to sleep. I'm not sure you can call it dinner if you've missed all the meals before it but I am not about to point that fact out to Papa.

People outside are squinting up into the sky. I can't see anything they're looking for, perhaps some swallows someway off in the distance, but that's all. No, wait. We have been transported into a moving picture. There is an enormous plane in the distance. Its lights are bright, two big circles of light. We are saved! It's going to bomb the enemy! It's going to bomb the stupid Hun!

But it's coming this way. I make a noise and Papa looks up and notices it too and he shouts and brakes and we all lurch forward. It swoops right down low and passes our car but up ahead we see the people scattering in its path and it is firing at them, firing on the people who are walking.

I can't believe it: it can't be happening. It is firing actual bullets and people haven't time to take cover. They are carrying bags and children and there was no warning. I see the boy with the neat hair standing right in the middle of the road looking straight at the plane; he is frozen, mouth open, as others rush around him, his younger brother isn't there. I lose sight of him as people rush past, and the lights of the plane pass over. I can't see him standing there anymore, I don't know where he's gone.

Papa tells us not to look and he drives the car right off the road and stops by a tree. He tells Maman to stay with us and runs off to help the people who were shot at. I can hear him taking control, like when he ran into the middle of our hockey game once when a boy at school got hit in the middle of his face with a stick and everyone was screaming at all the blood. Maman repeats that we keep our heads down so we all lean completely over ourselves, not wanting to look, and praying, praying, praying that the airplane doesn't come back.

Papa comes back and drives us back up onto the road. He steers us through the spot where the people were shot at. There are still things on the road and I moan when the wheels run over a doll, a book, a shoe. I see the face of that boy even though my eyes are closed now. I wonder if he found cover.

I don't think he did.

ISABELLE

My thighs protest as I climb, the muscles in my legs not used to walking this far. Keeping my head down I push on into the wind. I feel my ankle almost turn, the shoes I am wearing narrow and slippery on this surface. All around me the weather roars and I feel tinier the further I clamber. Behind me is the village, the shop and the world we live in, impossibly small from this distance.

Standing at the top of the ridge I feel my lungs empty, my breath snatched away by the wind, which picks up my hair, whips it across my face, strands cutting across my view as I steady myself, lean into it. The thrill of the air fills my head and I feel everything else pushed out: all my worries for Paul, my sadness for our parents waiting, Maman's nervous worrying leaking into every room.

Something nudges against the noise: Sebastian's face, his laughter, his hand hesitating for a second before taking mine, and then my head is full again, of him. I turn in the direction of Limoges, look out across the fields. The tram lines below me twist out of sight, a row of trees weighed down with leaves blocking my view, a fence, another field, green, but I still know it is snaking its way there.

I couldn't believe my own boldness, the suggestion to meet and the incredible moment when I crossed the street and realized that he was waiting for me. I felt heady and reckless walking along the street with him. We went to a café, shared a chocolate éclair, the price now extortionate but entirely worth it. I told him more about the village, my childhood, giggled at a memory I hadn't thought of for years: Paul and I building a fort in the garden, pretending the chickens were on sentry duty. I stopped then to watch him, his eyes sparkling as he laughed. I'd wanted to reach across and put my fingers through his hair, felt myself blush with the thought. Something shifted then, as if he had seen inside my head at that moment. The room seemed too small for the feelings I was having. He asked for the bill, paid in silence, looking at me quickly, a hand on the small of my back as we left.

We walked back to the tram in a sort of wordless bliss, the memory of his touch leaving me with nothing to say. He bought me a bag of *marron glacés* which I ate on the tram home, furtively, filling myself up with their syrupy loveliness. Scrunching the bag into my pocket I left the tram, feeling my stomach warm with the sugar, couldn't eat Maman's dinner. She protested – the veal was expensive, such a waste. Papa had looked at me, like he'd known. I'd smiled at him across the table, dabbed at my mouth with my napkin as if I still had sugar sticking to my lips, as if my new secret would spill out onto the dinner table.

I couldn't tell them, they would only worry. Papa seems to have more lines on his face since Paul left, spends more time behind closed doors. Up here I can think again, recall his expression, feel the same calm that seems to descend when I am with him. The wind whistles around me, blowing my whole body back so that I take a step to balance, laugh into the emptiness, my whole body light enough to lift right off the ground.

PAUL

Dear Isabelle,

You do write good, long letters. Two arrived on the same day a while back and one a week or so later that nearly made me cry. Will you make this letter sound a bit better when you read it to Maman? I don't have a way with words and I know you will add what I want to it. I can picture you all now crowded into the kitchen, Father with one eye on the newspaper, one giant hand holding a drink, Maman stirring something on the stove as she asks you questions about your day. You flatly refusing to answer them sensibly, and making Father look up from his paper and do that enormous rumbling laugh, like the tram has come into the village early.

I know you want a better picture of things but I can't talk about details really, and you mustn't worry if you haven't heard from me – I seem to write these things to myself. All I can say is the last few weeks have been a whirlwind of new experiences. I continue to learn things all the time, it is physical and you know I am always happier when I am outside. I was never any good in the fusty classrooms at home. We march and we clean and we eat and talk. I'm glad to have some of the other men from the village with me; we play marjolet and I am getting much better at lying. You laugh but it's true. Looking back it is clear you had some kind of supernatural power and all those wins were therefore completely unjust. You tricked me, quite literally, and on return I shall prove it by roundly beating you.

Now, on a serious note, you cannot call Claudette a startled duck – that is my future fiancée you are mocking and I won't have it... Oh, I can't be serious with you and you're not ever here to laugh with, and I know half these letters don't arrive anyway.

At the moment, in truth, I don't think of any girls or marriage or love, all I want to be is a soldier. I want to be here in this place, preparing. I want to fight for France and do something with my life. This feels big, bigger than anything I ever thought I would be involved in. I stood in the fields in the early dawn on that last day in the village, saw the long strips of soil churned up ready for planting stretching out before me, the low mist hanging over the woods in the distance and I felt good, good to be fighting for our country. I feel France is in my blood and under my nails.

That sounded rather romantic, didn't it? Maybe you can make a poet of me yet.

Shake Father's hand for me, sister, kiss Maman and take care of yourself.

Until I return,

Paul

ADELINE

1952, St Cecilia Nunnery, south-west France

Sister Constance nods her head at me as I sit on the bench by the old well. It is in a quiet corner of the garden, its moss-covered walls dark with age, insects climbing hopefully over the surface. I lift a hand to acknowledge her. She is walking with Sister Marguerite who looks at me shyly, her mouth moving quickly, Sister Constance placing a hand on her arm. She stops talking.

Marguerite has pleaded with me to join them for a daily service. I know that I cannot. She says that others still do not think I should stay any more, insistent that I should be made to leave if I don't start attending services. She walks over to me now. Her face kind as she sits side by side.

'Sister Constance has told me we might have a few more weeks,' she says, her voice hopeful. She cocks her head towards me. 'I love this corner of the garden,' she breathes, leaning down to pluck a long piece of grass from the ground.

She runs it through her fingers. 'Sister Bernadette needs more help in the garden – perhaps we could work there tomorrow?'

She doesn't wait for an answer, tips her head back and closes her eyes. A couple of strands of hair have broken free of her veil, are golden in the light.

A fly lands on my lips; I wave a hand at it, a quick panicked gesture. I raise both my hands, wipe quickly at my mouth again. Golden hair. Sister Marguerite places a hand on my back in the present but I return: the smell of the earth is in my nostrils, the darkness, the insects.

The peas dangle above me but my eyes can't make them out in the inky night sky. The sounds of men roll out: voices, bicycle wheels bouncing over cobbles, a bark of laughter. They're replaced by the chatter of insects, untouched by the day, that make their way over the landscape. The men may return.

Flies land on my nose, eyelids. I blink, spit at them, not daring to move from the bed I have made. Beneath the damp soil my leg is numb, the throbbing pain dulled, the chill sweeping through my whole body. I tense, waiting for the shouts to start again but there is nothing now.

I am frozen in the silent hours until I am nudged awake, alert, by the lowing of cows in the fields next door, joined by others, so many, restless, tramping, unmilked, straining in the black. Their voices melt together like a terrible choir. They surround me, frustrated, persistent and they stay that way forever. I am stuck in the shadows, unable to escape as they all moan for help.

PART II

TRISTAN

The trip from Paris might never have happened – almost like a horrible nightmare that you wake from and then forget. As if Maman has given us warm milk and a piece of chocolate and sung us back to sleep. Sometimes in the day, though, I am caught out. I think about a broken doll on the road and remember the noise and the feeling of our tyres slowly bumping, bump, bump.

We're staying in a farmhouse now, just outside a village, and we have lots to do and see so I do often forget. It is only in my sleep that I have to face a blurred witch through a window, a wrinkled old woman who tries to claw at me. Her fingers look like Grand-mère's but the nails are dirty. I always wake up then and lie still as a statue, trying to remind myself she never gets through the glass.

Our motorcar broke down south of Paris and Maman cried. We waited in the longest line of people I had ever seen for a train to take us. When we got on we had to have all our belongings piled high on our laps. We couldn't fit it all on and some things were left in the trunk and Papa sold one man his jacket for food for the journey. Maman cried again.

It was quite fun on the train as there were a few other children and Dimitri and I managed to make a friend called Grieg. He also lives in Paris, not near us but in a district miles north, so we didn't know his school, and he was an only child which I think is probably dull, although it might be nice to have the first choice of everything.

We stopped for a while as they were fixing the tracks or the signalling; I was only half listening when the conductor told Father that the train behind us had been 'strafed' and Papa nodded solemnly at the news and I guessed this was not good and hoped it wouldn't mean more delays.

We slept all curled up, leaning over bags and boxes. Elèonore was being a bit weepy and so had to sit next to Maman for the whole journey, which didn't seem like the best plan as they often set each other off. Dimitri and I managed to build a sort of den out of a bag of clothes and a thick, knitted jumper which made for quite a good pillow. The train was so busy and more people arrived at every stop. One man stood in the aisle for the entire journey as his pregnant wife tried to sleep in a seat next door. He apologized to people who wanted to get past him, and had to pick up an old suitcase and move it every time they moved through. He was standing when I was awake and eating a biscuit, and then I slept. When I woke up it was dark outside and I could see the man's outline still in the aisle. It must have been the middle of the night. He was still standing in the morning. He'd stopped saying sorry to people who wanted to get past.

We're staying with a couple who know Papa; Monsieur Villiers was at university at the same time as him and is now the mayor of a town near here called Limoges. He has a wife who was quite friendly when we first arrived but has since been rushing around like a whirlwind, and can get angry if you slow her up or get in her way. She is a different sort of woman from Maman – her hands are red raw and her nails are splitting. I also saw her chopping logs outside with an axe that was practically as tall as me. Monsieur Villiers is as wide as she is with a stomach that spills over his trousers. He has lots of dots of hair on his chin, not like Papa's moustache which is always so neat.

We are staying here until Papa has worked out what to do. I would happily never travel again. On our first night here I realized that we hadn't slept in beds for a week. It isn't the same as home though, as I have to share the bed with Luc and Dimitri. It's quite a squeeze but better than the train or car. It felt so good to smell the fresh sheets and stretch right out so that, even when I was pointing my toes right down, I was still ages away from the foot of the bed. Dimitri got the bolster and put that underneath our pillows so we had extra padding. Luxury.

After breakfast, Madame Villiers asks her husband to get the coal in from the shed. He tells her he doesn't like being ordered about and slams the door as he leaves. He returns (with the coal) and she says something about his boots. I think they must have been muddy, and he stamps all through the hallway. Maman and Papa never shout like this and we are seeing everything.

Madame Villiers marches out of the kitchen, waving the frying pan around her head, and threatens to brain him. He starts shaking a fist at her and uses language that makes Maman shuffle us outside with her hands over our ears. It's truly dramatic and I can still hear them going at each other from our room upstairs. We have to sit quietly on the bed as the voices bubble below. Maman is sitting with her hands in her lap, every now and again twisting her handkerchief and saying, 'Oh dear, oh dear.' Elèonore copies her, sitting in shocked silence, while Dimitri and I struggle to hide our giggles. Luc just keeps looking out of the window at the sunshine.

Once the voices stop (did she brain him? – it seems quiet) we are told to put our coats on and be ready by the front door.

'We'll go on a walk,' says Maman, clapping her hands and standing up.

Madame Villiers appears in our bedroom doorway, red in the face and still looking thunderous.

We race right past her, no one daring to raise their eyes to meet hers.

'That bloody man,' I hear her say to Maman, who mumbles something about a glove in reply.

Maman's coat is barely on as she walks down the stairs, through the front door and down the garden path.

We all follow her in a line. She goes down one road and then looks left and right when the road stops, uncertain as to where to go next. I think it's unusual, Maman in charge of us all like this. Normally we have Clarisse or a nanny. Madame Masson had been the latest in a long line of nannies, she smelled of peppermint and used to talk about her only son who had died in the last war from a disease – something called gangrene, I think, which Dimitri told me was when your limbs fall off. It sounds disgusting.

No one is really in the mood and it starts to rain a little so now we are all just hoping Maman might let us go back and sit by the fire and play with some toys. Elèonore found an old set of dominoes in the cupboard in her room and we played with them this morning, making a line of them run right under the bed and out the other side. Dimitri starts kicking at the pebbles in the road and Luc starts saying that he's getting wet and even Elèonore is looking put out, although she would rather die than complain to Maman. Luc tugs at Maman and she takes his hands and rubs them and starts to sing him a little song about a bird in a garden but Luc shakes her off before she gets to the chorus and runs on ahead. Maman comes to a stop and announces we have walked far enough and we all just turn and walk back again, towards the house.

We don't know what's going to happen. Maman doesn't know any of the answers to the questions about Paris or when we are going back or if we're staying here or going to go and live by the sea. She has an Aunt Augusta who lives there but I'm not too bothered whether we do go there, as although the sea is lovely Aunt Augusta is less so. She makes us take baths every day. She says children are always dirty. Once she made Dimitri strip down and wash his entire body from top to toe at the outside tap when he came in from a walk, and it was October.

I don't dare ask Papa who has been in and out of the house every day. He keeps talking about his offices and whether they should all relocate, which means move I think, and I'm not absolutely certain what Papa does but I know he had lots of people working for him in Paris in banks so I suppose he is trying to find out the news from there. Everything is up in the air, and with the arguments between Madame and Monsieur Villiers added to that, we don't know whether we're coming or going.

I'm starting to think I wouldn't mind going back to school.

PAUL

Dear Isabelle,

I can't say a lot about our plans but I wanted to write this evening. I am not sure how tomorrow will play out and I wanted you to be able to read these words and know that I am ready for it. We are all willing to stand side by side and defend our beautiful country. Whatever happens, I chose to be here in this moment and I am proud of that choice, of the men who stand with me. Please know that, and please explain that to Maman if you have to.

As I write, the moon has emerged in the failing light, a thin crescent, and I wonder if you too have seen it in the village tonight. I wonder whether we are both looking at it at the exact same moment. Take care of our parents and know that I love you all. I don't say it enough but I am saying it now,

Paul

ADELINE

1952, St Cecilia nunnery, south-west France

Sister Constance approaches me as I work on the stone bench outside the door to the nunnery. Tucked around the corner, set back into an enclave, it must seem perfect for her purpose. The sun is directly overhead, and her body forms a temporary shade as she greets me.

Nodding her head at the space on the bench next to me, I shuffle up in a gesture of welcome. As she moves towards it, I squint at the burst of sunlight from where she had stood.

She sits slowly, one hand on her lower back. I work the needle through the tapestry, a shock of yellow thread.

'No doubt Sister Marguerite has told you a little of my plans,' she states.

I lift my head and nod an acknowledgement, not wanting the younger nun to be reproached if I lied.

At this movement Sister Constance sighs and looks across the lawn, no doubt noting the uneven tufts of grass, the dozy sheep grazing in the corner beyond. She places one hand over the other, the sleeves of her habit showing off thin wrists. Her skin seems greyish-blue in the bright light.

'There are places where I believe you might be better suited, somewhere in Toulouse that…' A pause as she worries at the bare skin of her ring finger. 'It has been eight years,' she says, perhaps attempting an explanation.

I move the needle through the holes.

'Some of the community feel that a change of scenery would perhaps suit someone in your condition.'

The needle slips and I feel a sharp pain as a bubble of blood appears on my finger. Lifting it quickly to my mouth I suck at it, the metallic taste making my stomach leap and then settle. I don't want the blood on my clothes or on the scene I am creating.

'Your refusal to attend any of our services, to even enter the chapel… well, that is…' She stops herself and stands.

She hovers there, once more looking to the tree in the corner, sweeping her eyes across the grounds and then down at me. When I look up at her she has cocked her head to one side, lines deep between her eyebrows.

'I will talk to the doctor,' she says, one hand moving to touch the chain of the crucifix around her neck.

I nod once more at her as she walks back around the corner, back into the nunnery, her footsteps on the stone there and then no more, as the heavy wooden door closes behind her.

Sister Marguerite ushers the doctor into my cell and pulls up the chair by the side of my bed. I am waiting, propped up on two thin pillows, sitting awkwardly on top of the bedclothes. I smooth my skirt down as he comes in and realize I am nervous... hopeful?

He smiles at me, his eyes crinkling to nothing, and thanks Sister Marguerite.

She leaves the room, taking one last glance back at us before she shuts the door.

The doctor gestures to the chair and sits expectantly. He doesn't fill the silence, simply looks at me. I shift a little under his gaze, my hair brushing the back of the headboard as I turn away from him.

He goes to open his case, the ageing leather testament to his long career, and then pauses. 'Today you look a little different,' he announces.

I feel my eyebrows meet, lick my lips.

He shrugs and turns to reach into his case, pulling out a familiar wooden stick and his miniature torch. 'Well, madame, let's check your throat and we'll do some of the exercises we practised the other day.' He leans over me as I dutifully open my mouth. 'OK, say ahhh,' he says automatically, then blushes, the wooden stick still pressing down on my tongue, 'I'm... well, yes, say, I'll...'

I continue to look at him, my mouth still hanging open as he stutters. He returns to peering into my throat, squinting and umming as if my problems might be quickly diagnosed, treated and cured. He finishes, throws the wooden stick into the wastepaper basket and returns to sit on the chair by my bed.

'Right then, if you remember, as we practised,' he says, gesturing to his own mouth. 'O,' he enunciates, making an exaggerated shape of an 'O' with his mouth that makes him look not unlike a small child sucking on a straw. 'A,' he continues, his mouth moving into the exaggerated smile of a circus clown. All his teeth are shown in the process, a neat little row, slightly yellowing, but uniformly straight. 'I,' he demonstrates, nodding at me eagerly as I attempt to mimic the movements.

I feel mildly ridiculous, as I do every time this routine is performed. I continue though, always spurred on by the eager look in his eyes as he waits for a breakthrough.

He shows me how to say 'E.' I copy.

It seems so easy. Why won't the words come? Have I simply forgotten how to speak? I stop copying his movements. The doctor continues for another few tries, determined to make some kind of progress with his patient.

He gives up in the middle of an 'O', snaps his mouth shut. He presses his hair down. I know his first question: 'When did you last speak?' he asks, as he does in all our meetings. He waits an appropriate time and, when there is no response, asks another: 'Can you remember what event might have triggered your condition?'

I shake my head.

He sighs. More seconds tick by and he shifts in his chair. 'Have you ever been able to speak?' he asks.

I nod.

'Good, good,' he responds, almost as enthusiastically as he did the time before. 'Can you remember when this ceased?'

More seconds tick. I shake my head. Seeing a doctor's bag, a bottle, the odour of anaesthetic, I feel a sharp stinging in my legs and flinch as if it is not imagined.

The doctor doesn't appear to notice as he smoothes his hair once more and then places both hands in his lap. They are the hands of a professional: clean, fingernails clipped. He starts wiggling his fingers, perceptibly irritated by my focus on his appendages. 'We'll continue with some exercises. Now, slowly breathe in and breathe out...'

. . .

An hour later, I see the cloud of dust in the road in the distance as the doctor's motorcar speeds away. I'm sitting on a wooden bench in the garden stitching the hem of a brown skirt to give to Sister Marguerite – we are mending clothes donated to us for a family in the village.

Sister Marguerite and Sister Constance are talking a little way off across the lawn, looking across to me every now and again. The stone walls of the nunnery rise up behind them, throwing half the lawn into shadow. A statute of St Clare in a stone niche just behind them kneels as if she is pleading to be heard too. Sister Marguerite points a finger towards me as she talks. I know she is keen to ensure the doctor's visits continue in the hope that I will one day find my voice.

I think I want that too.

In the last few weeks I have started to feel alive again, aware of my surroundings, like putting on spectacles and having things come into focus. Whether I can talk or not I don't know, but my thoughts are less fuzzy now, more distinct, and I can stay in them longer. Perhaps it is talk of moving me on. Sister Constance's threat lingers in the corridors, on the faces of the nuns I have come to know. It is in Sister Marguerite's worried looks.

As I work I watch the hens claw at the soil, their great bottoms wobbling as they strut about the little square of ground allotted to them. Behind the wire that has been have put up to keep out the foxes is their entire world, and eight of them are happily pecking at the ground, scraping their feet along the earth, delving and scratching about the place, exuding a contented calm.

We kept chickens.

I was amused by their strange little habits, touched by their incessant babble of communication. One hen used to follow me right into the house, clucking expectantly as if she was continuing a conversation I had begun. At the end of the day Paul would often be sent out to herd them back into the little wooden coop we had at the bottom of the garden. Swearing and sweating he would chase them, back bent, arms waving at his sides, his large hands snatching at the air, desperately homing in on them as they raced off every which way. I would stand at the kitchen sink, peeling vegetables or idly stirring whatever was bubbling on the stove, and laugh at his efforts. He would return with straw in his hair and mud on his shoes to sit and talk to me in the kitchen as the sun set over the fields beyond. It would be just us, the waning light, the easy talk that happens between families, and the sure knowledge that this would all happen again tomorrow.

A new memory, drawn to that moment by the still air in the garden. I'm not sure, but it stays, I can see it.

I am in our garden. I am crouching down, alert, my skirts hitched up, eyes watching her every move. She is cornered. I can feel the sweat collecting on my hairline and the sun beating down on my back as I remain absolutely focused. She is trapped. In a breath it all happens: her wings flutter, she sees a gap and runs towards it, head jerking forwards, backwards, feathers bending a little in the breeze, her feet raised high with every step. I gasp and plunge and grab at her but she is too fast.

I swing about again, feeling like a gladiator in an arena. I don't have time for these games, but this chicken will not defeat me. Back bent over once more, I slowly advance, holding her eye contact, willing her to stay still. It is just at the moment when I am to pounce that I hear a shout of laughter – the chicken races past me, I dive, arms out-stretched, I hit the ground and Isabelle is running over to help me.

She pulls me to my feet. 'Maman, what are you doing?' she asks.

She sees me glaring at the hen, dusting my skirts down.

'She,' I say, pointing to the offender, who is now strutting backwards and forwards in my herb garden, victorious, 'will not be caught.'

Isabelle looks me up and down, at the marks on my clothes and the dusty scuffs on my face, and grins. 'I'll help.'

'She will be going in the pot if she continues to evade me,' I warn.

'Maman.'

Isabelle joins me, we look at each other. I nod. We rush. The chicken is confused, unsure where her best exit lies. She is being backed into a corner, noisily protesting as she steps into the shadow of the wooden fence. Her eyes dart left and right as we keep coming at her. Isabelle is breathing heavily, enjoying the game. The chicken decides to make a last bid for freedom and scrabbles between us both. I move swiftly, feel her bony body in my hands as I grab her running between my legs.

Seizing her firmly on both sides, hands clamped down on her wings so she cannot flap and free herself, I hold her at arm's length and carry her over to the coop.

Isabelle throws herself into the little wrought-iron chair with its rusting arms and delicate patterns, resting in the shade of the wisteria that has grown out of control, her blonde hair shining in the sunlight. I shove the chicken back into the coop, see the grateful flap as I release her wings and slide the door across quickly, shutting her in with the rest. She turns, eyes me, resenting her loss of freedom and the chance to tear up my garden, feast on the plants, and then with a blink starts to scratch at the soil beneath her, all forgotten.

Turning to the table I take in Isabelle. We meet in that moment, and I feel a smile spread across my face.

Our garden, the scene of so many of the memories. I snatch at them, want more. My finger plucks at the skirt I am stitching, tracing a line on the material, but the present dissolves as more faces crowd onto the wooden bench with me. My family, fresh, tanned: Vicente with his rumbling laugh and large hands, Paul nudging me in the ribs, teasingly. And she is here, as if she really was at the table nearby.

Isabelle traces a line on the garden table, expression peaceful, enjoying the warm wash of sunshine that is trapped in our little courtyard. I go to hang the clothes out, humming off-key, relishing the smell of the garden: rosemary and clean laundry. She gets up to return to the shop, waving at me to stay and enjoy the sunshine a while longer. I thank her and watch her return inside.

She is replaced by another at the table. An argument returns.

Vicente is sitting in the same seat, his expression furious, his eyes on me as I sit opposite him, my mouth half-open. I suggested Monsieur Coudran as a possible husband for Isabelle, a recently widowed farmer with at least fifty acres and a big farmhouse in need of a woman's touch.

He didn't let me finish the sentence. 'You would marry her off to that old man, who has barely any of his own teeth left?'

'And how do you expect her to live? What are we going to be leaving her?'

Vicente is silent. I see my chance.

'It is true that Monsieur Coudran is a little older than she is...'

At this Vicente snorts.

'But he has the farm and...'

'Do you remember when Renard had to sell his land? Monsieur Coudran only offered him a third of its real worth and the poor man

accepted. Broke him. No, no, Isabelle won't be offered up to him as a second wife.'

In a quiet voice I persist: 'Who is she to marry, then?'

'There is time enough to think of that,' he says, ending our conversation.

As the daughter of a shopkeeper, we can't hope for a particularly advantageous marriage. Vicente doesn't seem able to grasp this fact. I know he wants to keep her close for as long as he can; ensure that easy smile never leaves his sight, keep hold of one child. A large part of me wants that too, but she can't stay with us for ever, she deserves something more. And yet there seems to be no one suitable in the village – or no one up to Vicente's exacting standards – and with so many men gone, the whole village seems to be a gaggle of women, no husbands in sight.

I bite down my reply, reaching for the glass of water in front of me.

Vicente is looking out at the fields beyond, mist stretched out like a wispy hand on a lilac horizon, a lone bird of prey hovers nearby, a sudden dive as it sees something in the long grass. His face has closed off to me, the knowing sparkle in his eyes dimmed. There will be no point continuing to nudge him. His enormous hands rest on his thighs, like he is posing for a portrait; traces of mud seem worn into the knuckles, testament to helping with the harvest. We will stay in this village until those hands became lined and cracked.

Can he really expect her to stay here, too?

I simmer, one finger sliding across the top of the glass. Beads of water cling to the outside. Staring at them, I take another sip. If only we could find her someone. She is blossoming before us, walking differently, straighter, wearing clothes in new styles, her hair loose, next to me in my aprons and wooden shoes she seems from another place entirely. I worry for her working in the town, the action and temptations of her new life.

'Limoges,' she had scoffed. 'Hardly.' This from a girl who was so

excited by the opening of the tram stop that she waited three hours to see the first carriage go by, pointing to the trail of tracks leading out of the village, out into the world.

Where would she end up if she could?

I want Vicente to be right: perhaps she will be able to attract a man with exciting prospects – a wealthy landowner who had a good eye for beautiful things.

I am still in the courtyard but this is another scene, a different day; the time when things all shifted for us.

I am watering the plants, watching the water trickle into the soil, form a pool on the surface, spray the leaves with fine droplets. The clouds sit fat and low in a greying sky but rain hasn't fallen in days. I shiver and wrap my cardigan around me with one arm.

Vicente stands inside looking out at me over the top half of the stable door. I am not sure how long he has been standing there. His face is grim, his normally ruddy skin washed out. As our eyes meet my mouth goes dry. He doesn't need to say it, I see it in his hand.

A square of paper.

He announces it anyway, holding the telegram up. 'Something's arrived.'

I have the same pit of dread in my stomach sitting in the sunshine on this bench, the nuns quietly working around me, as if I am back there living it all over again.

But now I also know what came after.

The hope drains away, my voice is lost to my past and no amount of doctor's prodding will be able to find it for me.

TRISTAN

I arrive at the house to find Maman and Papa talking in the hall; their bodies form a semi-circle as they mutter to each other in low voices. 'No, no chance at all, all five of them, apparently.' Maman jumps as I appear and looks at me as if I'm no more important than the coat rack I'm standing next to. Her fingers are playing with the cross she wears around her neck.

She comes forward and greets me in a loud voice, patting the top of my head. I run through to the kitchen to see if Madame Villiers has cooked anything, looking back at them briefly before I turn the corner. They are both staring at me, still. They look so serious. I skid to a halt, the rubber soles of my shoes squeaking as I stop.

Have they been talking about me? Have I done something wrong? I rack my brains to think of something I might have done that could get me into trouble. Was it from a couple of days ago when I pinched Elèonore for taking the last of the *clafoutis*? She squealed and ran off at the time but, knowing her, she probably ran weeping to Maman with more stories of how I'd done her harm.

I forget I'm hungry at all when Maman says, 'Darling, your father wants to see you.'

I gulp.

Papa calls me into the study and sits me down in the leather chair Monsieur Villiers told us was for guests, so I know he wants to talk to me about something important. My hands get hot at the thought of all the things I might have done wrong and I note a cane right up on the top shelf. A plan forms. I will open my eyes wide and say that I would never do anything of the sort. I am going to remain brave as last time I cried and it only made him angrier.

But Papa isn't looking angry and I am not absolutely sure I have done anything wrong. He is talking to me in a different sort of voice, the sort of voice Maman sometimes uses when she's trying to make us go to sleep or make us swallow medicine. Normally, when he's angry his voice gets low; Elèonore always claims this is enough to make her start weeping. He is taking his time getting to the point. I remain silent, eyes on him, everything else forgotten.

He smoothes down his thin moustache with a finger. 'Tristan, do you believe in heaven?'

I don't understand.

'Of course,' I answer because it is true – of course I believe in heaven. It is where I will go if I am good and say my prayers every night and clean my teeth and look after my brothers and sister. I feel a little bit guilty about the last one and vow to be a little nicer to Elèonore; it would be most annoying not to get into heaven just because I have been horrid to her in the past.

'I am glad,' Papa replies. 'And do you know when you go to heaven?'

I nod, confident he doesn't want to hear about cleaning my teeth and saying my prayers. 'When you die.'

'Exactly, when you die,' he agrees. 'Now, Tristan,' he says, leaning forward a little to look me in the eye. 'I'm afraid that I have some bad news.' His eyes don't leave my face as he takes a deep breath, mouth half-open. 'Clarisse has been ill and died last week.'

'Clarisse,' I repeat.

'I'm afraid so.'

Clarisse is dead.

I don't know anyone who has died. Marcus at school told me he saw a dead man, a man in the park near where he lived who died on a bench and had been there for hours. He said that he had his eyes open but they weren't looking anywhere and his tongue was poking out and he'd been puffy and pale. His nanny got the police but when the police went to move the man from the bench they couldn't make him go flat on the trolley so they had to cover him with a sheet and wait for the ambulance to drive into the park.

Clarisse is dead.

I look at Papa, who is waiting for me to say something.

'So then she has gone to heaven,' I say slowly.

'Yes, yes, that is where she has gone.'

I can't imagine Clarisse in heaven, although I imagine she would be pleased as it is probably very, very clean and she always hated cleaning. She used to moan at me when I left mess in our playroom and was always going on about how I trailed mess around me like some kind of wild animal. I would roar at her and scamper off which made her laugh the first time but hadn't worked the rest. Clarisse was always full of energy; she didn't seem the sort that would get ill and die.

I picture her now at the oven in the kitchen in Paris, red-cheeked and sweating a little from the heat of the food. We crowd around her as she spoons out helpings for all of us. 'Sit at the table,' she shoos, wiping her hands on her apron and pointing to the places all laid out.

Maman is standing in the corner, a list of instructions for tomorrow in her gloved hands. 'Thank you, Clarisse.'

'Thank you, Madame Soules.' She ruffles my hair as I reach for the gravy boat.

She's not in the kitchen anymore, she's in heaven. I suppose it's good to think of her somewhere, but it seems strange that we'll never see her again, that she is now somewhere else, a place we can't reach because you can't visit heaven. That thought makes me feel funny; I have a bit of a lump in my throat. I swallow but it won't go. I think of Marcus's dead man again and worry that Clarisse might have died with her tongue poking out, all puffed up and pale with her eyes wide open. I blink a couple of times but the image is still there. I hope Papa will tell me to go now as I suddenly feel afraid that I might cry and I don't want to show him that I am a drip.

'Elèonore might be a bit upset by the news so I want you to be extra nice to her over the next few days as she was close to Clarisse. Can you do that for me, Tristan?'

I come out of my daze and then blush. Had Papa read my thoughts earlier? I nod and promise that of course I will look after my sister and then I leave and go upstairs to the playroom wiping the tears from my eyes with my hand. Clarisse is in heaven after all, so there is no real need to be upset.

Elèonore clearly does not agree and spends the afternoon wailing on her bed. I bring her up a cocoa that Maman has made but when I go back later to see her she hasn't touched it and I have to bite my tongue just in time because I can't tell her off about that. It does seem a waste though, particularly as

I know that is the last of the cocoa and we aren't allowed another lot until next week.

Clarisse liked cocoa, she used to drink it out of a mug with a rabbit on the outside. I think of Clarisse in heaven with lots of cocoa and her feet up. That cheers me up and I tell Elèonore of my thought. She smiles a little and reaches up to hug me. We don't talk about Clarisse after that but now, whenever I think of her, I think of her in heaven just like that.

ISABELLE

Darling Paul,

The village has heard some terrible stories now. They arrive, refugees from the north and east. Some of them travelling miles, often on foot. Homes are left for looters, belonging are lost, sold or stolen.

A woman broke down in the shop. Surrounded by a circle of sympathetic shoppers she told us how she was forced to leave her village in the middle of the night. Her husband had urged her to go for days, as the Germans were moving in, but she remained resolute. Her mother was confined to a wheelchair and couldn't leave the house. They had no car, no way of moving her, no neighbours who could take her in. One night shells fell, rattling the windowpanes, and she left. In the madness and fear and noise and panic of others, they seized what they could and fled, leaving her mother behind.

She said her mother might starve to death, alone, wondering why she was abandoned by her daughter. Her letters go unanswered. She doesn't know if her mother has received them or even if her house is still standing.

Where are you, Paul? Maman misses you, everything she does is in honour of your return. Never has the shop floor been swept more fiercely, every speck of dirt whisked out of every corner, every can standing poker straight, labels all facing outward in a uniform line.

We got the telegram, know you are captured, but we have heard nothing from you for weeks now. Are you safe? Is there anything to be done? We don't say it aloud and I don't even think it but writing this now makes me frightened. Tell me I am being dramatic; tell me I am hopeless and of course you are all right. My brother who seems impossibly strong. I feel the French air throbbing with your life. Write to us.

I have started at the school now, adore seeing the children, their energy, their innocence. I want to be a good teacher, try to encourage them. Then on days off I sit in a café in Limoges, feel the sun on my face... can you imagine? While you are off in this war I am still eating pastries and reading books about nothing. This waiting for news though, so many of us just waiting, is so peculiar. I know I mustn't complain, I know so many others have been affected so terribly by this dreadful war but know that we love you and miss you and are always planning for your return.

Isabelle

SEBASTIAN

In the past week Father has refused to discuss the plans to open the new branch in Couzeix. He seems to be shrinking into himself, a ball of knotted worry. Jean-Paul has noticed and finds an excuse to visit the office almost every day. As he goes over the plans with me, his gravelly voice and occasional guffaws of laughter are the only thing that seem to be able to raise a shadow of a smile on my father's face.

This morning he is not yet downstairs and Maman and I sit in the strained quiet of the dining room, the tick of the carriage clock seeming to fill the space. She tries to talk but finds herself fading away as she catches sight of his chair and the head of the table, the indent in the cushion, the dark oak of the armrests. I pick up my bowl and drain the coffee, dabbing the side of my mouth with a napkin.

Excusing myself from the table to escape the depressing atmosphere, I take the stairs two at a time, one hand on the banisters, the other on my thigh, blocking out the dull pain in my joints with thoughts of what lies ahead. I feel the solid wood underneath my hand, its surface smooth, the smell of wax lingering in the air. My feet don't make a sound on the runner, its faded middle showing its age, the edges still a clash of reds and orange.

I pass the door to my parents' bedroom, wonder if my father is padding around inside. The thought doesn't stay. My mind is jumping ahead, knowing what lies in store for me. Unable to keep a smile forming on my lips – my mother's sad face already forgotten, any thoughts of Father dissolving into dust – I push open my door and an explosion of images of Isabelle overwhelm me. Today I will be seeing her. Today, today, today. I know I am young, and naïve, and in love, and all the other absurd phrases that are bandied around in songs and poems that mock a man in my position, but I can't help myself.

I disguise my feelings in front of her – I don't want to scare her and I know, with certainty, that I don't yet want to know if she feels the same. Because if she doesn't I don't want to face it. I want to enjoy these moments in the sun, bask in the impression that my feelings are reciprocated, that she lies on her bed in idle moments wondering where I am, what I'm doing. That somewhere, out there, she is thinking about me.

I have yet to tell my parents about her. At any other time Father would have noticed and wormed it out of me, but he is so distracted I could wander around the house with a bull-horn announcing my feelings for her and he would probably not look up from his cold *café au lait* and half-read newspaper. I know I should tell them, as it is not like me to keep these things a secret, and yet I feel the need to keep it to myself a little while longer.

Every girl I've ever known seems to move through this life with a chaperone in tow – a glimpse or smile scolded instantly by a disapproving look from the person trailing her. It is always just Isabelle, and that thought makes me grin again.

She assures me she doesn't need to tell her parents yet. They are worried about their son, have heard nothing for weeks, and she doesn't want to give them more to worry about. I don't press her, don't want to upset things. I know that there will be things about me to make them worry, things I can't change. I think fleetingly of my Father's face, know what he might say. I shake off the thought as I pick up my hat.

We don't plan to meet – it is always seemingly coincidental; no arrangements are made. But since that first meeting at the café all those months ago, and every time since, when I see her she mentions she will be in the book shop on rue Aristide Briand at two o'clock on Thursday or in the Parc Victor Thuillat around one o'clock on Monday. So I am drawn there and she is waiting. She looks up as I arrive, eyes widening a fraction, as if she doesn't really expect to see me. That look gives me such a jolt – an electric charge surging straight through my eyes to my heart, zap; she has me and I know it is improper, and I know it can't go on, but the weeks and months go by and we meet and we talk and then she says, 'I'll be at the Café Thérèse at three o'clock on Friday,' and I am incapable of staying away.

Today she will be at the library on rue Louis Longequeue and I will try to leave the office a little early for lunch as I must talk to her. I will try to muster the courage to move things along in the correct way; it isn't right to deceive others, or ourselves. Things must be out in the open. I am convincing myself of this as I walk down the street, umbrella up as it starts to rain in a rather half-hearted way, coating the pavement in a light sheen, little droplets clinging to my shoes and the bottom of my trousers. The weather has been as listless as Father's mood and the overcast skies seem to be storing up more rain to come later. The air is thick and stifling.

As I am shaking out my umbrella on the steps of the

library, a tall man with a pencil-thin moustache emerges. I nod at him, mouth twitching, amused by his facial hair, which doesn't fit his ample frame. He tuts at me, and I wonder if I have spoken my thoughts aloud.

I don't hear what he says the first time.

He mumbles at me as he adjusts his hat, looking me up and down slowly. He repeats his words to a besuited companion, as he too emerges from the library. 'Not fighting. Typical of *them*.'

I freeze, willing myself to be mistaken.

The other man, all bristles and gut, looks over at me, sneers as he turns up the collar of his coat.

I go to say something, to challenge the man, but I am hopelessly deflated. His words bite into me, make me want to explain to these people that I can't be a soldier, that I did try. *Their sons are probably away fighting,* I think, trying to reason with myself.

Them.

Had he really? Was it more than not fighting? Was Father right? Did people really see us in a different way?

'Sebastian… Sebastian?'

It is a moment before I turn, an expression on my face making the smile die on her lips.

'Is anything wrong?'

PAUL

Dear Isabelle,

Who knows which of these letters will reach you? You will all be worried, I know, so I write simply to reassure you, I am safe. I have been taken prisoner; we all have. It seems my war is over and I hope news of my capture has reached you all so that you are not left wondering. You must convince Maman that I am well – I know she will worry in that dreadful, quiet way of hers so you must promise. It happened so quickly I'm still not sure how it happened. It was with a whimper rather than a roar and for that I think we now feel ashamed. Lines of bewildered men marched all around me afterwards, flanked by cocky Germans, their rifles hanging across their backs, their broad smiles confident. They are crawling all over our country now and we are unable to stop them.

They say we will be released when this war is over and so we wait knowing that it can't be long: reports tell us that most of Europe has fallen with us. For now we are processed, held, divided into groups – the officers are sent to separate places.

It seems the lads I am with are all from quiet French villages like ours; most are outdoor lads like me, bored of concrete buildings and inaction. Confusion reigns and I almost wonder whether it happened quicker than the Germans expected it to. More arrive each day and there is talk that we will be put to work – some of the boys think we'll be in the factories or mines. I'll do whatever I'm told but I'll pray I can see some sky while I'm doing it.

I've stayed alongside Rémi who seems now like a younger brother: I feel hugely protective of him. He got hit in our attack, holding a bridge with some others, but doesn't tell me what happened to the rest. I haven't seen any of them. We try to find time to talk and get the news, but it is so hard to find out what is happening beyond wild rumour. His family's paper mill has closed down. He is determined to get it back up and running when this is all through.

Things are loud and confused. We slept on an athletics track those first few nights; I imagined getting up in the night, doing hurdles against the guards. We have been herded about like animals going to market and now we are being held in an old barracks. It is fine – I have my own bed and we are being fed. Some days are worse than others, I didn't know how an hour could drag before, how an afternoon could feel like a week, no purpose to anything. Enough of this though. The conditions are fine and the Germans are not mistreating us. The only thing you won't like is the news that my head has been shaved, all that floppy, sandy hair you said was my best feature: gone. But if that is the worst thing that befalls me I will take that.

Some talk about release as a real possibility so I pray I will return to you all soon. It all moved so quickly. And I thought we were ready.

God bless and love to our parents. I will write again hoping one will get through,

Paul

ADELINE

1952, St Cecilia nunnery, south-west France

Rain pounds against the windows. The water pours in rivulets down the glass and outside is a blur of greyish greens. The room is so dark it seems like there has been no new day. The rain has set off something outside, an unpredictable rattle of metal – something is loose and blowing carefree in the storm. The wind is making a low moan as it sweeps across the courtyard. There is so much energy and noise outside I wonder whether it will ever be calm again.

The sisters, seemingly oblivious, have continued their usual routine; in fact, Sister Bernadette has been loudly praising the Lord for the good weather because it helps the second love in her life: her courgette plants. Sister Marguerite's mood mirrors the weather today, sweeping into my room to bring me a tray of food. She barely stays a minute in the stool by the window before she is up, pacing. I follow her movements. She opens her mouth to say something, and then continues to pace to and fro. She is usually so light on her feet, an easy nature, a ready smile. Today I wish she was not in my room.

'Did I ever tell you about the day we found you?' she asks, abruptly turning to look at my face.

I slowly shake my head.

'The look in your eyes when Sister Bernadette brought you in… She had seen you in the village, wanted to help…' I try to remember my arrival here but my mind washes around, throwing up blurred images and scenes that seem to form one long day, nothing lighting on a moment.

'The others were fussing about your injuries,' she continues. 'The scrapes on your legs, down your sides. Your arm was a bloodied mess and you'd broken your wrist. I looked at your face for a flinch of pain, a response to the prodding, and there was none. You allowed them to take you in their arms, allowed them to disinfect the scratches, allowed them to push and pull you in each and every direction, and all the while you said nothing, and your eyes...' Sister Marguerite stops. 'You didn't care.' She is whispering now. 'I couldn't understand it – I wanted you to cry out, to whimper, to ask us whether you were going to get better. You nodded at their questions but gave them no answers. That was eight years ago today.'

This isn't an ordinary explanation of the day, I realize. This is the reason for her daily visits.

'I couldn't understand what could drive someone to give up all hope. I couldn't begin to fathom what you might have been through to look like that. For the first time in this nunnery it made me... it made me question whether there was a god.' She takes a step closer. 'To allow that much misery in one person.'

This pity, this open, unabashed pity for me, makes me start to shake. Why is she saying these things? She must stop.

'Sometimes you have that look again, I can't reach you, I can't...'

A scratchy sound, a gurgle rises up in my throat.

Sister Marguerite stops, strides over, puts both hands on my shoulders, forces me to look at her. 'Please.'

My eyes meet hers.

'Please... please, talk to me...'

I try. The gurgling sound again. I can't and before I can write her a note, scratch something as I sometimes do, broken sentences to reflect the gaps in my own mind I am pulled away.

It is *that* day – I know it is: I'm aware of the same strange pull on my insides, the feeling that I might expel the contents of my stomach if I stay too long in this memory. It is so clear, often repeated, when other things are barely there or stubbornly refuse to reveal themselves, when my own surname alludes me.

I am walking with Isabelle to the green. We pass Monsieur Lefevre – I remember I need to talk to him about ordering a joint of lamb. Not now. He is hurrying too, sweating as he looks around him, I don't stop. I see Madame Garande carrying bags of food, shouting after some local child for stepping on her skirt. She shakes it out, brushing at the mark. The child's hair is blonde, ringlets under a hat. Where is Vicente? I look for them and see my own confusion etched on the faces of others.

The number of soldiers is overwhelming, and my heart vibrates in my chest. The whole village is moving towards the green, clusters of children excited to be out in the sunshine. A couple of boys conjure up a yo-yo and take it in turns to practise tricks. Twins, faces covered in freckles brought on by the early summer's sunshine, long plaits down their backs; one of the girl's ribbons is loose. It trails onto her shoulder and the pale pink satin strip glimmers. They giggle together, swapping a note, a drawing of some sort.

They're oblivious to the men dressed in that dull grey uniform herding them efficiently to be registered. But a few of the boys are looking, unable to drag their eyes away from the sleek rifles slung casually over their shoulders, some with ribbons pinned to their top pockets. Soldiers are rare in the village and to see one so close up must be a treat for them.

The adults scowl, muttering in French about the Hun swine, some loud enough to tempt the soldiers to turn their heads and find the source. My clammy hands grip the bag I am holding, our papers inside. I will it all to be over quickly. I see Isabelle looking warily around her, attempting to smile at a couple of the boys in one of the classes she teaches. A wash of relief that we are together at least. One of the younger soldiers admires her, his gaze appraising. The sun beats down on her hatless head and her ringlets are a riot of yellows. She looks so slender and fragile in her short tea dress, as she clutches her bundle to her chest.

If I had stayed with them, refused to let go of Vicente's hand, would it have turned out differently?

He was there too, his solid mass, his low voice, his hand enormous as it enclosed mine. He turned. It was a profile I knew without needing to see it. He looked across at the mayor, seemed to relax, shoulders dropping a fraction, his jaw unclenching as he watched the men talking in a tight circle.

I didn't stay – my hand left his before I had stopped to think about it. I would have kept clinging to it if I had the moment again. He'd stepped back, was talking to Paul, gesturing across the green to something out of my eye line. There had been no words as we parted, a look back, another and he'd gone; they had both gone, and I could still feel the warmth from his hand, wanted to seize it back and make sure we never let go.

I study Sister Marguerite's face as she searches mine for clues: a moment of frustration glimpsed briefly, and then gone. The drab greys of the room, and Sister Marguerite's uniform of black and white, are a gloomy haze. The colour from that day, the village in full bloom in the heat of summer, her face and the faces of the children, are all blurring into nothing, fading into the recesses of my memory once more.

She pulls the stool over to the bed and picks up my left hand. She holds it to her lips and gives it a simple kiss, then bows her head so that she is almost doubled over my bedclothes. 'You must keep trying. Please. Try to talk. You must. They will send you away but I know you are in there. Please, have faith...'

We breathe in and out. The room grows even darker, the sky fat with clouds. I can do nothing but sit there. I cannot force the words out.

She leaves shortly after. Her tired footsteps fade on the stone flagstones and I feel a surge of guilt that I had a part in slowing them.

SEBASTIAN

We step into the library, the air filled with the smell of books and furniture polish. It tickles the back of my throat. There is a long table in the corner under high latticed windows, with reading lamps down the middle and empty, scuffed leather chairs around it.

Isabelle cocks her head towards it and moves through the turnstile, giving a small sideways look at the librarian behind the desk as she passes. I tip my hat and am rewarded with a pink close-lipped smile. I follow her across the room in silence feeling lighter already, the stillness of the place blocking out the noises and rush of the high street outside. I pull out a chair for Isabelle and settle opposite her. There is a lone, light cough and the sound of pages being turned, of delicate movements, quiet industry.

Isabelle removes her gloves, producing a book from her bag, some notes in untidy blue ink. I let my breath out slowly and ease back into the leather. She leans over her desk, her blonde hair falling over the book she is engrossed in.

My chin is resting in one hand, the other wavering over the page of the journal I had been reading. I can't look away. The light from the high, thin windows casts long beams onto the scratched wood of the desk, slicing across her, highlighting strips of skin of softest gold in the late afternoon light. I love the silent way in which we are working. She often comes here to plan her lessons, researching the books she is going to teach the children, recounting what she has learnt in whispered snatches, or during breaks on the bench in the alcove in the corridor outside.

I plan to tell my parents about us but weeks and months pass and I don't find the words, know that I need to somehow. This is wartime and we are Jewish. For now though I don't want it spelt out, I don't want father thinking of a dozen reasons why I should call it off. So there is next week. In this moment I am certain - I don't want anything to change. Someone sneezes and the noise brings me back and she looks up, catches my eye and gives me a slow smile.

Beyond her, the librarian moves past, pushing a wooden trolley in front of her, her pursed painted lips the only colour to her face, her thin frame obscured by piles of books in different colours, some with spines coming away, nondescript titles etched in gilt. I get up to search for a book, one hand massaging my leg as it sears with pain from resting so long in the same position. Isabelle doesn't look up and I move away, wanting something to lose myself in before I fall asleep reading about banking. I head to the Classics section and wander aimlessly down the aisle, skimming over the titles.

I can see the back of her head over the tops of the books on the middle shelf and feel my mouth lifting at the sight. Her shoulders are hunched, one hand resting on her cheek, her elbow on the desk. Her pale blue summer coat hangs from the back of her chair. I think back to how my life had been before Isabelle. My mind is filled with her and, despite everything happening in Limoges – father's worry, the mutterings dripping down from the occupied zone, life there so different to ours, everything scrutinized by Germans – there she is at the centre of my thoughts, vibrant and alive: she seems to personify hope, the future. Her light laughter, her kind exchanges with strangers, the way she can raise a smile from the surliest person – this energy that she exudes seems to block everything else out: all my worries, made worse when I see Father's greying hair, the slight stoop in his shoulders like the world is weighing on him and he is waiting for it all to collapse; Mother, her knitted brow, the new lines in her face as she looks across at Father, tries to intercept the paper, prepare him… all of it is forgotten in the moment when Isabelle rests a hand lightly on my arm.

Isabelle is living only a few kilometres away in Oradour, and yet it is another world, a world seemingly unaffected by the changes. She tells me there is rationing, refugees, farmers who have lost sons and whose elderly mothers are bringing in the crops, but she speaks more often of lazy days wandering through the meadows, the old guys playing *pétanque* by the champ de foire, the woman gossiping over the clothes lines, the oblivious carefree screams of children racing around the school playground. I want to be part of that world, I want to stroll through the streets, sit and smoke with Father outside a nice hotel, hear Mother's carefree laughter tripping over our conversation, have Isabelle by my side, her hand resting in mine.

My whole body aches for that moment, the impossible moment, when two worlds collide.

And suddenly she is in front of me, standing at the end of

the aisle, one hand loosely on her hip, her pleated cotton skirt thin in the light, the faint silhouette of her thighs through the material. Her face is quizzical, one eyebrow slightly lifted. She places a finger on a shelf, begins the pretence of searching the books as the librarian, her pale face all eyes, wheels past once more as if waiting to pounce. I turn a laugh into a light cough as Isabelle looks at the librarian and then up to the ceiling, feigning exasperation.

Trying to focus on the titles in front of me, I realize I am unable to make out the lettering: the authors' names a mix of consonants and vowels as I feel her presence, watchful, playful, as she moves slowly towards me, eyes still on the shelves, head held to the side so that she can read the spines more easily. A quick glance to me as she approaches and one side of her mouth lifts. She is now an arm's length away, so close I can make out the small, neat mole on the nape of her neck where she has swept her hair aside, the stiff white collar of her shirt in stark contrast to the peachy softness of her skin, the pale pink of her cheek. In the shafts of dusty half-light she looks like she has emerged from the pages of a romance novel. An arm's length and yet a world away . . . could I pull her towards me?

Catching me staring, she points a finger at the shelf and asks, 'Anything good?' in a half-whisper.

I shrug quickly, heat surging to the ends of my fingers, pulling out a book at random; it slips in my hands so I have to save it, then turn it the right way up.

She appears over my shoulder as I read the first page. Her breath is on my neck and her body is centimetres from mine. I freeze, muscles tense, not wanting this moment to end. She smells of soap and roses. My eyes remain still, the first line repeated again and again until I hear her say quietly, 'Sounds far too depressing.' And she has broken the spell, sidled away from me, still looking at the books in regimented lines. I breathe out in a rush, roll my eyes at myself and seize two more of the nearest books, hastening back to the table to trawl through them.

TRISTAN

The rough fabric of my grey shorts itches and Luc runs ahead of me as I stop to adjust them for the fourth time that morning. I call to him but he says he can't stop because he is being the wind. If Maman was here she'd tell me off for dawdling. She often joins us in the morning but today she is looking after Dimitri who has been in bed with the flu for forever, so it is just us and I am in charge because I am the oldest. I think that means I have to hold his hand when we cross roads and things but there is only one road between our new house and the school so I'm not sure it is entirely necessary here.

Luc's favourite part of the walk is around the next bend – a field on our left of brown cows, today all lying down in the shade of the trees. He tells me to hurry up. I think I'm still waiting for a cyclist to race around the bend, or hear the sound of crowds walking to work, or a lot of cars beeping as I cross the road, but there is nothing. The long grass on the side of the road is curling into itself it's so hot, and there is no breeze so the trees are all still.

It feels good to be out of the house. We lived at the Villiers' home forever but last month we moved into the nearby village, called Oradour. Our new house still smells like the cellar did in Paris. Apparently the couple who lived there won't be needing it for the time being; they have gone abroad somewhere as they don't like the 'political climate', which is different from not liking the weather (I knew that but still Elèonore had to point it out to me). Anyway, clearly no one had lived in it for a while as we had to take lots of sheets off the furniture and all the dust in the air made us cough and cough and blink it all out of our eyes. Maman set us all to work scrubbing every surface like Clarisse used to do. I see now why she used to complain about her back hurting as Dimitri and I were set to work cleaning the bathroom and after an hour or so of trying to get orangey streaks off the bath we had to sit down for a rest. It's like the workhouse. Maman says not to complain and that we're lucky we have a house at all but I think she is being silly because everyone has a house.

Father goes into Limoges a lot as he has banking business there and Maman says he is talking to Monsieur Villiers about new opportunities. Maman isn't alone though – a girl from the village has come to help her. She is called Claudette and she has two very big front teeth and sometimes when she speaks a little whistle comes out. She talks to Maman a lot which I think Maman likes as in Paris she had lots of ladies to talk to but here she is often by herself.

Luc is mooing at the cows now. I let out a great whoop and go chasing after him. Luc looks about, startled, but then joins in and we go racing down the street. I feel like I've been let out into the wild after years of being a pet. Maman would never have allowed us to walk to school in Paris – too many automobiles, too many dangers.

We get to the school gate and split up. Luc gives me a

wave. I hope he doesn't come up to me at break time again, as last time a couple of the other boys laughed.

We started the new term a few weeks ago. Elèonore's school is further down the high street, along from ours, but she likes to leave earlier than us to be on time. Papa announced we would all be spending the 'foreseeable future' at our schools and that we were to work hard until we could go back to Paris after the war. It seems to have gone on practically for ever already and Paris has become all faded in my head like that picture in the nursery where the colours went all pale.

School is nothing like my last school in Paris, which was built with heavy stone walls which made it cold in both the winter and the summer and had huge echoey rooms and stained-glass windows everywhere. This one is smaller and sits between the other shops and houses on the high street. It has flowers in little boxes on the windows and it has been whitewashed on the outside. Quite nice. For a school.

The teachers put football goal-posts up on a grassy bit at the back last week and the master in charge, who looks a bit like the Villiers' dog (a sort of flattish face and a look that says: 'My bite *will* hurt'), has organized shooting practice later today. I will probably make the team but first I have to get through a whole day of lessons.

It seems silly to be inside in a classroom learning algebra and reciting Latin. There is a war on. When a German soldier is running at you there's no point quoting Virgil at him, better to kick a football at his face. We sit in three rows of four desks in a room with wooden beams and a massive map of Europe on the walls. Monsieur Pincet, who teaches us Geography and Science, has drawn a line all through it in red pen, showing where the occupied zone is. You don't have to go very far north to get over the line. He got cross when Michel said it seemed a little strange – why would the Germans only want part of France?

Our form teacher is Mademoiselle Rochard and she isn't like any of the teachers in Paris. She looks so small and delicate seated behind the huge desk at the front. I didn't know teachers came like her at all: she's softly spoken and her hair smells lovely, like honey. I once asked her to check a piece of my work just so I could catch the smell again. She has the sweetest voice which rises above all of us when we all sing in the mornings under the photograph of the old man whose name begins with a P. I had to punch Dimitri on the arm last week when he teased me about her. He claimed I loved her but that is stupid. I don't love her, she is a grown-up. The punch left a good purpling bruise.

The good news is that Mademoiselle Rochard thinks I'm wonderful. She told me that I am very clever. This is not a view shared by my old teachers from Paris, where Monsieur Hébert was quick to get his cane and punish me for any small thing. He definitely didn't think I was '*très intelligent*'. My heart skips a beat at the thought that I will not be seeing him at all this year. No more Paris is quite sad, but no more Monsieur Hébert – my backside rejoices.

Being new is fun too. We get a lot of attention. We're the newest people to join the school and the only ones from Paris, and a lot of the other pupils love my stories about the Eiffel Tower and the busy honking of the Champs-Élysées. I am a glamorous city boy and I try to keep people happy, telling tales about Parisian life: women dressed in scarlet silk dresses and long, buttoned evening gloves, smoking cigarettes and drinking champagne; films; the newest automobiles I saw advertised; music I heard.

I am yet to decide on a best friend. They ask funny questions here – one boy asked me if everyone in Paris could see the Eiffel Tower from their house. Also some of the boys here have never been to the pictures, haven't even heard of some films and some of them don't have telephones in their houses! I have promised Michel to show him ours. He says he wouldn't know who to call on it.

The small hand on the clock hanging in the corridor shows that the first lesson starts any second. A couple of others arrive, puffing, behind me, and I am glad I'm not last. Unlike in Paris, I want to be there at the start of the lessons, I don't dawdle when break is over and I've stopped making up illnesses at home to get out of school. I've been doing very well in my classes and enjoy the feeling of being right for once, winning a lot of merits and praise – not just from Mademoiselle Rochard – and only sometimes wonder whether I should admit to covering some of the things at my school in Paris.

As I sling my satchel over the back of my chair, Michel nods a hello in my direction. The sun is pouring through the windows onto our desks and the butterfly wall display is as happy as I am. From the windows I can see the wide blue sky, dots of birds far, far away. The caretaker of the school is fixing a hole in one of the goal nets. The sunlight bounces off his bald head. I turn to point this out to Michel but Mademoiselle Rochard arrives and everyone scrapes their chairs back to stand up.

There are a few whispers as a small boy walks in nervously behind her.

'Good morning, class.'

'Bonjour, Mademoiselle Rochard,' we chant, but everyone's eyes are on the boy.

'We have a new addition to our class this morning. Boys, can you all welcome Samuel. He is new to the area too, so I want you to make room for him and be helpful and polite.'

I notice André – the tallest boy in our class and an excellent goalkeeper – steer the new boy to the desk next door to his. He takes his seat and opens his bag quickly to try and hide his red cheeks behind it. I wonder if he is old enough to be in our class – he seems impossibly small, his feet dangling above the floor.

Our homework was to read a story. I quickly looked at it last night but then I got bored and Luc and I played a new game we made up and the winner got to wear Dimitri's glasses, which make the whole world go blurry. Anyway, we read the book last year in Paris.

We are looking at where fairy tales come from. Some are based on true stories that actually happened, and this story is one of those. Mademoiselle Rochard asks the class to describe the central character, Bluebeard, and I close my eyes to try and see him. I think his beard is blue but can remember little else about him. I turn to a page that I think talks about him but Samuel has got there first. He raises a hand and the class looks at him curiously.

'Yes, Samuel,' Mademoiselle Rochard says.

Samuel describes Bluebeard perfectly; he floods into my mind in colour. He is massive and tall and scary, so strong he can smash the door to the tower down.

'Well done, Samuel, beautifully put.' Mademoiselle Rochard smiles at him. 'So, can anyone tell me a story that reminds them of this fairy tale? What is the relevance of the door that she should not enter?'

Fast as light I put my hand in the air.

'It is like the fairy tale "*La Belle et la Bête*", because the beast in that is very nasty to the woman and that is the same in this story,' I say, waiting for her praise.

Mademoiselle Rochard looks at me. 'That is not quite what I was asking.' She looks round the classroom.

'Anyone else?'

When no one moves Samuel raises his hand again.

'It's similar to the story of Adam and Eve when God has forbidden Adam to eat the fruit from the Forbidden Tree. When Bluebeard tells her not to look in the room, it is tempting her to.'

'Well done, Samuel – a merit. Excellently put.'

Suddenly, as if God has switched off the sun, the classroom seems darker, clouds form outside, it might rain. The new boy is blushing. André pats his arm.

The new boy is sitting in the seat next to mine, pouring some ink into the well in the desk, getting ready for our next lesson: dictation. His book is filled with neat pages of writing, no ink blotches or smears. Mine is in a bad way after I dripped ink right across my last piece of work which then got stuck to another piece of paper, leaving a blurry mess on both sheets.

He sticks out a hand and says hello. 'I'm Samuel.'

'Tristan,' I reply.

We shake hands awkwardly.

'I've heard you're from Paris,' he begins.

I nod, looking around the room.

'Which district?'

'Sixteenth, Villa Herran,' I say, taking the books out of my bag, removing my little pot of ink, taking out my pen from its case.

'Where is that?' he asks.

'Quite near the Seine,' I mumble, knowing this would be little help as lots of Paris is near the river that runs through it.

I don't ask, but he continues: 'We had a house in the third.'

Papa has mentioned the area in the past and not in a nice way. Maybe some of his workers lived there. I imagine it's nothing like where we used to live. I think back to our huge town house with its shuttered windows, rooms three times as high as my papa, the hallway as big as any room we had in our new house, the wide staircase always polished, the chandeliers throwing light into every corner, making everything shine. The park outside our house was also what Maman called 'the height of elegance', with great trees stretched out, lots of paths and places for people to picnic, and a sort of little house made of wood where a band played.

I look at Samuel, 'I haven't heard of that part.'

'It's nice.' He pauses. 'It's home.'

He says this in a way that makes me think he won't be going back to it. Like it's already in the past. And for this I dislike him even more.

'Why did you leave?' Samuel asks, still looking at me curiously.

'I don't know,' I admit, realising I didn't. Not really. 'Because of the war, I suppose.'

Samuel nods. It is obviously the reason he left too.

I remember when we left then – all the people on the road. I remember the boy.

'Are you going back?' he asks.

I blink and then shrug, cross that he is asking the same questions I have asked Maman for months. Questions to which I don't have the answers.

Luckily, Monsieur Garande appears in the doorway. He is so enormous he makes me feel like a little toddler. There is no greeting or instruction; his big, booming voice begins our dictation: '*Je me trouvais sur le champ de bataille...*'

I jump into my seat and lean over the page, concentrating hard. I start to write.

For the next forty minutes the only sounds are quiet scratches on the paper and Monsieur Garande's footsteps as he walks slowly up and down the classroom. I remain bent over the page, careful to make it as neat as I can, keen to avoid any attention from Monsieur Garande. He calls, 'Sit up, boy,' to Michel and the whole class sits up straight. André said Monsieur Garande used to be high up in the French army and has a bullet hole in his leg. No one has seen it but on some days he rubs his left leg so it's probably true.

Two pages are covered in lines and I think I have spelled things right. My hand feels like it might drop off. Monsieur Garande announces that the dictation is over. He walks slowly around the room, leaning over our desks, his shadow blocking out the light as he corrects our spelling mistakes, grammar and punctuation. When he gets to me I stand behind my chair. My hands twist nervously as he scans the page. Finally he writes a big 'M' on my work. It is my fifth merit since arriving at the school.

'Neat hand, boy,' he growls, as he passes me back my work. The book is small in his hand.

'Thank you, sir,' I squeak.

He turns to Samuel's work, barely looking at it. Instead he looks straight at him. Samuel looks anywhere but up at his face. Monsieur Garande waves a hand at him like I have seen Papa do at waiters when he's cross and walks off, muttering something about 'more of them'.

Samuel's face falls. My smile grows a little wider.

SEBASTIAN

Lilies are my mother's favourite flowers so I have bought some artificial ones for the living room. She was heartbroken when the florist closed his doors a few weeks ago. Although they aren't quite what she wants, I know she will appreciate the thought.

The apartment is strangely quiet when I arrive home from work and I close the door softly behind me, placing the flowers on the side table in the entrance hall. A little pile of letters, addresses written in thick blue ink in my father's sloping handwriting – one to an address in England – are waiting to be posted. I shrug off my coat, flinging it onto a hook on the hat stand. The streets were wet outside from a light rain shower earlier and I know Mother has spent some back-breaking hours cleaning the carpets, so I do the polite thing and remove my shoes. I don't want to give her any ammunition.

Padding over the carpet, past the archway to the sitting room, I can smell a soapy scent still in the air, a light breeze from a half-open window in the sitting room wafting the smell around the apartment. Not for the first time I see my mother's pride in our home: the ornaments, delicate figurines of musicians, are dusted on a regular basis; sideboards are polished; cutlery is cleaned; clothes are magically brought from the back room after being scrubbed at and ironed. The whole place is immaculately presented and when people arrive at the door they are instantly charmed, commenting on the prints Mother has selected for the walls, the crocheted cushion covers, the lamps she has picked up in little shops in narrow alleyways. Father and I do not compliment her enough on our surroundings. Suddenly, the lilies seem horribly out of place. I must get hold of some fresh flowers, but it is not easy during a war.

I take the stairs two at a time. As I put a hand on the banister to turn the corner to my bedroom, I notice the door to my parents' bedroom is ajar. In the thin gap through which I can normally make out the cream bedding and large linen chest at the foot of my parents' carved wooden bed, a figure sits. Pushing the door open slightly, I see it is my father, sitting on the edge of the bed in his dressing gown, his feet dangling inches from the carpet my mother laid down a year or so before. His feet are bare, and he is smoking a cigarette. The room smells stale, the curtains are still half-drawn, the bedclothes rumpled.

I clear my throat to signal my presence.

He looks up wearily at me and I shrink back a little. The ashtray overflows with spent cigarettes and the shadow on his chin suggests he hasn't been up at all today.

'Are you ill, Father?'

'Apparently,' he states, dragging on his cigarette and then grinding it aggressively into the ashtray. His left hand grips the mattress but his voice is steady, a little higher than normal. 'God only knows,' he continues cryptically.

This dishevelled man in pyjamas is not my father. He is usually fastidious about his appearance, and not because he is vain. His combed hair is always in a neat side parting – baldness is not a family trait and he used to remind me that his thick head of hair was at least one piece of inheritance I could be grateful for. He wears braces over spotless shirts and polishes his shoes as if he were in the military and turning out for parade. He keeps a clean handkerchief in his top pocket and is never seen without his hat once outside. He ensures his clothes are laundered and kept flat and has admitted to me that he would never do business with a man who had dirty nails. He bemoans my mop of hair that never quite rests flat and has, on occasion, left a tin of shoe polish outside my door that he obviously thinks I should use, or trip over.

This man, sitting on the edge of the bed, grey hairs poking up sporadically from his collar; this unshaven man who doesn't appear to have the energy for slippers, is not him.

'Where is Mother?' I ask.

'Out.'

'Father, what is it? What's happened?'

'Don't you read the papers?'

I take in the newspaper at his side, pick it up, shake out its pages to scan the print.

'*It*'s happened,' Father says, drawing another cigarette from its case and searching for his matches. 'Shit,' he swears, uncharacteristically, as he realizes he has used up the last one. 'Match?' He looks at me hopefully.

I automatically shake my head. 'What does this mean?' I step backwards, taking a seat on the little stool by the dressing table.

'It means everything.'

We sit in silence, my thoughts whirling.

'Jean-Paul can help,' I say.

'Perhaps.'

'There has always been this hatred of the Jewish race. Banned from public office—? I mean, of all the...' My eyes glance at the paper again.

'And teaching, running newspapers, running cinemas...' Father rattles off. 'Just think what they're doing by this one act.'

'They can't do this.' My protest sounds pathetic.

'People can do anything.'

We sit, listening to the only sounds in the room: our own breathing, irregular in contrast to the gentle tick of the carriage clock.

'It has always been there. They don't want us here, Sebastian. They don't even have the excuse of occupation. They simply want rid.'

'That's not true,' I insist.

'Is it not?'

'What does it mean for us?'

'The business?'

I nod.

'The beginning of the end.'

'But it doesn't say anywhere that we can't continue to run the bank—?'

'No, not yet.'

'What do you mean "yet"?'

'I don't know what I mean, Sebastian.' Father rubs his eyes. He seems to have aged ten years in the last ten minutes. My head is spinning with it all, what it means.

'What is "Jewishness" anyway?' I continue. 'How are they to know?'

'We've told them, haven't we?' Father laughs, a dull sound. 'We've trooped along like good little citizens and signed their census, admitted to the great sin of being Jewish.'

I'd ticked the box without a second thought.

'Soon they'll be testing our facial features, measuring our noses, our ears . . . like sizing up cattle for market. We'll be herded in the same way as those animals, shunted off to somewhere in France, out of the way.'

'Surely not in Vichy? They can't touch us here. It's not in their interest – we're fighting a war, so why turn on their own men?'

'This was passed in Vichy,' Father points out.

'But...' I am flailing now.

Father sighs. 'No one will stand up for us, Sebastian. No one will come to our aid.'

'But *we* won't be affected,' I stress again, wanting confirmation, wanting something, feeling the floor disappear from under my feet.

Father is talking as if to himself. 'We should have left months ago, but the business, I didn't... your mother...' He trails off, staring at the cigarette he's snapped in half as I pace the room trying to help, to solve, to control this.

A cold, creeping fear squeezes the edges of my heart and I shiver.

There is a scrape of a key in a lock and the sound of footsteps up the stairs. Mother has returned from shopping. She clutches a little posy of pink flowers to arrange in the vase by the bed, a smile on her face as she enters the room.

'Mother bought flowers,' I point out stupidly.

Father hasn't heard. He is still staring hopelessly at the halves of his cigarette.

ISABELLE

From the bench outside the town hall I watch a family nearby: the little boy, who can't be more than six, is playing with his older sister. The game involves a lot of complicated hand-clapping and chanting some made-up song. Their parents are scanning the tram timetable, the mother looking over every now and again to check on them. The pace increases and I giggle as the boy loses the rhythm, his older sister cuffing him gently before ordering him to start again. Children are so wonderfully uncomplicated. This kind of game is popular in our village school.

I have loved the last few months as Mademoiselle Rochard.

I remember my own childhood with Paul. I think I bored him for years but was still always a playmate when no one else would do. I watched him and Papa fish down by the river and spent hours dangling upside down from tree branches, something that always got me a telling-off from Maman. We fought of course, ridiculous arguments that embarrass me now, but we became closer in our later years. I miss him now.

The family is leaving. The mother, taking the hands of her

children, smiles at me as they pass. I wish them a good day and go back to my book, a rather dull book that I haven't the energy for, encouraging my restless mood. It's a relief to finally see the familiar figure of Sebastian walking along the pavement in the distance, heading in my direction.

This bench has become a regular meeting place, mostly due to an excellent café around the corner that still manages to produce pastries, of varying qualities, despite the shortages. He hasn't seen me yet. He is wearing a suit and hat, his thick brown hair just visible above the collar of his jacket. He's an ideal height, just over six foot, which is tall enough to make me feel suitably dainty and feminine and short enough that I don't have to crane my neck backwards to look at him. He is a man you can't help noticing: even if I try to focus on something else, one eye will peek, just to see what he is doing. There is something in his movements, fluid, like water, his face open, like hope; an easy raise of his eyebrows or a twitch of his lips that makes me want always be in on the joke.

I see another girl, a redhead, pass him, head snapping back to take another look, and I feel a rush of pride. He is oblivious to the attention, nodding an acknowledgement to an elderly gentleman in the street, his brown eyes, edged with thick lashes, crinkling as he smiles.

I sigh like I'm starring in my own romantic novel and feel warmth spread through me when he sees me and breaks into a grin.

He removes his hat and leans down to kiss me on the cheek. 'Have you been waiting long?'

'No, not really. I've been pretending to read this.' I hold up my book. 'It's terribly dull, so please distract me from it.'

He laughs, turning it over to inspect the jacket cover. 'Remind me never to borrow it from you. I'm desperate for a drink... you?'

'Absolutely.' I stand up, put the book in my bag, notice a patch on my cardigan, dart a hand to cover it.

I know it's shallow and silly to be so concerned with my fraying clothes but I want to dazzle him.

He tucks my arm in his and I am unable to resist leaning into him, our bodies centimetres apart. His wide shoulders carry a heavy weight: I know he worries about his parents, the business, and I know he finds it hard being young, male and at home, unable to go to war.

I feel a rush, the start of an addiction, as I say something that makes him throw back his head, his teeth flashing as he rocks appreciatively. Glowing, I feel there is a light inside me, starting in my stomach, bursting into the edges of my skin, heating my organs, and when it starts to sputter and go out, I want to say something else, prompt the reaction all over again. I want his hand to brush mine, want him to lean towards me conspiratorially, as if it is only us in the whole country, only two of us against the rest, and the light is sparked all over again.

We push into the shop, waiting briefly to be seated, step back to let another couple leave. I adore the feel of the little café – the scattered tables, the assortment of chairs and the crockery with faded china patterns.

We sit and I order almost immediately. Sebastian laughs at my enthusiasm.

'They're not going to run out of pastries,' he states.

I roll my eyes at him.

Over Sebastian's shoulder I notice two middle-aged men. One man is staring at us, brow furrowed. I make a mental note to be a little quieter. Something niggles at me, something familiar.

The waitress brings us our drinks, a substitute for coffee, roasted chicory and grain, and a thin apple tartlet in a pool of cream. As I stir the mixture I briefly imagine I can smell real coffee. I open my mouth to share this thought with Sebastian.

I am vaguely aware of a scrape of a chair and then the man from the table behind us is standing, looking down at Sebastian. He is towering over our table, a man who needs to duck before entering a room.

'You're Pierre's son - at Maribanque,' he states gruffly.

Sebastian pushes his chair back and stands, 'I am.' He dabs at the side of his mouth with his napkin and then holds out his hand to the man. 'Sebastian.' He is clearly trying to place him too and, as I see the man look at the proffered hand, ignore it and shrug on his coat, it hits me.

His thin moustache twitches. 'I don't bank there,' he says, buttoning up his coat.

'And I never will,' mutters the other man who appears beside him, putting on his hat, his mouth nothing but a straight line on his face.

A look passes across Sebastian's face and I don't know whether to stay sitting or stand too.

'I'm sorry, do I know you?' he asks.

'No, we just know your type,' the second man says, turning around before pulling on his coat.

At this I stand. Sebastian says nothing, but one hand flies out as if to stop me, or protect me – I'm not sure which. His mouth is half-open in surprise. The waitress glances over at us all huddled around the small circular table. Other diners are curious too.

The man continues. 'We were just sitting there listening to you laugh with your lady friend here. How nice everything must be – your cosy little tryst, no matter that other young men are off fighting a war on your behalf.'

Sebastian flinches, hurt in his eyes. I know he'd hate it if I said anything but I'm fizzing with rage; it's bubbling to the surface, threatening to spill out. My hands clench into fists at my sides. How dare they? And then I can't stop myself, because Sebastian is just taking it, standing there, allowing them to say these things.

'You don't know anything.'

'Isabelle...' Sebastian looks at me.

'But...'

'We should leave,' he says. His shoulders sag and his brown eyes have lost all their sparkle.

'No, no, please stay and continue to enjoy yourselves. You and your money-grabbing kind are used to living the high life, I imagine.'

His kind?

I take a step forward and the table wobbles, spilling the dirty liquid over the tablecloth. The waitress hurries over.

The man leaves with a last look over his shoulder. 'We'll be sure to be looking out for you and your family.'

Sebastian lowers himself slowly back into his chair. He looks at me wiping fruitlessly at the stain as the waitress fusses that I mustn't worry. I can feel it in her voice, the need to try and reach out to us, to assure us she doesn't think like that, and I want to hug her for it.

Sebastian has lost all appetite, the tartlet abandoned. He is staring at his plate.

'I'm sorry. I should have stopped him, it's just... I... I've never...'

I reach a hand across the table. He looks at it and after a pause, takes it in his own. I squeeze it.

'Don't think about it. Really. They are just vile people with their own problems.'

'Their sons are probably fighting somewhere, or prisoners,' he says generously.

'A lot of sons are fighting somewhere and that doesn't

excuse it,' I respond, knowing that Paul would have said the same to him.

And it had been more than that. We both know it.

'Shall we go?'

I want to stay, to rally him out of this sudden black mood.

'Of course. We can walk to the park, go and feed those fat ducks or...'

He cuts me off. 'I think I'll go back to the office.'

I nod quickly, feel my throat thicken, swallow. Ridiculous.

Back along the street, Sebastian doesn't say a word.

'This is me,' I say, pointing to the tram stop, knowing I probably have an age till it leaves for Oradour. 'Thank you for the drink and the pastry.' I falter, feeling cross with myself, cowardly, for not saying more. 'I'll be at the library on Thursday for lunch,' I try.

He nods, his mouth turning up a fraction.

I should throw my arms around him. I should tell him the man is an ignorant fool and should be instantly forgotten. How can anyone think like that? I don't know what to do though, so I pat his forearm and let him leave me.

He walks slowly down the pavement, head bent down, one leg stiff, affecting his gait. As I turn to check the timetable I see the men again across the street. They too are watching Sebastian leave.

ADELINE

1952, St Cecilia nunnery, south-west France

Sometimes I am captured in a memory so clear, punctuated by a warmth that flows through every sinew, making me feel for a moment that I can run out of this place, that I am still there and that it is all possible. And then it shimmers, flickers, twists.

I see Vicente's face, every feature perfectly recalled. He is sitting in the armchair in the small room we keep as a study, a book open in his lap, the reading lamp beside him casting an orange glow. The fire has long gone out, just feathery ashes. I close the door quietly behind me, move to the other chair, picking up my tapestry as I pass him. A slight incline of his head in my direction, barely there but vital. He reaches out his hand, huge as I place mine in it. He squeezes it briefly and, without looking at me, starts to rumble with laughter at whatever it is he is reading. His face has new lines where it has creased and I can't help but smile as I sit. His laughter ends and he looks up at me, his mouth turns up so slowly, and I feel wholly at peace as I settle back on a cushion.

I wish I could see his face once more. I never said goodbye to him, I never said I was sorry. His face distorts, then fades, his mouth turns down, his eyes leave me. Too dark to read, I desperately try to catch them once more.

He is only ever there for a moment.

SEBASTIAN

Isabelle has persuaded me out to her village, to see where she was brought up and get some rest from banking, paperwork and, although she doesn't say it, the melancholic mood of my father. Ever since the Jewish statute banning Jews from various positions, he seems half the man he used to be, stooped and weary. Ever since the man in the café, I suppose I have, too.

We meet at the tram stop in the village and Isabelle looks furtively left and right before greeting me quietly.

'I'm so glad you came. Follow me.' Her voice is light, the words almost lost as she turns, walking a few steps ahead.

Three young boys are behind the tram stop, two are kicking a football, the youngest, adorably blond and not part of the game, sucks his thumb, watching me through a thick fringe as I walk past him. I tip my hat at him and he removes the thumb to give me a big smile, showing uneven front teeth. The oldest boy – Tristan – blushes furiously as Isabelle calls out his name, mumbling a greeting and looking at me with narrowed eyes.

Isabelle trips lightly across the street, delicately picking her way over the tram lines in her low-heeled shoes, her skirt swinging just below her knees; a thread has come loose at the hem. She wears her hair half pinned up, thick strands falling between her shoulder blades. Looking over her right shoulder she smiles briefly at me, a thin line between her eyebrows, before dropping down a side street and then into a small path to the left.

Once there she slows, waiting for me, shadows making patterns on her skirt and cream cardigan. I squeeze myself by her side. The path itself is narrow and brambles poke out at various angles, breaking free of the hedge. I lower my head as we walk along, dodging the thin branches spattered with early buds. The air smells earthy and the ground beneath us is soft, tiny puddles of rainwater captured in the runnel of churned-up mud that runs down the middle of the path. A fly hums around my head and I swat at it uselessly.

Isabelle seems less tense now: her shoulders lower a fraction, an easier smile lights her face, no glances around as we walk across the meadow. Long grass prickles my calves through my trousers, daisies are dotted around, dandelions form clusters and, beneath it all, the river moves effortlessly through.

Shaking out a rug she lays it carefully on the grass and motions for me to sit. I feel creaky and awkward as I lower myself down. An insect skitters across the fabric making his escape. The grass beneath the rug tickles the hand that I rest on, uneven. The river narrows at this point and the water forces its way around larger stones in its path, dampening the slime-green edges and leaving the tops of the stones dry. Weeds and grasses grow in the cracks and some pink flowers have clumped on the bank beneath twisted tree roots that disappear into the stream. We seem almost hidden from the village here. Isabelle sits down; I crackle with nerves. There is colour in her cheeks, a peach blush as she looks off into the distance. I wonder if she feels it too. I realize this is the first time I have been truly alone with her.

'No one comes here,' Isabelle announces, as if confirming my thought. 'Paul and I used to spend hours here in the summer, further down there.' She points to a wooden bridge someway off. 'It's more popular, but I've always loved this spot.'

I lean back on my elbows, watching the waterflow making the reflections of the plants that drape over the edge quiver as it eddies. Shadows from clouds above darken the water in places and the river is a mix of browns and greens.

Silent and peaceful I feel my muscles relax, feel the warmth of the sun, weak but there, through my clothing, and listen to the occasional chirrup of birds, the rustle of an animal and, all the time, the backdrop of the quiet trickle of the river as it continues to move past. Closing my eyes I breathe in deeply, holding the breath, my senses heightened, then release and open my eyes again. The fields beyond look like a vivid watercolour painting; my mother would love the view.

Isabelle is watching me. She has kicked off her shoes, the suede heels lying sadly abandoned on their sides, and her stockinged feet resting on the rug. I find myself fascinated by them, the gentle arch, the curl of her toes, the soft pink of her nails just visible beneath the flesh-coloured fabric.

'Join me,' she laughs, wiggling her toes and making me look up, a heat creeping up my neck.

'I wouldn't want to lower the tone,' I tease, brushing one hand over the rug.

'I'm glad someone is concerned with standards,' she says, her face solemn, removing a flask from her basket. 'Water?'

she offers. She hands me a small tin mug and pours from the flask.

I sip the water, feeling the cool liquid run down my throat.

'How is the school?' I ask.

She nods eagerly. 'I really enjoy it, every day is different. My classroom is decorated with poetry and pictures and I adore their faces when they understand something for the first time. It's magical, that moment.'

'It always sounds much more exciting than the business of a bank.'

'Ah, but not as lucrative.' She laughs. 'Now, wait here.' She disappears somewhere behind me. 'You're not to follow,' she calls over her shoulder, and I wait for her to re-emerge. When she does, I can't help but laugh as she throws her stockings in a ball at her bag and makes her way over to the bank.

'You know, you can be quite shocking, Mademoiselle Rochard,' I say.

'I do hope so,' she sighs, gasping as she steps into the shallows.

Taking another step to plant herself, the water forges past her calves, splitting and meeting again, as she stands there, her skin pale in the light, paler beneath the water. She dips her hands down into the water and trails her fingers along the surface.

'Amazing.' She looks back at me. 'You have to,' she says, no teasing in her voice.

She is right, of course, and without a second thought I find myself removing my shoes, untying the laces hastily, pulling off my socks, rolling up my trousers, the hairs on my legs dark against my skin. Standing up, I walk over to the bank, place a toe into the water, my expression earning a laugh from Isabelle.

'It's colder than Alaska.'

Stepping onto the flat pebbles I exhale in a rush. The shock of the water stings, like cold jaws have clamped themselves around my feet. At that moment the sun is obscured by a cloud and the scene becomes muted, faded to dull green and muddy brown. Small goosebumps break out on my skin and I give an involuntary shiver.

I soon get used to the feeling, wading out a little deeper, feeling the light tug of the current, enjoying the ripples I create moving in wide rings away from me, disrupting the darker parts of the water.

Looking back towards Oradour, I place my hands on my hips and feel the sun emerge, warming my back like a hug from Mother when I was younger. The whole village can be seen above the line of trees: the tiled rooftops, backs of houses, windows left open to welcome this weather, washing hanging out in the gardens and then the church, rising up at the end on my right. Its rectangular tower, topped with a spire, seems to act as a watch guard to the village. The stones look like they have been there for ever, solid in a shifting landscape. A pale trail of swallows in the sky beyond it dives en masse.

'I want to invite you to meet my parents,' I blurt, turning to catch her eye. I worry that this admission will scare her but I realise then, as I see her expression change, that I am the one that is afraid.

She opens her eyes wide. The greens seem to reflect the mossy colour of the water below. 'I would love that.' She smiles, closing her eyes and lifting her throat so that the sun shines on her face. 'I'd love that.'

We spend the next hour on the bank, bait on a simple piece of string dropped into the water. I sneak glimpses of Isabelle over the book I am barely reading. Her long hair falls towards her lap in blonde waves, a small leaf caught in it; her arms are turning brown, small faint freckles sprinkled over warm skin.

I will return and talk to my parents, finally. I know I want to be with her, like this, for the rest of my life.

I look back towards the village. I can't imagine a more peaceful place.

ISABELLE

Dear Paul,

I've fallen in love.

I wish I could see your face – see that disapproving look you get when I announce I've bought a new hat ('How many hats does one girl need?') or met a man. I have to share it here and miss the creasing of your brow… it's not a hat, Paul – I have actually fallen in love!

Honestly and truly I feel it deep within me. And don't go saying it's just indigestion or some such, or that it's only because he's handsome (he is, of course, but you know that can't be all of it – Marcus Porcher is good looking and I find him so dull).

You would like him. He is gentle – an optimist. He's kind in infinitesimal ways and he's thoughtful. He brings me things – of course, you'll think he's just buying his way into my affections, but I mean small things, like a strudel (you know I adore them; well, anything covered in pastry) and flowers he has picked or an article he has read that he thinks I will find interesting.

Although I suppose all this is wasted on you – what you really want to know is if he is any good at sport? I shall have to find out. He certainly can't fish.

Is this trivial? I'm sorry but I don't know what else you want to hear from here. We miss you as ever and the village seems to be waiting for something to happen. We hear of the fighting in other places but we hardly ever see any Germans and it's quite unreal still, as if it is happening to other people and we are just hearing about it all second-hand. As I write this I feel so foolish – of course you won't want to hear it.

How can anyone be falling in love when elsewhere such horrible things are happening? I am sure you are staying strong and making others laugh and being brave. How you must hate working for them. Is it better than being idle or do you loathe the fact that you must help them? I'm glad you're with the others, grateful you're not alone – is that awful? Wishing the same fate on others? I think you know what I mean.

I am thinking of you every day: we all are.

We love you.

Isabelle

TRISTAN

Papa's eyes narrow as he reads Monsieur Garande's note and then he looks at me, waiting for me to speak. The note felt hot in my hand the whole way back from school.

'It was Samuel,' I begin. 'He's a liar, he got me into all this, he started it.'

'He made you fall on him like a savage in the playground in front of everyone, did he?' Papa asks. It is a hard question to answer and so I pause to think of a clever reply.

'He's a liar,' I repeat, realising I have failed.

'Can you enlighten me then, Tristan?'

'He accused me of cheating on a trick,' I say, not feeling confident that I am enlightening him to anything, as I don't really know what that means.

'What trick?'

'A card trick.'

'Well, did you?'

'What?'

'Did you cheat in the trick?'

'Well, it's a trick...'

'So you did.'

'Yes, sir.'

'Why that boy in particular?' he asks.

I frown at that. How can I explain why I don't like Samuel? He just makes me so angry.

My father looks at me. 'Monsieur Garande tells me what he is and I would expect nothing better from their sort, but I don't want you to be so out in the open with it. We must *always* be cleverer than them.'

I don't understand that bit either, but I don't want to say anything in case I add to my punishment.

'Do you really not have anything else to say?' he asks.

I do not.

Father sighs and starts the lecture about the war and bigger things to worry about and Maman and him under a lot of pressure and all this makes me squirm. But much worse is when he gets a long stick out of the coat stand and I know I am going to have to bend over and receive a punishment. He asks me one more time if I want to tell him exactly what happened but I know he will probably punish me anyway so I think it best to just take the beating.

I try to stay still as it hurts so much more if you tense, and I try to offer him the most plump part of my behind in the hope he might hit me there, but as the first blow falls the familiar sensations flood over me and I don't feel like staying still and taking it. There will be extra strokes if I move, but each stroke of the cane makes me wiggle even worse.

I don't know what Papa means about Monsieur Garande telling him what Samuel is – I can say what Samuel is, and that is a know-it-all. Of course I know exactly why the argument began but I don't want to share it with Papa as I'm not confident he will see things from my point of view.

It was my new trick. Perfected over the weekend. At school

break, André chose a card, I did a series of complicated flicks and things, a quick tap, a lot of magic words, a shuffle and – *voilà* – I pulled his card from out of the pack as he stood there with his mouth open. It was brilliant.

Samuel came and sat down in front of us both and then another boy with a birthmark down one side of his face, who is in the year below, joined too. They were both eating the vitamin biscuits that taste like cardboard. I smiled at the boy with the birthmark but turned my back a little so I was facing away from Samuel. Annoyingly, he didn't get the hint and stayed right where he was to watch. I didn't really mind though, as this seemed to others to be quite a crowd as I noticed a few other people looking over at us.

André selected a card again and I did all the flicks and things like I had learnt before asking him in a low voice, 'Is this your card?'

He nodded again, clearly impressed.

Samuel piped up, swiping crumbs from his jumper, 'You didn't even put the card in the pack.'

André looked at him in surprise, then back at me.

'Yes, I did,' I said, gritting my teeth and closing my eyes. How dare he question my trick?

'No, you didn't, did he, Pedro?' he asked the boy with the birthmark, who nodded.

'I did,' I repeated, feeling my face get hot.

'You kept it out of the pack, I saw.'

'You can't see clearly from where you are,' I said, shaking my head at André as I said it. 'And anyway, no one likes tall stories,' I added, quoting from something Papa said to me once.

Samuel looked hurt at this, clearly faking, which made André feel sorry for him so then André sided with him in this and claimed that I must have done it as why else would

Samuel have said that? I threw the cards on the ground but then, to prove that he was just a liar, I picked them all up and repeated the trick one more time, this time super-fast, with extra-large taps and twists and things and I made sure that the card was out of sight.

Samuel didn't say a word at the end and I turned to André. 'See, I told you,' I said, holding out the four of spades. 'That is your card.'

'It was,' André said, shrugging at Samuel, who nodded then and turned to go.

I hadn't had enough of this yet, though. 'Ha! See! He is just a liar. A silly, little liar.'

Samuel froze on the spot. Then he slowly turned, looked straight at me and said, 'It was up your sleeve.' That made me go quiet and André just stood there. 'You put it up there once André had chosen it,' he said.

He ruined everything with his showing off.

'He keeps it up his sleeve whilst he's shuffling,' he said to André.

Before he could continue, I launched myself at the stupid know-it-all, who ducked out of the way. I caught him again though, and we both fell on the ground. It was at that moment that Monsieur Garande saw us and his booming voice stopped both of us dead still.

As I lie on my Papa's lap and feel each stroke I blame it all on Samuel. This is not over.

PAUL

Dear Isabelle,

Are all my letters getting through, I wonder? I write to you in the hope they are, I love receiving your news. I am glad you have found a kind man, you deserve someone warm and I promise I won't tease. It is a brief glimpse at some colour when a lot of my world is grey.

The weeks and months are dragging on and sometimes I find it hard not to despair. The mood is wild and chaos reigns in the Stalag, where officers surrounded by mounds of paper shout one thing, then another in their nonsensical language. All the while we wait on bunks and cots playing endless games of cards.

I wish I had some joke or story for you, but it seems at the moment that there is nothing but waiting. We seem to have told each other everything there is to know, and sometimes a little bit of what we didn't. It is like a family, I suppose. Nerves are being stretched and rumours are always circulating. It is the inaction that brings it on – tempers shortening and at times I crave the quiet of the River Glane. I hope you wander down there often, sit on the bridge and drop a line into the water. I think it is one of life's simple pleasures and it makes my heart ache at times to be back there.

Some of the lads here go off to lectures and seem to forget there are fences at all. I don't want to sit through lectures or read books, I want to pound the earth and wrestle with the others. Here we can remember that we are men and when I take the head of a friend and rub at his hair I feel the blood pumping through my arms and legs and I don't feel so utterly useless.

In some ways I will be relieved to start the next lot of work – hope the Kommando is outdoors. Some of the lads are being sent to nearby farms, others to the factories or mines. They say life can be easier out there and I want to be doing something. Farm work will seem wrong somehow, when the fields around Oradour are to be neglected, but I don't want to be swallowed by the earth or stuck on a production line. Rémi is nervous about the work, he is about half my size and knows nothing about farming, only paper. He joined an amateur dramatics group in the camp and is playing a woman. He isn't built for farm work and has bitten his nails right down and asks me constant questions about crops and all sorts. I've been telling him about the work we do in the village – what will you all do for another harvest time with no men, I wonder?

Please keep writing, dear Isabelle. Your letters take me out of all of this,

Paul

ADELINE

1952, St Cecilia nunnery, south-west France

We're in the forest, you and I. The woods I visited as a child. The trees are so tall. We are near the top, where everything thickens and the light fights its way through the cracks around the leaves leaving shadows speckled on the soil under our feet. Vicente and Paul are behind us at a distance but we have decided to set off down a path. We duck under branches, get tangled in cobwebs and walk ahead, talking, forgetting our way. It is so good to hear your voice.

You suddenly draw up short, your breathing laboured. I almost knock into you as I come to a halt.

He is there. A large shadow of an animal, a huge body hunched over strong legs covered in matted fur. His slanted yellow eyes are watching us closely. A wolf.

He lunges at me. My breaths are hard and fast but I'm frozen to the ground. You jump in the way.

'Run, Maman, run!' you cry, batting at the wolf with a branch.

The jaws snap and you are grabbed. I can only watch as his jaws close around your jumper, trapping you. You are still trying to swipe at him with the branch. He is too strong though, and drags you by your collar to the ground.

'Run, run, run, run, run.' So urgent. That's all you're saying, all I'm hearing.

I turn and I run as fast as I can. Branches scratch and tear at my face and clothes as I head back down the path. It gets lighter; I can see the forms of Vicente and Paul as if we were never gone. They are not worried. Vicente asks what is wrong.

I'm crying and I can't get the words out right but I know I have to be quick. 'It's Isabelle, Isabelle's been taken by a wolf. We have to help her. I have to go back!'

Vicente looks at me calmly. 'Adeline, there is no one there. Don't upset yourself.'

'No. Isabelle, she's there, and the wolf has her!' I'm repeating. Why doesn't he understand? I tug on his arm but he is still.

He cocks his head to one side. 'Come on, Adeline. There's no one there and we are going home now.'

'No, you can't, the wolf, Isabelle, the wolf, he's...'

'There is no one there.'

'He's got Isabelle,' I scream, imploring them to turn around to come with me, to save you.

My words merge into whimpers and I'm bundled down the path away from the forest. Paul and Vicente are taking me home. The woods fade into the distance. I leave you there with the wolf. And somehow, as the journey goes on, I unfurl, my breathing steadies and soon I forget. I walk with them both, enjoying the sun on my skin.

When I'm home I say to Vicente, 'You were right. There was no one there.'

I open my eyes and stare straight ahead. The moon is bright outside and bluish fingers of light creep through the window, making long patterns on the bedspread; as the minutes tick by, they slowly move up towards my neck as if to strangle me. The nunnery is sleeping, breathing in and out, at peace. There is a slight rustle from the courtyard and then, far away in the distance, an animal cries.

Sister Marguerite has lit a fire and we are both sitting in two chairs by the hearth. The snapping of twigs and the gush of the flames as they are drawn up the chimney are the only sounds in the room.

I am darning, carefully pushing the thread through the holes and tightening the gaps between the wool. It is mundane work that I often do, but I feel grateful to be giving something to the life in the nunnery.

Sister Marguerite has her Bible in her lap but her eyes seem unable to focus on her reading. She takes the poker, prods the coals a little needlessly and the fire glows red. 'So, what are we going to do today?' she asks, looking up at me. 'I would suggest a walk but it's been raining so hard Sister Bernadette says we might have to start building a second ark.' She smiles feebly at the joke and returns to pushing and prodding the wood about, pieces breaking off and falling into the glowing mass with a hiss. 'We could read a little, or we could work on a new tapestry. You could help me pick out colours again – I have nearly finished the last scene.'

Normally Sister Marguerite continues in this way, answering her own questions out loud and maintaining the pretence that I have contributed in some way. She will chime, 'Right, well, we will begin a new reading from the New Testament,' or 'I will mend these cushion covers and you can rest a little.' Today, however, she does not answer her own questions: she simply looks at me expectantly, waiting for my response.

I continue to darn and allow her to make up her mind.

'What do you think?' she persists.

My hand wavers a little before I plunge the thread into the material. It is a bold red, the red of Isabelle's favourite jumper; the red of fresh blood.

'Sister Constance thinks you are being wilful.' She says this quietly.

The thread knots itself and I rest the material on my lap, looking down at it as she goes on.

'Why do you not speak? Why do you choose this silence?' she continues.

We stare at each other. I can see her doubting, see her incomprehension. She has spent endless days sitting with me, weeks, months, years, in fact, and still I say nothing. Her frustration is obvious, but there is something else in her expression.

Sister Marguerite stands up quickly, brushing her arm across her face. 'They will tell you soon. They have a place. Sister Constance has spoken to the doctor. He isn't sure you're ready but she is making arrangements. If you stay this way, refuse to attend services, refuse to speak, to try, then…' She chokes and runs out of the room, leaving me in front of the fire that still dances gaily in the gloom.

SEBASTIAN

'Mother,' I call out. 'I'm home.'

Shutting the apartment door I smile to myself, my mood light, another afternoon with Isabelle like a warm, secret stone resting in my stomach. I know the habit of calling out irritates Mother, wishing me to arrive like a gentlemen, greet her at the door in a calm and poised manner. I move through the entrance hall to the sitting room. Mother wouldn't reply but will most likely be reading or knitting in her armchair in the yellow room, readying herself to admonish me.

The long mullioned window she sits next to throws enough light around the room to make her little side lamp obsolete, even in the day's fading light. I will catch her as she turns the page of her book. She cannot read without maximum animation, gasping when she is surprised, chuckling a little at unexpected moments. She adores books, consumes stories, has always spoken of her delight in novels and memoirs, diaries. She pretends to like non-fiction the best but I know she would rather sink her teeth into something far more frivolous.

She used to read to me until I told her I'd grown too old for the habit. I regretted it for weeks afterwards. I would whisper the familiar words under the bedclothes, remembering the feeling of being huddled next to her with our favourite books, the heavy blankets tucked right up around us as she brought those tales to life. I would fall asleep listening to her and dream of journeys to far-off lands: the scented air of Arabia, the heat, the spices in the air, the dust and bustle of the market or trekking across a snowy landscape, a world of white, the sting of the wind, hair whipped up. My dreams were a hundred times more times more colourful than our simple life in the city, in the little three-bedroomed flat we kept above the main road stretching through Limoges.

Today she is not reading; she is perched awkwardly on the edge of the sofa pouring hot water over herbs into our finest china cups from a silver cafetière with a spout shaped like an eagle, left to her by the imperious Grand-mère a couple of years before. She has dusted down a spindly old tiered cake stand and is offering a guest a selection: miniature éclairs, little triangular sandwiches, the scones she bakes, so delicate they can be popped into the mouth in one go – a move that will cause her to raise an eyebrow and chastise me later. She must have used every ration ticket she had or called in a favour.

'You remembered our guests,' she motions, the smallest frown touching her face because it is clear I have not.

The guests are a youngish girl, perhaps nineteen or twenty, looking awkward holding a china cup, and her elderly chaperone. They both turn to look at me as I enter, and I am struck by the sudden urge to turn on my heel and flee, get away from that room and the absolute knowledge that this poor girl has been invited here in a desperate attempt by my mother to ensure I settle down, and fast. The older woman, with an expression on her face as if she has just consumed a lemon, is sitting, thin lips smeared with grease, dabbing at her face and eyeing me from her vantage spot on Father's favourite armchair.

I nod a clumsy acknowledgement to the girl, who is introduced as Anne by my mother, and nod my head at one Madame Feigl, the disgruntled other party.

Mother is obviously keen to leave us alone as she instantly rises to fetch more water, practically tripping up over going past me with a jug that is almost filled to the brim, calling to Madame Feigl to come and look at the print she bought recently at a gallery, which hangs in the kitchen.

Madame Feigl dutifully follows, a sallow glower at me as she passes.

I walk slowly across the room, aware I might smell of dust, books, sweat – flashes from my afternoon in the library with Isabelle making me more awkward. Standing with an elbow up on the mantelpiece, I realize I will need to start some kind of conversation with Anne. Catching my flustered expression in the cloudy mirror above the mantelpiece I realize I need a haircut. Anne sips her *café au lait* and looks up at me, shyly, through long, thick lashes. She is pretty, with glossy dark hair, flushed pink cheeks and a friendly, rounded face.

I smile at her, feeling a little silly in my fireside pose. 'So, Mother hasn't yet told me how she knows your family.'

Madame Feigl is back, clearly unmoved by Mother's print – she doesn't seem like a woman who is moved by much, and dives in. 'Your mother and I play bridge together.'

Anne smiles and nods along, nibbling at an éclair.

'Ah.'

This conversation is dragged out as long as I can manage. I

have never been one for small talk, am much more comfortable around the old scrubbed pine table in the kitchen, or in the café with a few friends. With no sisters, I have struggled to find much to say to women; until Isabelle, they seemed completely foreign to me. I grope for my bridge jargon, and try a little harder to engage them both, so that Mother gives me an eager expression on her return. I am feeling generous and disarm her completely by giving her a smile, taking the water jug from her, and offering Madame Feigl a top-up while complimenting her on a rather startling brooch of a tiger. She readjusts the little stripy ornament on her ample bosom and gives me a glare as if to accuse me of being interested in the latter.

Mother suggests a game of whist and I am paired with Anne. The palaver of bringing out the card table with its faded felt top, the removal of the tea things, allows me to chat freely with her. She is obviously a literary enthusiast and, for the first time that afternoon, lights up as our talk turns to books.

Anne is a perceptive card player and we beat the older couple easily. I find myself grinning straight at her on our final round, a look of sweet triumph on her face. After the game, Madame Feigl bustles her out in front of her, airily kissing Maman on the cheek and sending her regards to Father who is, I imagine, probably hiding in the bank rather than putting himself in her line of fire.

They leave, and Mother turns and says, 'I shall invite her again.'

She looks confidently at me, at my reaction, and is confused when I answer quickly, 'I am sorry Mother, but I'd rather not.'

'Why not? You two seemed to get on so well.'

My face flushes as I realize I must admit to the reason. I cannot continue to deceive my parents. The declaration must be made formal, for Isabelle's sake. I picture her in the dusty light of the library earlier, her hand flicking the pages of a book, her eyes holding me.

Mother looks hurt, and I open my mouth to try and explain.

TRISTAN

Samuel is late for school. He comes running in, panting apologies to Mademoiselle Rochard who, after a pause, waves her hand and tells him to sit down. Normally Mademoiselle Rochard is very strict about being on time: 'Time waits for no man,' she often says. No one really knows what it means but no one wants to find out. She says nothing to Samuel and he just takes his place at the front and pours ink into the well as Mademoiselle Rochard continues to speak. She has a big bump now, and when she talks she often rests her hands on it.

There are whispers and everyone is looking at Samuel. All I can see is the back of Samuel's head: no mystery there – his brown hair is uncombed; his jacket is a little tight across his shoulders. Aside from a few marks on it – Maman would be appalled if I allowed my jacket to become that dirty – I don't see anything special at all.

We are going over some Geography and we have a test on the capitals of the world at the end of the week. I am quite confident about it as I know a lot of capitals, like Moscow for Russia and London for England. Mademoiselle Rochard is pointing to the map on the wall, her back to the class for long periods as she points to the various capitals we have been learning about. It is clear that only a few of us are still with her as she pauses over Rio de Janeiro, sighs and looks around.

'Concentrate, please.'

Usually this is enough to have everyone poker-straight in their chairs, eyes following her every move. But not today. Aside from myself and Hugues Martin, a goody-goody who spends most of the time waving his arm in the air, everyone is still staring at Samuel.

He is glowing; his ears are bright red. He is squirming in his seat; he looks like Grand-père looked when he got the illness that Maman said made it uncomfortable for him to sit still. Then I see it. When his arm goes to dip his fountain pen into the well, a flash of yellow. A symbol, a sort of star, is stitched onto his clothes. It isn't part of the school uniform and it seems an odd thing to do, to sew it onto your arm, when no one else has one.

Mademoiselle Rochard has her back to the class again and is writing on the board. What will she do when she notices?

No wonder everyone is whispering. She can't have seen it when he arrived, although it seems so obvious now that I look at it. As it isn't school uniform he is bound to be in trouble. You can't just sew things onto your uniform without any kind of punishment. He'll probably be sent to Monsieur Garande. I almost feel sorry for him.

Mademoiselle Rochard carries on the lesson but I can't help sneaking a look over at Samuel any chance I get. I want to see the moment Mademoiselle Rochard notices.

Samuel shifts in his chair at one point and is looking out of the window of the classroom. He looks a little like the white mice I've seen at my friend Paul's house in Paris – all pale face and red eyes. André gives him a smile, and a gesture with his head to the front and Mademoiselle Rochard. Samuel seems to come out of his daze, turns back to the front.

'Excellent answer, Samuel,' comes the clear, sweet voice of Mademoiselle Rochard moments later. My head whips over to him once more and, sure enough, there is Mademoiselle Rochard leaning over his work, right above the symbol.

I scowl, no longer sorry for him at all. I hope Monsieur Garande is in a bad mood. Perhaps Mademoiselle Rochard is going to take it up with him at the end of lesson. Staring at the hands of the clock, it seems to take for ever – I swear, sometimes the hands go slower when I look at them. I get my South American capitals confused, earn a sigh from Mademoiselle Rochard, and add it to the list of reasons I don't like Samuel.

The lesson ends without a word. Mademoiselle Rochard simply leaves the classroom. No one has time to say or do anything as Monsieur Pincet sweeps straight in and sets up for his lesson. He has a big box of something with him so there is silence as he sets it down on the table, everyone trying to get the first glimpse of whatever is inside. We can make out some peculiar noises coming from it, and everything else goes right out of my mind.

We have the most brilliantly disgusting Biology lesson, pinning a frog out, all open, to look at his insides. It all looks like glistening pink worms. Monsieur Pincet shows us how to pull bits out and examine them to learn more about the frog's entrails and how they eat things. Their organs are so small, Monsieur Pincet says, that my heart is at least ten times bigger, and I have some organs in me that a frog doesn't have at all.

In break there is no avoiding the talk about 'the star' and lots of the pupils whisper about it. Samuel has taken himself off to the corner of the playground alone. Even André isn't there, kicking a football with him. Apparently, there are two other pupils with the same symbol stitched to their clothes. One, a boy from somewhere near the border of Germany, refused to wear his jacket to lessons, and one boy in the year below me thumped another boy for pointing at it in break.

'*Juden*.' I roll the word over in my mouth. I think I have heard this word before. If Samuel is a '*Juden*', I imagine I won't much like them anyway.

'What's a *Juden*?' I ask.

Papa's eyes widen and Maman calls for Elèonore to start clearing the plates. Elèonore takes her time leaving the room, slowly dragging one foot after another, looking back at us before finally exiting.

I repeat my question. 'What's a *Juden*?'

'Tristan,' Maman snaps.

'What?'

Papa rests his hand over hers, smoothes his moustache as he thinks. 'A *Jew*' – Papa clears his throat, turns to look at me – 'is a person of the Jewish faith. That is to say, they are not Christians but follow a different religion.'

'What religion?'

'The Jewish religion.'

'How is that religion different from the Christian religion?' I ask.

'There are a lot of theological differences between the two but I suppose, in essence, they are still waiting for the Messiah.'

I look at Papa blankly, unsure what 'theological' means and struggling to remember exactly who the Messiah is. I think he is a bit like the Lamb of God but I might be muddling things.

'That is to say that they don't believe Jesus Christ was God's only son sent to take our sins away.'

'I see,' I say. I don't. 'So, why do they wear badges?'

'So we know who they are,' he replies.

'Oh.'

I sit in silence, not sure what to ask next.

'Why do you ask?' Papa asks.

'There is a *Juden* boy at school.'

My Father speaks in a low voice, 'I know.'

'Davide...' Maman fiddles with her napkin and closes her mouth again.

I'm still not absolutely clear on what a *Juden* or a Jew is, but think if Samuel is one then that makes him different from us as I know we believe that Jesus Christ was God's son because we always have to pray to him.

Maman has been looking at Papa a lot during our talk and now Papa is staring at me.

'We know about these things Tristan, and you are not to be frightened,' he says.

Mother turns her head sharply. 'Darling!'

Papa waves a hand at her. 'I don't want him to worry. We should not have allowed it to go on this long. They must go. All of them. They are not welcome.'

I don't understand and I don't want to ask anything more and want to go and play now; it all seems complicated. Thanking Maman for dinner, I ask to get down from the table. She mumbles something that sounds like a yes and I hop down and out of the room, listening to their voices as I start up the stairs.

If it is all about religion, what is Samuel doing stitching stars onto his clothes? I know Grand-mère always wore a cross around her neck to show she was a Christian but I don't really think that's the same thing. Although maybe Samuel just wants everyone to know, although I don't think the school will allow us to start wearing funny little symbols everywhere;

it would look rather bizarre if we all turned up with little moons and planets and pictures of the sun on our arm.

Typical Samuel to show off like that.

At bedtime, Maman kisses me good night and she reaches across to close the curtains. Before she draws them I look up. All over the sleeping village are hundreds of little stars in the sky squinting down, wishing me a restful sleep.

ISABELLE

Dear Paul,

You must hold on, Paul. Life in the Stalag does sound bleak but you will be out of there soon and perhaps back on a farm. You won't be sent to a factory – why would they waste a man like you pulling levers? I hope it is safe for you wherever you go.

It's all got so grey these days, hasn't it? There are so many whispers people are afraid of their neighbour now, and so quick to point fingers. It's just all going on so long isn't it, and people get bored and want the end. I hadn't noticed some of it before, but now it chills my skin hearing people be so cruel.

Claudette now works for the family up in the big house and she has taken to following the mistress of it around the village like a particularly irritating pet. She tells me things about them as if to impress – her fancy talk of Paris and politics, it is quite pathetic. Monsieur Soules, an odious man with a ridiculous moustache, is friendly with the mayor of Limoges so I think he thinks he owns the village now. He can be seen striding down the street to the garage opposite, pestering for a motorcar apparently, as he runs about a dozen banks all over France. He looks so out of place here, his suits sharp at the edges and her in expensive furs looking like a queen, descending on the shop. He would seem ridiculous but he changes people, Paul – smiles to sneers, they're gripped by him. And yet their son is in my class, not grand at all, simply another boy with shorts and freckled knees. He makes me laugh.

Why can't we all remain like children and not see any of the ugliness? I don't want to get fired up about these people. I just want to spend the days after the war in the sunshine, under a parasol eating truffles on a picnic rug, then fish for our dinner next to the bridge as insects hum in clouds around our heads and butterflies skitter past. The men will be working the patchwork of fields as far as the eye can see and we'll drink warm cider as the sun sets on another day.

Hold on, darling brother – it will be that way again soon, I am sure of it.

Isabelle

ADELINE

1952, St Cecilia nunnery, south-west France

'Ah, madame!' The doctor seems happier today, walking tall. I nod a greeting at him and his face crinkles into a smile. 'We meet again,' he announces, as if we are at a cocktail party about to sup champagne and discuss the weather, rather than in a nunnery waiting for him to stare at my tonsils.

He pulls up the stool from the corner of the room and sits at my bedside, pausing to look at me briefly before plunging into his suitcase to find his tools. He sits back up, pats his brown hair. It seems to have more flecks of grey these days. He has grey hairs in his eyebrows too.

Perhaps my searching look embarrasses him, as he brings his little torch up to my face with a nervous cough. 'Right, open wide, madame.'

He makes a cursory effort to look into my throat. Within seconds he switches the little light off and announces there is no change.

I'm not sure he knows what he is looking for, any more.

He leans over to put the torch back in the bag and returns to his seated position, smoothing his hair once more as the effort of leaning down has obviously been enough to make him believe he must. He shifts a little on the narrow stool. He is a man who needs a chair: his legs poke out at awkward angles as he tries to balance.

'I've been thinking about your case recently and discussed it with a colleague. Obviously, we are all keen to help.' He waves his hand so that I could infer that he is including the nuns in this. It doesn't seem like a coincidence when Sister Marguerite walks by, putting her face up to the grille at the door to peer into the room. 'And, well, I thought it might do you good to undergo a sort of therapy… more than these check-ups, a way of sorting through some er... psychological barriers you might have put up.' My face obviously changes, as he quickly goes on: 'My wife says that I wasn't really made for therapy. Probably right. She normally is, but don't tell her.' He barks either at his own joke, or the uncomfortable realisation that I can't. 'And I thought I could perhaps ask someone in to aid you in this way. We know that obviously you can't communicate verbally and we know you write notes and things to the nuns—?' I nod slowly. 'And, well, we thought perhaps a solution might be to write things down, about… before,' he suggests. 'Anything – any thoughts or stories or memories, anything about the time when you could talk perhaps? Or now? Any time that strikes you as important.'

I reach out and put a hand on his arm. He flinches, only briefly; it is the first time that I have touched him, but it's enough to make me blush and draw back my hand.

'A good idea then?' he asks.

I think back to that afternoon by the fire, Marguerite's

pleading for me to try, her warning that I was to be moved on. Will they really send me away?

He holds a finger up in sudden thought, as if he had just come up with a new invention. 'Oh, wait, I forgot.' He dives back into his leather briefcase, and there is a clash of metals as he searches for what he is looking for. Triumphantly, he locates the object and stretches up again, not waiting to smooth his hair before saying, 'I thought perhaps you could use this – my wife has a similar one, painting of Renoir on the front that I've never liked, couple in a boat . . . this is a Monet, same sort of artist but I prefer this one. Looks like they're having a good day out.' That laugh again.

He is holding out a bound notebook with a miniature print of a painting of a woman and a child walking through a field of poppies, the scene rather dream-like.

'Going to give it a go?' he asks, pushing the notebook a little towards me.

I stare at the child in the picture. The doctor coughs.

Nodding slowly at him I agree to his request. I reach out and take the notebook.

'So pleased, so pleased.'

I run a hand over the notebook's surface and start to think of what I might write. A memory nudges.

We are at the annual village fair. Paul is eight and Isabelle still has that gap where her front tooth should be. She is on Vicente's shoulders, holding on to his neck, his big hands trapping her legs and making her squeal when he lifts her to put her down. It is summer, below us little sections of the river sparkle in the early spring sunshine, trickling over stones and pebbles, making a steady course downstream. Everywhere we look people are descending on the chateau: *on foot, on the back of carts. There is little Claudette Dubois, all teeth and solemn eyes, hanging off her mother's hand.*

Madame Thomas greets the villagers outside the chateau. *One hand holding her cigarette, the other playing with a long string of pearls that drip from her neck. Isabelle stops to stare at her, chin raised, eyes wide.*

Madame Thomas ruffles her hair, mumbles something, a puff of smoke tickles my throat. Isabelle's laugh, quick, light.

Colourful tents, the tinny noise of a slow-moving carousel, the painted horses moving up and down in time, merge with the chattering laughter of the village. There is a man selling chestnuts, the smell mingling with the scent of spring and freshly mown grass and rain. Isabelle pulls on my arm, desperate to explore. I watch as Paul and she are swept up in a cloud of other children.

I move between crowds of familiar faces – many farmers from the fields have taken a rare day out of their work to throw their children up into the air and onto their shoulders, instead of hay bales. Monsieur Renard is surrounded by a dozen nieces and nephews, all clamouring for his attention, the chance to go on another ride, a chance to show him what they had spotted in the corner: a colourful float, flowers hanging off every surface; the strongman, his muscles glistening as he preens and poses; some men wearing large papier-mâché heads, parading about as caricatures.

Madame Garande waves me over to a corner of the sloping field, away from the commotion. She stands by an old-fashioned tent, swathes of velvet over the flaps to enter, tassels in rich oranges and reds hanging from the top, flapping at her ample bosom with a fan. An old woman stands in the shadows of the entrance and Madame Garande bustles towards me. 'Go on, Adeline, I insist – this woman here can tell your fortune.' She passes a handful of coins to the woman. 'Your turn, truly she seems to know everything. I've paid for you.' Before I can protest she has pushed me inside. 'Go on.'

The sunlight is obliterated as I move to follow the old woman, the canvas giving off a smell I can't place, a musty stench of straw, people and damp. A pot of incense fails to cover the stink. The flaps close behind me and the only light comes from a lantern on a table at the back of the tent. The woman points to a chair covered in brightly embroidered cushions, tiny mirrors sewn into their surface, and sits on a stool opposite. The gloom weighs on me, the distant noises of people moving around outside, the whistle of the breeze, all muted by the tent.

The woman smiles at me, wide enough to see black fillings, and tells me her name is Madame Mystique. Her skin falls from her face like ripples on the river, her hands wrinkled and covered in liver spots. She observes me for a while and I shift under her gaze. She seems ancient in many ways and yet she gives off a youthful energy and vigour.

'Hold out your hand.'

Her voice is strong and her eyes are wide and alert. I slowly hold out my arm, palm upturned, and shiver as she touches my fingers with hers, tracing a finger with a yellowed nail across my palm, following a line.

'Strange,' she says.

I retract my arm, hold my right palm in my left, bringing it to my chest protectively. 'Strange?'

She points to the ring finger of my left hand. 'You're married,' she comments.

I nod, not impressed with her grasp of the unknown quite yet.

'You are religious.' It is a statement not a question. The cross around my neck another giveaway. I nod. I am a Catholic. I believe in God. Doesn't everyone?

'There is a church. It's...' Silence. The air is thick with heat and incense and I strain to focus. I lean forward a fraction. A look passes across the old woman's face. My eyes flit to the entrance of the tent.

Madame Mystique appears to be talking to herself. 'So many.'

The dusty heat of the canvas, the stale smell and the urge to get back out into the open air with my family grips me. The chair topples over in my haste to leave.

The old woman doesn't respond, staring at something I cannot see. She is mad, or this is part of her act. I want nothing to do with it any more. I reach the entrance to the tent and pull back the velvet.

'Wait, my dear madame, please...' She is walking towards me, skirting the fallen chair and, with no warning, embraces me.

She is shaking. I push her off and back out of the tent, turning towards the familiar shouts and sounds of the village at play, the sun beaming at me from overhead, the breeze lifting my hair. Tripping on the uneven ground I set off back up the field. I imagine her watching from the entrance of the tent; my neck burns.

When I reach Vicente he picks me up by my waist and kisses me on the cheek. I feel foolish for my reaction to an old woman's tricks. The sun plunges behind the only cloud in the sky. I can't see my children.

PAUL

Dear Isabelle,

It is much better out on the farm. The work is hard but it's good to feel the limbs burning, feel my muscles screaming when I haul things up. The guards here are more relaxed, willing to share a cigarette and turning a blind eye to our ball games. It's outdoor work unless we are working in the kitchen, the stoves operate about six hours a day and we go in groups to prepare potatoes, boil cabbage. Potatoes for 150 men. Rémi and I found a pigeon newly dead, plucked it and cooked it. The smell took me straight back to our kitchen and Maman standing over the gas, burning off the last, small feathers from a chicken. We dined well that day and then Rémi went and threw it all back up in the field that afternoon.

The air raids happen in the daytime sometimes but they are heading to the city – the poor lads back in the factories. You can look up and make out the bombs dropping like pebbles, glinting in the sunshine as they fall. Then you hear the bangs, a curl of smoke in the distance and the imagination does the rest. They are worse at night, humming overhead, making your toes curl in, your back stiffen. It's a hopeless feeling and sometimes I want to sit up and roar through the building, hammering on my chest and feel like a man in charge of his own destiny. Instead, I make my way to the shelter where we are told to sit up not lie down, and the next day I'm resting on my spade, exhausted.

The guards let us near the fences and the German boys come near and stare in at us as if we are zoo exhibits. We ask them their names. They smile shyly and run away. They don't look any different to French boys, really.

Perhaps I can bear it, if I can stay here, if this can last, perhaps I can survive it all. A man escaped from the farm last week. I've heard they are still searching for him. He slept in one of the outbuildings, they found a bed of straw in amongst all the machinery. They haven't found anything else.

The sky and fields here look less than at home but I am safe, which I know will please Maman. I think of you all often,

Paul

SEBASTIAN

She is early.

Descending the stairs as the bell to the flat rings I find my parents milling around the archway to the living room. My mother gives me a warm smile. She is wearing a green patterned cotton dress that Father bought her for a birthday years ago. She is wringing her hands as we hear their footsteps approaching the apartment and when the doorbell rings again she hurries out to go and receive them. Father gives me a grim smile and readies himself.

I take a deep breath, plastering a welcoming expression on my face whilst trying to steady the nerves that are biting at me. Father pats me on the back once. 'Let's not jump on them as they arrive,' he suggests, pointing to the living room. I nod and follow him in.

Isabelle arrives in a whirlwind, the energy in the room instantly responding to her presence, whipped up, electric, all eyes focused on her as she shakes hands with my parents, comments on the scent of the flowers to my mother and smiles at my father as if she has known him for years.

Her father, Vicente, seems automatically relieved to see a small library of books in the room, and the chance to engage Father on the tome he can see lying on the little table by the armchair. They fall into an easy conversation about literature as my mother quietly gets on with pouring our drinks. Isabelle's mother has not come and Vicente makes her excuses: no one could cover the shop. This is entirely plausible, but a look passes between our two guests and Father.

As Mother pours and Father talks, I am left to face Isabelle. She is dressed in a cornflower-blue dress, her cheeks a little flushed. My breath leaves my body in a rush; it hits me that she is here because I am going to ask her to marry me. Once this meeting is over and done with and we have gone through the formalities, I can ask.

Mother thrusts a cup at me. It feels impossibly small in my hands. Isabelle nods towards our fathers, her eyes mischievous. I can't help but grin at her. The liquid slops over the edge.

We spend the next half an hour skirting around some mundane subjects: the tram ride to Limoges, the on-off weather we've been having, the effect on the harvest and the shortage of workers. Isabelle chips in, laughing easily with her father, seeming so confident and bright.

How am I ever going to get this woman to agree to marry me?

Isabelle looks up at my mother and says, 'Sebastian tells me you are an excellent pianist, and I imagine he is, too.'

'I am a plonking amateur, but my mother is wonderful.'

'Wonderful,' agrees Father, his eyes warming as they turn to pay her the compliment.

My mother is blushing now. 'They exaggerate,' she mumbles, looking at the table, trying to find something to do that might require her attention.

'Perhaps,' Isabelle ventures, 'you might play us something at a later date.'

A pause, as if the whole room has breathed in and is waiting for the response. Isabelle's daring has stunned everybody into silence.

Mother tries to recover quickly. 'I'd love to,' she states and gets up quickly. 'I must boil more water.'

I watch her leave the room, then glance at Father, who doesn't meet my eye. Isabelle shrinks a little into herself, the earlier bravado forgotten as she sips her tea.

Mother returns and we talk about music a little more: the opera that my parents love, while Isabelle talks about the new jazz phenomenon sweeping America. I glance again at my father worrying that he might disapprove. His expression is unfathomable as he listens, hands clasped together as if in prayer.

A little while later, as they get ready to leave, I catch Isabelle's hand in the hallway as my parents fuss over Vicente's coat and she meets my eye.

Hearing the street door to the flats closing downstairs, I flop onto the sofa and wait for the barrage of talk in the aftermath of the meeting. Instead, there is silence. My mother begins to load the tray with the paraphernalia from the table, scraping the crumbs from one plate onto another in careful movements, catching the eye of Father as she does so.

I await Father's verdict. He likes her: I saw the appraising look when she talked, and I want him to say it out loud so that I can revel in the sound. Instead, he opens his paper and my mother leaves the room, a backwards glance at the doorway, and then gone.

'Father?' He continues to read, his eyes frozen in one place. 'You didn't like her?'

More silence and then he sighs and closes the paper,

folding it in half as I continue to look at him. With a snap of his wrist he flicks imaginary dirt from his shoulder.

'She is very pleasant.'

My shoulders relax and I am keen to start a list of the many reasons why Isabelle Rochard is frankly perfect. Father is staring at his hands and I nod at his statement eagerly, trying to rouse a few more words on the subject from him.

'She is good company, don't you think?'

'Yes, good company.'

'She is amusing.'

'Yes.'

'But not silly,' I qualify.

'No, I think not.'

'She is well read, too,' I tack on, knowing this might help him expand further. 'Her father is friendly, is he not?'

'Very.'

I pat the top of the sofa, smoothing the delicate wool rug that hangs from the back of it, worn away in places by numerous heads that have rested on it.

'But...' Father starts.

I suck in my breath.

'You see we...'

My grip tears a tiny hole in the rug.

'Sebastian, it is impossible.'

'What is impossible?'

'All of it,' he cries, his arms wide. 'Life has changed, *your* life has changed.'

'Not this again.'

'"Not this, not this." What do you know of "this" – you are like a small child with both hands to the side of his face and his eyes closed! It would be unfair to bring her into all this!'

A surge of anger, that I would put Isabelle at any risk,

makes my words harsher than I intend. 'What do you know of it all? Really, Father? What do you really know?'

'You cannot ignore the current situation, Sebastian. You cannot bury your head in the sand.'

'Things haven't changed that much,' I continue.

'You're a fool if you think that. Everything has changed. Whose name is the bank in now, you think they'd let me keep it? What are the stars we're meant to wear on our clothing? Changes are happening every day and we can't just carry on as usual and pretend that we don't have to make plans.'

'I *am* making plans.'

'No.' Father shakes his head. 'As a family – we have to make plans together. Isabelle cannot be part of this.'

'Part of what?'

'Your mother and I have discussed this and we are leaving, Sebastian – we are making arrangements to go to England, to stay with the Macharts, who have established themselves there. We can't leave you here, we won't leave you here. And you can't ask her to come. It wouldn't be fair. Perhaps when this is over we can see, but for now, I'm sorry my boy, it isn't going to happen.'

We're leaving? I drop my head into my hands as his words sink in. 'England,' I repeat.

'England.'

I look at his face, search his eyes for the lie in his words, but can find nothing.

'What do we know about England?' I ask.

'We know that they're not being over-run by Nazis, and,' he adds, 'we know we have friends there.'

'We have friends here.'

Father sighs.

'I won't come,' I say. 'We're not even in the occupied zone.'

'Which is why we need to leave now,' he urges, 'while we still can.'

'We could go later, once we know how this all works out. We don't know what might happen. We don't know this won't all end tomorrow.' Father sits in silence as I continue. 'We could work somewhere else, we could set up another business, or work through somebody or...' I run out of steam entirely.

'I'm sorry Sebastian, but it is settled. We should have told you sooner. We have just received a letter from the Macharts in England.'

'Father, I can't! I can't leave.'

'You must.'

'I love her,' I announce, too wound up to worry that I sound melodramatic.

He gets up from his seat and comes over to sit next to me on the sofa. 'If you love her, then you can wait for her.'

I change tack. 'We don't need to go to England. We could move further south – a quiet village perhaps, sit it out. Or we could...'

'Enough.' A gentle voice but enough to make me fall silent. 'It will be the same everywhere.' He sighs. 'We can't stay here anymore.'

Mother appears in the little archway. A look passes between them. I know then that they are serious, and I don't want to stay and listen to any more. Seizing my coat, I push past my mother and slam the apartment door behind me so that I block out her voice pleading with me to stay.

I run down the stairs to the street, not knowing where I am headed but knowing I have to get out. Two men, a little way off in the street, talk to a stranger, pointing towards our apartment. Even in the dark I can just make out a thin moustache on the taller man. The little group don't see me leaving.

A brief thought flickers and is gone.

TRISTAN

The Villiers stayed last night having come for dinner. The table was all covered in wine bottles this morning and Claudette kept sucking on her teeth when she tidied them away for breakfast. The air smelt like the window needed opening and my baguette tasted funny.

It is sunny today and I want to play *boules*. Monsieur Villiers lent us an old set when he arrived last night. He said they belonged to his son. He said this in a sad voice, like when Papa talks about his brother who died in the First War, so I think that his son is away fighting somewhere, or is dead, but I didn't dare ask, we just promised to take very good care of the *boules*.

This morning, though, Maman announces that we will all be going on an outing and Papa says he is coming too. Apparently there is a man who has a goat farm nearby and we are going to visit him. The farmer has a goat who is as big as him and Papa says that apparently he can make the goat look like he is dancing with him as he can stand on two feet. I practically fall off my stool to run upstairs and get ready.

Maman has left her stockings and heels off today and she looks so funny in thick boots, like Madame Villiers often wears. A scarf is knotted in her hair and she is wearing a baggy coat too. I like her new costumes, like someone else's Maman who lives in the country. I give her a big squidgy hug as we wait for Elèonore to put on her shoes. She laughs at me and I am so happy with the whole day.

We all leave the house, being quiet as we pass Monsieur Villiers, who fell asleep in the hammock after breakfast. Madame Villiers, though, goes straight over to him, reaches out a hand and tips him right off it. He rolls straight off, landing smack-down flat in a muddy patch, his eyes open, a yell, no time to work out what has happened. Papa lets out a low chuckle and helps him up. He has dirt on his bristly chin.

We go away from the village, straight through the back of a farm and into a field behind. I don't often walk this way with Dimitri or Luc. In the distance is a forest of trees and Madame Villiers points out some different species, which Maman finds interesting; Monsieur Villiers and Papa talk about crop cycles and the harvest then, and I switch off.

As I swat at the long grass with my hand I look up and notice a thin trail of smoke just over the trees ahead. Before I can point it out Dimitri nudges me, pointing to a massive oak tree nearby with very low branches – a perfect tree to climb. I nod at him, reading his mind. Somewhere for our next trip out.

We loop around the edge of the field until we reach a gap in the hedge. Papa helps Maman and Elèonore down but Madame Villiers pushes his hand away with a 'Psch' which makes Dimitri and me smile at each other again. We scamper off ahead, away from the adult talk, and tag Luc, who can't possibly keep up.

Along the lane Madame Villiers points out all the blackberry bushes. The whole lane is full of them and she says we can pick them later and she will show Maman how to make a pie. She says they make your tongue go purple and Luc doesn't believe her. My mouth starts watering as she describes the taste. I will pick so many so we can have a lot of pies. As I'm thinking about how many I will need, Papa has pointed to something. It's the wispy trail of smoke coming out of the trees, and he asks Monsieur Villiers who lives in the forest.

Madame Villiers' head snaps right up and she is rude and cuts Papa off and says, 'No one.'

Monsieur Villiers' mouth is half-open and he looks like a letterbox. He shuts it again. Papa raises one eyebrow and there is a pause and I wonder who does live in the forest as the smoke must be from a chimney, but maybe it is a bonfire, and I wonder why Madame Villiers is so cross.

We hear Madame Villiers whispering to her husband: 'We've talked about this,' she says.

'Maybe it's time – now he is here, some of us can do something about them. They all live there, everyone knows.'

'They're people too, remember,' she says, sort of through her teeth.

'Barely,' he scoffs, and that makes Madame Villiers give him one of her looks, where she gets all red in the face and you know she wants to say more.

They are talking about the house with the smoke – Madame Villiers keeps looking back at it.

Dimitri gives me a funny look and then leans over and whispers to me, 'They must be spies, living out there. That's why it's a secret.'

Of course! We've learnt a lot about spies at school, how if some people sell secrets to the Nazis then they come and take you in the night and you are just not seen again. And no one knows who the spies are because they could look just like you or me.

And now they are living in the forest.

If the spies were caught then the war would be over and we could all go back to how things were and we could go back to Paris. *Why would Madame Villiers not want them found, though?* I wonder. Unless – my eyes widen – she is a spy too.

I whisper to Dimitri, 'We should do something.'

And he nods solemnly back at me.

ADELINE

1952, St Cecilia nunnery, south-west France

It has been hours, days, and I am dreaming again of the shallow waters of the Glane, longing for it. My mouth is dry, ragged, the earth in my mouth makes me want to choke. I have to be quiet. The noises have died down and I feel alone, in this patch, my skin now part of the soil. I reach up, feel earth fall away like sand as I reach for one of the pods, snap it off and raise it to my chapped lips. Push the little rounded balls into my mouth desperately. Hard as I bite into them, they release a fraction of water. I suck at it, snap another from above me, repeat, pause to listen through my layers for sounds, snatch again. They are not enough. My throat is earth, my tongue sticking in my mouth. I think of the river, the water flowing cool, clear over the smooth pebbles, too far for me, or I would crawl there, reach from the side and with cupped hands swallow the water, push my head beneath the surface, drink in the water until my mouth, ears, hair and lungs fill with it, until just the chill of the water overwhelms me and I can be free.

. . .

Taking a great breath I gasp, struggle to sit up, a hand to my chest; scuffing at the sheets, trying to get them off me like they are the soil that sticks to me in sleep. I see the grille, the greyish still of the room, the crucifix.

My chest rises and falls, slower now.

The greyish still of the room, the crucifix.

Wearily, I shift my leg over the edge of the bed, wincing as I push at the scar: my mouth lifts a little. Sister Marguerite will be along shortly and I stand, move across to wash myself, gasp as the water from the jug splashes over the edge of the bowl onto my bare feet. Sponging my face, the water drips into my mouth and remnants of my dream return. I hold the water in my mouth and then, closing my eyes, plunge my face into the bowl, open my eyes to see the bottom, a wash of blues and creams: just a bowl.

SEBASTIAN

The last train to Oradour has gone but I must find a way there. With the rain, great puddles are already forming. The streets are empty of people, lights are on in the first floors in many of the houses, people upstairs in the dry and warmth, all together.

My resolve fades and with a heavy sigh I turn and trudge back up the road. The rain eases off, as if congratulating me for my choice. I pass a smart house and notice a bicycle resting against some railings outside. I waver.

Most people are quick to put away their bicycles, so many thefts since the start of the war. Before I can change my mind I seize the handlebars and wheel the bicycle out into the road. It rolls off the pavement with a bump. I swing my leg over, knees sticking out at the sides as I place my feet on the pedals that are a little too high for me. Keen to get as far out of sight of the house as possible, I start to pedal. The bicycle is only borrowed, I assure myself.

The rain starts up again, punishment, and everything becomes a miserable effort, every incline a struggle. My leg, unused to the movement, is jerky and unwilling, pain searing through me. Sweat merges with the rain and the tyres bump over the uneven road as the light fades.

Hours later, every limb aching, the village of Oradour rears into view. The high street is deserted. I drag my feet on the ground either side of the bicycle to stop a little way from Isabelle's shop. My legs nearly fall away from me when I get off. Shaking myself out like a wet dog, I wish I looked more presentable.

I rest the bicycle on a lamppost and, with Father's words ringing in my ears, I push my way into the shop, limping slightly as my knee protests with every step.

A middle-aged woman dressed in a rather drab brown dress looks up as I enter, frowning as I traipse pools of rainwater into the first aisle. She has the same shaped face as Isabelle, the same startling eyes. Her mother. At that moment, a door at the back is pushed open and a blonde head appears. Using her foot to keep it open, Isabelle backs into the room holding a crate of tomatoes. I watch her turn and stop and look straight at me. The crate wobbles in her hands and I rush over to help her.

Isabelle looks stricken, glancing first at me then her mother then back at me again. Her mother does not know about us. I try not to let that thought fester, she will have her reasons.

'Thank you,' she says, in a formal way.

'I must talk to you.' My whispered words clash with hers and she merely nods a quick response. 'Not at all,' I say, louder.

Her mother is watching us. Isabelle is not going to introduce me. I pretend to browse the aisles and wait until her mother is serving another customer before daring to try and get her attention once more.

Isabelle crouches on the floor, as if to do up a shoelace – despite the fact that both are neatly tied – and whispers, 'The alley down the side of the house, the gate on the left.' She straightens up and disappears through the door from which she came.

Isabelle's mother looks over at me and smiles briefly. I scoop up one of the tomatoes and a newspaper.

Her mother looks at me as I produce my money. She is too polite to make any comment. I must look ridiculous – drenched, red-cheeked. Her eyes burn into my back as I leave, pushing the bike down the alley with one hand, tomato and paper in the other, the print already running.

There is a gate on the left and their garden is beyond. Isabelle is there, waiting for me.

'Sebastian, what is it? Why are you—?'

'I can explain.'

She slips past me. 'Come on. I know where we can go.' She beckons me to follow her further down the alley. 'Leave the bicycle here,' she says, pointing to a narrow break in the alley. Dense foliage creates a perfect spot for hiding it from view.

I hurry to keep up with her as we burst into the wide expanse at the end of the alley, the fields beyond and the sliver of the moon up ahead in a deepening blue sky. It has stopped raining and the air smells damp and earthy. The grass shimmers with raindrops as Isabelle guides me towards a tree in the corner of the meadow. A curtain of leaves shields us from view and she ducks beneath it. I follow.

'What?' she interrupts, disbelieving, as I start to gush an explanation. 'You cycled all the way here?'

I nod. 'I had to see you.'

Even in the failing light I can see her smile.

I can't put off this moment anymore; I have to tell her.

'When you left, Father, he... the thing is that...'

'He refused to let you see me anymore,' she says. 'So did mine. He says it is not wise because' – she looks at the ground, faltering – 'of these times.'

Tears sting the back of my eyes. 'We're leaving,' I say, my voice cold.

'Leaving?' Her eyes widen. 'When?'

'Imminently.'

'Why? I told him he was being silly. I don't want to stop seeing you. Where are you going?'

In a softer voice I say, 'I wanted to ask... I mean, I thought, perhaps, when our families met and...'

Her eyes have lost their usual glint. She looks so forlorn as she wraps her cardigan tightly around her.

'Well, I can't ask but I will come back to you. I promise, Isabelle. I promise I will come back to you,' I repeat.

She looks at me then, nodding slowly. 'I believe you.' Tentatively, she moves towards me, closer, so close I can see tiny gaps in her eyelashes and the flecks of colour in her eyes, feel her breath on my face making my heart race so fast I think it might jump out of my chest. Her hand reaches for mine and I close my fingers around hers, close my eyes to stop my head spinning. I breathe in the smell of her, the earth, the hint of spice on the air. The river running past us provides a gentle backdrop to our scene. The moment is made for this and I pull her towards me, kiss her.

A little moan in my ear practically ends me there and then. She whispers words, encouraging, and I allow her to take over. She guides my hand down her body, all the while whispering in my ear and coaxing me to continue, welcomes me. Peeling off her stockings I look up at her and she nods, her legs sliding apart, an invitation. My head is screaming that I must stop but my body has long since taken over and shut it out. I am hers and she is mine and here under this tree, in this little patch of another time in another world, we lie down on the earth together.

Afterwards we lie there, breathing heavily. What have I done? Have I taken advantage of this girl? I won't forgive myself. I rear up on one elbow, startling her. 'I wanted to ask – I'm asking you now. Will you marry me? Please wait for me...'

She leans up and kisses me softly. 'Yes, I will – I will, of course.'

And I settle back down beside her, feel her head nestling under my chin, her hair tickling my face as I hold her. She will wait for me and we will be together and we will marry and have children: we have a future.

PART III

ADELINE

1952, St Cecilia nunnery, south-west France

His steps on the flagstones outside my room are familiar to me by now. He moves into the room, glancing quickly at my bedside table. The notebook he gave me during his last visit is there by my side, next to a little kerosene lamp and a half-empty glass of water. It sits there, and he must see that I have thumbed through it – its pages look as if they have been turned over on numerous occasions, its spine is wrinkled with these efforts, a pen rests by its side. Does he imagine I have written my story out in a neat hand? That he can just read it and unlock the secret?

I have battled with the notebook, knew I owed it to them to try. This was different to making notes, brief requests. The blank first page stared accusingly back at me for days and I hadn't known where to begin. So I recorded the fragments, the thoughts, some memories as they came. At times a rush, at times painstakingly. I knew the answer was not yet there.

'How are we today?' he asks, his voice filling the room as he drags the stool over to the bed. 'I've been doing a little research and there is a doctor in America who had a case study who responded well to a new treatment for your sort of condition. These Americans always seem to get there first. Well, aside from in a war, and then they sweep in at the end.' He stops to chuckle at his own joke, but I'm too distracted by his talk of treatments and conditions.

He pats at his hair, flattening the strands that had once covered the crown of his head. 'I'm making more enquiries. There is a chap in England I have been in touch with who seems keen to come across and visit you. He's quite a forward-thinker, involved in researching new ways of helping someone in your position. He does something that involves electric currents' – a pause to cough, did he see my head snap up at this? – 'but rest assured, it sounds quite safe.'

He is hasty today, distracted. There is a little mark on his tie, as if he missed his mouth with his toothbrush this morning.

'Today, let's try to stimulate some of those old feelings, prompt a noise. You must try and focus on the feeling and perhaps then you will be able to respond.'

I don't want treatments, fuss. I don't want people coming over from England. I don't want people talking about me in America. I don't deserve this special treatment. My foot moves away from him and he catches it and rests it on a cushion.

'There now,' he says, wielding a little rubber hammer. He gently strikes the sole of my left foot, peering over at my face, as if his hit might instantly cause my mouth to open, might make words come pouring out. I can always see it in his eyes: *Today might be the day.* That he might be the man to open the box, to listen and learn.

He finishes with my feet and rummages in his bag for the next prop, drawing out a long feather as if he is unsheathing a sword. He moves a little uncertainly to the end of the bed once more and starts to stroke the underside of my foot. When that fails to get a reaction he moves the feather up my lower leg, pausing just below my knee. I know a blush has crept up my neck at the same pace as the feather has moved up my leg. I stare at the ceiling, noticing every crack, every fleck of dirt on its surface. My leg twitches at the light touch and the doctor himself has become a little uncomfortable, coughing at sporadic moments as he trails the feather higher up my leg.

'Worth a try, I suppose,' he says, returning to his bag. Feathers, hammers – nothing ever works. My voice will not return; it belongs to another time. I am a shell, the insides scratched out. The scars are thinner now, a part of me as, over the years, my body has tried to heal. There are gaping holes inside me and yet still I breathe in and out and in and out.

Breathing wasn't always so easy.

I hold my sleeves up to my face, covering my mouth with the cloth, sinking to my knees to find the gap in the floor where the oxygen still flows, trickles, along the stones. Noise piercing, every pore raging, filled with it, the firey sounds and haze of panic. The floor, a thread of air still there, and I am moving, not thinking of anything else, my lungs filling with it.

My dreams and memories have merged and I know the next part.

The reason that I am silent.

There are no explanations, no excuses, just the weight of

guilt and shame and memory taking another scrape of my insides so that soon my skin will be paper-thin and then I will finally crack and die. I force myself to think again, flinching as I feel another strand splicing, stretching me even thinner.

Where is she now? Is her step as light, her smile as wide, her hair as golden? I wonder whether Vicente still writes, dreams, whistles when he walks. Whether they both glow from the inside out. Does Paul miss me as I miss him? Do they wander through their own memories, sifting and holding up what is dear to them, clutching it to try and keep out the cold and the dark? I hope there is light and joy and happiness for them, as I have always hoped.

PAUL

Dear Isabelle,

I've read your last letter about ten times now, I want to read it again so the words form pictures and I am with you all in the village. I miss the small things – a beer with Father in the garden, lazy dinners, kicking a football in the meadow by the river, bringing in the harvest, sitting on the back of Old Renard's cart, the scratch of hay at my back, hands blistered, back aching, gripping the side as we jostle along, watching the sun sink behind a bank of cloud, streaking the sky with oranges and reds.

We have been moved again. The officers in the Stalag sent us to a different Kommando and we are in a factory, an hour's walk away from the main camp. We sleep in a long room next door to the machines that sit silently in the darkness. Outside the guards patrol the courtyard contained within a barbed-wire fence, so we are truly hemmed in. This lot seem bigger than the last, barking rather than talking. Mocking everything we do, so we feel laughed at and pathetic.

The everyday seems smaller and greyer now that we are in

the middle of this mesh of buildings. I miss being able to see into the distance, not wonder at what is behind a blank wall or a fence. We can't see the horizon, only patches of sky through grimy, high windows in the factory where we work, making out distant vapour trails and feeling a shudder as something drops too close. We've been in the city now for a few weeks and the work is colourless and never-ending. Worse, I feel that we really are now part of the machinery of war, that we are helping them.

There is talk of escape as we lie on stained bedclothes above an alley that seems to always be piled high with festering rubbish, breathing through our mouths. Rémi isn't sure, he wants to sit tight and wait for it all to be over but I don't want to sit and wait for a war that might take years to end, to lose my life on the whim of someone else. We hear stories – it has been done before, and successfully too. Even talking about it makes my heart hammer harder, pumping blood to my limbs, making a foot twitch, hand resting on my thigh stopping it rise and fall, rise and fall. Father would not want me to sit here, he would want me to fight, to stand up and bloody a man's nose.

I know I can't post this now; will no doubt have to destroy it – another reminder of my submissiveness, and I shouldn't worry you about these thoughts anyway, but I will try to get out. I will not just sit on my hands and nod at them. That is not me. I am not sure what the future holds for me but it can't be here. I hope Rémi can be persuaded by others – I don't want to leave him behind but I will go-

TRISTAN

Luc and Dimitri agreed that we should go back to the big tree and take a rope to make a swing. I think of the smoke and the spies living near it. It will be good to have a rope as we will probably catch them and then we can tie them up and end the war. We have made a pact not to tell Maman that we're headed quite so far away as she won't like the sound of a swing in a big tree; she'll think it's too dangerous. I think she would probably think spies are dangerous too, but I haven't told the others of my plan yet. Today we have got permission to take a picnic and go and play games outside as long as we always keep the house in sight. I think this is the day.

We set off through the lanes out of the village. The hedges have grown right up and the long grass is bending over into the road, tickling our legs as we pass. We take turns carrying the little basket Maman has packed for us. I am straying out into the middle of the road, the silence is all around us, apart from the cry of a bird in the distance or a little insect who is calling to his friends. I realize I haven't seen a motorcar in days and I grow more and more forgetful of our old life in

Paris where there were plenty of cars and noises, and not so much grass and sky. We get to a gap in the hedge where there is a little wooden bit to climb over, surrounded by nettles. You can see where hundreds of people have stepped on the wood in the past and the patch of mud around it is churned up with footprints. All the grass has worn away.

We clamber over, jumping into the field. I breathe out happily at the sunny day, the cloudless sky. A butterfly bobs past me, dips right in front of my face, his blue and green wings beating quickly. We can see the line of trees up ahead, the start of the forest, and walk along the bit where the grass has been flattened into a track. I'm looking out for the smoke but I can't see any. Dimitri runs ahead then spins round on the spot, making *rat-a-tat-tat* noises, firing shots from a make-believe gun at me and Luc. Clutching at my chest I fall to the ground, the basket forgotten. I then jump straight back up and give chase, arms outstretched, firing bullets in his path, diving into the grass to escape his shots, lying out of breath and panting. Luc tries to join in the game but is so slow he gets shot a dozen times. He keeps refusing to die so the game ends in me calling him a blockhead as Dimitri attempts to explain the rules to him for the hundredth time.

We see a massive hole in the ground by a fallen trunk. It looks like the home of a badger or a fox or something. Luc wants to leave a bit of his lunch outside the hole and lie in wait to see what will come and eat it. We can't even get him to move by threatening to leave him there by himself, and then Dimitri comes up with a masterstroke and claims the hole might be for a bear, as they are found in this part of France and they are known to eat children. When Luc protests the hole is too small to fit a bear, Dimitri simply shrugs his shoulders and says he wouldn't be waiting around to find out. Luc joins us without a word and spends the next few hundred yards looking over his shoulder. Dimitri can be terribly clever.

I'm confident I can remember where the tree is and lead the other two into the forest. The whole world turns a funny shade of green as we walk through and only little bits of light poke through the leaves above our heads. There are a lot of mushrooms and some mossy patches and fallen branches around so we have to watch where we are walking. Luc says we should take some mushrooms back with us but Dimitri has read somewhere that they can be poisonous so we decide it isn't a brilliant idea. Although I put one in my pocket, to maybe see later what might happen – I heard a few mice scrabbling around in the outhouse at our new house and think they'd be perfect for my experiment.

There's a crack up ahead and I think of bears. We stop still and listen. Then nothing.

I'm hungry and I'm glad we have a picnic to eat. Maman made the sandwiches from freshly baked bread and butter, and they're very good. Even the smallest scraping of butter now seems like heaven itself as Maman keeps telling us it is rationed, which means you don't get very much because of the war. I don't know why the Germans want all our butter but maybe they don't have it in Germany. I talk to Dimitri about the treats back in our dining room at home in Paris: pastries, *petit fours,* madeleines, éclairs, miniature cakes in different colours on the cake stand, with the icing with silver balls and little bits of frosted lemon, bowls of sugared almonds that never ran out. It still doesn't seem particularly fair, especially as I know Papa is an important man and is wealthy. He once gave Maman a ring made of diamonds that Clarisse told me was worth more than the moon and the stars, so I think it was very expensive.

Another crack, a twig snapping, and I turn my head quickly.

A wall of trees and silence.

Everything is getting darker and the sun plays hide-and-seek behind the clouds. There is an enormous tree lying on its side, its roots poking right up in the air, all of them covered in moss.

Dimitri has stopped. He sniffs at the air. 'Do you smell that?'

I drag my eyes away from a slow-moving line of ants walking along the bark to sniff too.

'Burning?'

It's the smell of a bonfire, that smoky smell that gets right inside your nose and tickles the hairs and makes you want to sneeze.

Smoke. The spies. I feel like my heart is beating twice as quickly.

A louder crack, this time nearby, makes both of us jump.

We can't see Luc.

'Don't scare us,' Dimitri says, as Luc appears from the other side of the trunk.

'What? I...'

Another crack and we all stop, frozen.

I turn my head and then see what looks like a house in amongst the trees, a field's length away. The windows are hanging off its hinges and its roof doesn't look right, like parts of it have fallen inside. There *is* smoke though, I can see it. The window's all smeared with dirt but... the spies! I can see the eyes watching us, I'm sure of it.

I think of the rope but this wasn't how I thought the plan would go. My ears are buzzing like there's an insect trapped in my head.

There's another crack and it feels like the whole forest can see us. Dimitri's face is green in the shadows, he's looking left and right, pushing his glasses back up his nose with one finger. The same snap again and he yelps, like the noise the Villiers' dog makes when you pull on his tail.

The wood is alive.

A cry.

We run.

We urge Luc on. The noises are gaining on us. Words – French, or is that German? A bark – an animal? There are footsteps, crackling, snapping. We aren't alone. My hands ball into fists, one holding tightly to the empty basket. Dimitri runs with the rug, squeezing it to him like the blanket he used to suck on in the nursery. Luc grabs my free hand. His eyes are so wide you can see all the whites. He gasps, 'The bears, the bears!' He makes little whimpers because he is running as fast as he can. A part of me knows I could get away quicker without him.

We burst back into the open field and hide in the long grass, the sun making everything less frightening. We lie down to catch our breath. Luc refuses to stop for long and drags us to our feet, his two hands tugging at both our arms. We keep low and move back through the field, then make a run for it on the road back to the village.

Luc talks the whole way back about bears and monsters. I start to feel silly now – I didn't even try. We could have caught them. We could have paraded them back to Papa. We could have ended the war.

I promise myself to tell Papa. I'll give him the rope to take. He'll stop them.

SEBASTIAN

The night sky is inky and the stars are peeking out from swathes of thick cloud. My parents will be asleep by the time I get home. Isabelle's face, the memory of what we have done, our words, promises, stop me feeling tired.

I leave the bicycle where I found it and walk through the streets, one set of steps when, in a few short hours, there will be dozens of people hurrying along.

I turn the key in the door as quietly as I can manage – I don't want to wake the formidable figure of Madame Dusang, an ancient widower whose husband must surely have died of nagging, who finds any excuse to hitch up her skirts, march up the stairs and rap sharply on our door to complain of the slightest noise. Creeping inside, I pad softly across the hall and then place one foot on the first stair. It makes a tell-tale creak and I glance at the door to Madame Dusang's domain. Making my way quickly up the stairs – best to do it in a burst – I see that our door is open a fraction.

I edge into the apartment, aware that my parents might be out looking for me, holding my key uselessly in my hand.

Pausing two feet inside, I listen to the shadows, straining to hear any sign of movement in the flat. My breathing quickens as I notice the hall lamp has been knocked on its side.

Not daring to turn on the light, I try to think.

The moon casts an eerie glow over our furniture so that I imagine I see figures everywhere. Peering around the archway entrance into the living room I see the room is empty. The chaise longue stands in its usual place; the table by the window where Maman likes to sit is undisturbed; the chess board still boasts the abandoned game Father and I began a few days before, its pieces waiting patiently for us to resume. He is winning. I catch my own frightened reflection in the mirror and start.

Taking the stairs quickly and quietly I pause at the top of the first flight. My parents' bedroom door is closed. Leaning against the door, I try to detect their breathing inside. It feels ridiculous, as if I'm a young boy again, woken from a nightmare and going to seek solace in the warmth of my parents' bed. I can't very well run in on them now, make Mother scream at me in her cotton nightdress, can I? They left the apartment door open, that is all . . . and yet something feels wrong. My hand reaches for the doorknob and I slowly turn it.

Desperately trying to remain silent, I push open the door and poke my head around it, so that only the top half of my body can be seen – a smaller target for Father and his slippers if they are there.

As my eyes adjust to the dark I realize the bed is mussed up, the duvet thrown back, and that there are not two sleeping figures. They are not here. Yet they went to bed. Mother would never leave the bed unmade. My hands grow sweaty, my heart hammers.

My head is buzzing with questions. I don't know how

many moments I stand in their doorway dumbly, but after that I sweep through the apartment, calling their names. Perhaps they are looking for me. I can't imagine Father would be wandering Limoges with Mother in the middle of the night but perhaps she insisted? Perhaps they couldn't sleep and went to find me? I wish we had a telephone, a way of contacting someone. Jean-Paul might be able to help – maybe they are with him? Why wouldn't they have just waited in the apartment?

Every corner is searched before I return to sit on the end of my parents' bed, helplessly putting my head in my hands, feeling so small in their bedroom. Wherever they both are, only one thing is certain: they will be worrying about me.

The sliver of hope I have that they are out and all this is in my imagination comes crashing down as I approach my mother's dressing table. Lying on its smooth glass surface is her wedding ring, a simple band of gold. She always removes it at night and puts it on again in the morning, after layers of hand cream have been applied.

The memory of her smiles in the tri-mirror, all three faces beaming at me, make me grab the edge of the dressing table, suck in a breath as I think of her face now. My hand closes around the wedding ring and I stand there, in the semi-darkness, lost.

A noise. Spinning around to face the door, I seize the first thing to hand: a silver-backed hairbrush on the dressing table. I surge to the doorway, hairbrush raised. There are distinct footsteps on the stairs.

This is happening.

This is real.

The light is switched on and I roar. I hear a high-pitched squawk – not the squawk of an intruder but the squawk of a terrified woman and there, standing in the light, is Madame

Dusang, hair in rollers, bare feet in slippers, holding a saucepan aloft, gaping at me and my hairbrush. We are both panting.

'I heard noises,' she says.

I can do little but look at her.

'Your parents? Where are they?' she asks, looking about the apartment.

'Gone.'

'Gone where?'

'I don't know, I wasn't here, they are... gone.'

'Perhaps they're with friends?' she suggests.

I shake my head.

'There were noises. I thought I heard your mother, but I was listening to the wireless, the noises stopped.' She wrings her hands and looks at me. 'I didn't investigate.'

'Her ring.' I hold out the small band of gold. 'She always has it, she would never leave without it. Something has happened to them.'

'Who would want to do your parents harm?' she asks gently. I know her and Mother have tea together sometimes.

It is this last question that allows some doubt to creep in. Who indeed? Who would want my parents taken away? My father perhaps – he knew the bank made him vulnerable, had taken steps to put everything in Jean-Paul's name – but my mother? A small voice inches in. Maybe it can be explained. Maybe they will sweep breathlessly through the door, back late from a concert or a friend's dinner; maybe Mother will flit into the room, reach up and brush the bottom of my cheek as she kisses me good night, her familiar perfume washing over me as Father complains about the tough meat, smiling at his wife, removing his dinner jacket with a flourish, rubbing his neck with tiredness.

I blink, but it is still me and Madame Dusang in an empty bedroom and the certainty that they are gone.

'The *gendarmerie*? I… I don't know, but they are gone,' I say. 'Father was worried, said that we were in danger here, that perhaps the *gendarmes* were watching. Things were happening elsewhere; he'd heard rumours of others but I'd never really...' I stopped then, choking on the last few words. 'I must go.'

I realize that whoever has taken my parents might come back.

Father had warned me, all those times. I needed to get out, to think.

Madame Dusang stops my pacing with a hand. 'Do you have somewhere to go?'

I nod.

'I have not seen you.' She smiles at me. 'Your parents will be safe. You will see,' she says, looking at me earnestly. 'You will see.'

I nod again. 'Thank you, madame.'

I write my parents a note, barely explaining anything in case it is found but needing to write something. I wonder where to put it, to hide it from prying eyes. Father's beside table. He keeps a roll of money hidden there, in an old glasses case. For emergencies. 'In case,' he said. I open the drawer.

There is a thick envelope addressed to me in my father's hand.

Creeping along the roads, I return to Oradour, not thinking where else to go, just automatically returning to her. It is an interminable walk, all the while racked with guilt. I hadn't taken my father seriously, I need to tell him how sorry I am. I must find them. I think of my note telling them where I have gone, that I will wait to hear from them there. I think of his letter, instructions, money.

He had planned it all, just in case.

The moon, a thin whisper of a line in the dark, impedes my progress: the light barely enough to see by. I wish I had bought a candle. Every now and again I light a match that flares up for a moment, shows me the earth a few feet ahead of me and then, with a fizz, it is out and only its smell remains.

After hours following the lines of the tram I arrive in the high street, move towards the shop, my limbs aching. I trip on the side of the pavement and quietly curse.

Feeling my way along the wall of the shop, I make my way down the alley, pausing before I reach their gate, realising its creak might alert neighbours to an intruder. But there is no turning back. There is nowhere else to go.

I can't wake her now. She pointed to her window once before, but in the darkness I can't be confident of the right one. I'm convinced that if I wake her parents I'll be drummed from the village before I can explain.

Crouching low in the garden bushes, I hear a rustle as one of the hens re-adjusts her spot in the coop. I too feel like an animal: dirty, tired, bedraggled. Like a rat. The sun will be up in a couple of hours, the hopeful disc will surely lighten my mood.

I stare at each window of the house, imagining Isabelle lying beyond in a dreamless sleep. Wrapping myself into a ball, a familiar pose from childhood, I try to get comfortable, try not to imagine the insects crawling nearby, every tickle of grass or hedge a possible bug. The night air makes me shiver as my body begins to feel the cold. I don't quite sleep and, in my waking dreams, I see only Mother and Father, their faces grim, in a long line of other faces I don't know. Hundreds of them, all appealing to me for help.

It is still night. Unsure of how much time has passed I sit up and brush myself down, feeling itchy and uncomfortable. My mouth is dry and stale. I will Isabelle to wake up, to come to her window, to lean out and breathe in the air, to see me below, that she will come to the window and find a way of bringing them back, of making all this stop.

The panes of glass are totally black, the curtains drawn hours ago. The sky stretches for miles, no hint of dawn on the horizon; the whole world seems to be sleeping with her and, somewhere out there, I wonder if my parents are sleeping too.

I must have slept a little. I am woken by the urgent morning cry of a cockerel who has spotted me and with a wary eye seems to be alerting the village to my presence. I slink back a little further into the bush and watch for the opening of her window, not knowing what else to do. Finally, the curtains are pulled back and the window is half opened.

I dart out before I can think and call up to her at the window: 'Isabelle.'

No response.

'Isabelle,' I venture again, panicking that it isn't her window at all.

A startled head pokes out. Her hair is loose, falling around her shoulders. She's wearing a nightdress.

'Shhh,' she hisses, urging me back to my hiding place. 'I'll come down,' she promises, turning back to the room and closing the curtains on me again.

I do as I'm told and hunch low, feeling a brief rumble of hunger gnaw at my stomach, worry eating it up.

'Sebastian, what are you doing here?' she whispers when at last she appears, glancing back towards the house. 'If they see us they will...'

Of course she could not be found in the bushes with a stranger, a stranger with twigs in his hair and dirt on his cheek, a morning shadow grazing his chin. She takes my hand and asks me what is wrong. She sits, listening wordlessly, as I tell her what I found the night before.

'We must talk,' she states. 'Properly. Go down to the river. I'll meet you on the other side of the bridge, on the right – there are bluebells out now, you'll see them, I'll meet you,' she says, pushing at me urgently.

With a glance back, I see her. Staring at me, biting her bottom lip.

Does she now see what everyone else seems to see?

ISABELLE

Darling Paul,

He is a Jew. And this means something in this horrible new world. Such an absurd thing, I have seen things with my own eyes that make me shiver. I've hidden so much from Maman.

She's terrified of doing anything that will jeopardize you out there and please, don't think I would want that too. But I'm scared of people's fear, what it makes them do, and I don't want to be like that. I don't want to live in fear. But I have jeopardized things, and maybe I have done things that will endanger you.

I'd do anything to keep you safe – don't think that I wouldn't.

There is a place out in the forest, it's the worst-kept secret in Vichy. Paul, a Jewish family are living there, having moved south to be safe. Their boy attends the school. He's a tiny thing and so quiet, seems much older than his eleven years. My heart breaks when I look at him, his shirt dirty at the collar. His mother comes quickly at the end of the day, then they go, Monsieur Garande muttering at his back. A man like

Monsieur Garande, soft as anything under all the bluster, looking like that at him. Imagine – a little boy. I worry for them, hear things. They say there are others there now too.

I haven't heard from you in weeks, are you still at the factory? Are you getting my letters? I can't send this, filled with secrets, everything seems to be a secret now.

Come home to me, come home and remind me that people are good.

Isabelle

PAUL

Four of us will be going: Rémi has come round to the idea, and two brothers, farmhands in their life before the war, have joined. They're all thick shoulders and arms, big guts. The older, Maurice, a dimple in his chin, reminds me of Father. He has the same slow rumble of a laugh. The younger, Laurent, skinnier and darker, would follow him anywhere.

Rémi has approached the task in typically fastidious fashion, dismantling his chair to make a sledge for our belongings and bartering with prisoners for the things we might need. I think I thought I could just punch my way out, but then what? Rémi has planned it, an earnest look, one finger on the dusty floor as he charts our moves. The brothers have arranged to pay the guard on the gate, a man with a weakness for beer and a certain brothel in the town, who can be trusted to be asleep, or on patrol elsewhere: we have the timings. It feels real and, as the day approaches, my whole body fizzes with anticipation.

We are getting out, returning home, re-joining the war.

The evening has been spent in twitchy silence, barely

daring to look at each other, as if the guards might be able to translate the slight widening of our eyes, the knowing nod, the small raise of an eyebrow. We are heading to a nearby farm building and from there south as quickly as we can.

The night is thick with expectation, muggy and close. I lie on top of my bedclothes staring at the uneven lumps of the ceiling, one hand resting under my head. Rémi sits on his cot, foot tapping, eyes now flicking to the door as if he expects a guard to appear as a black silhouette, light behind him, hands on hips and discover us. Footsteps on the wooden floorboards, a distant sound of keys, has his eyes darting to the door, him starting to his feet.

When the whole bunkroom is breathing evenly, the only sounds outside the odd hoot, a rustle, it is time. I get up, stripping the sheet from my bed in one slick movement. Rémi's has caught and he tugs at it, his thin arms pale in the darkness. I touch his arm and take the sheet from him; he gives me a weak smile, fear shining in the whites of his eyes.

Silently pushing the bed against the wall to get to the window, I barely need to touch the rotten window lock before it disintegrates in my hand. The brothers have joined us in silence, rising from their beds without a noise, their faces set, identical expressions on their faces. Standing on the bed, we place the makeshift sledge on the ledge, a knotted bed sheet acting as a rope, and gradually lower it inch by inch, listening for sounds outside, feeling the slow bump, bump of the sledge against the stone outside. Pausing to peek out over the edge I am shocked by the blackness of the night, barely making out the white of the sheet only a couple of metres below.

I help hoist Rémi up to the ledge. He balances, my hand on the small of his back, his legs dangling down as he looks at the ground below, then back at me. I nod at him. His Adam's apple bobs once, twice, before he makes the leap. My stomach plummets with him as his close-cropped auburn head disappears. A small cry as both feet hit the dirt, followed by a whispered *'ca va!'*

The youngest brother goes next: we haul him up and watch him disappear too. I don't need to help Maurice: he lifts his body onto the ledge in one fluid movement, hunching to get out of the window that now seems so tiny against his bulk.

Palms sweaty, I follow them, hauling myself up onto the ledge, my arms noticeably weaker – how easy I would have found the same move a couple of years before.

Rémi has skirted the side of the building and is now moving out into the courtyard, a scuff of stones as he gingerly makes his way across. Lifting my leg onto the ledge, pausing to strain and listen, I make out his figure in the patchy dark, his outline barely there, one skinny arm pulling the sledge to the gate beyond, a thin segment of moon not enough to give him away. The night air is still and rain falls like a gentle mist. Turning back I pick up my bag and look over the room: our beds, hastily stripped of the sheets, now just ghostly lumps; the door, an uneven crack showing the faintest light beyond which a guard might be sitting, slumped, head in hand on the night shift. Can it really be over?

I go to jump, Rémi now a hundred yards away. As I do, a light suddenly fires up from the fence to my right. Then another. And Rémi is lit up in the middle of the courtyard holding the knotted sheet of the sledge in one slack hand as a third torch finds him. Frozen, I can only watch as whistles blow and he looks left and right as the guards descend on him in a rush of frenzied shouts. They *knew*, they knew we were going!

As the brothers make a dash for it across the courtyard shots ring out; I hear shouts – Rémi's voice – and as I look over the ledge again I see two bodies, half in light, half in shadow, legs crooked, heads bent, dark stains collecting around them.

I feel all the air leave my lungs as I duck back down. A torch sweeps towards me, a foot above and below me, the moving light flashing past the square of window and highlighting the long cracks in the plaster of the ceiling, scars in a bluish light. I lean my forehead against the wall, waiting for a moment, and then look over again. Rémi is being taken away by a guard, the cone of light from the torch on the ground in front of them. The guards have brought stretchers for the other two, so still.

I persuaded him, this boy who wanted to go back to work, make paper, who played women in plays and laughed like a twelve-year-old with no cares in the world; this boy, who hadn't wanted to leave; this boy, who in this moment is so much braver than I. He is marched away, not even throwing a look over his shoulder at me, his chair sledge a grey silhouette left out in the dark.

TRISTAN

'Do you think we'll have to fight in the war?' Dimitri asks.

'We're too young,' I say.

'Not now, silly. I mean when we're older.'

I shrug, not really sure.

'I suppose we'll have to,' states Dimitri glumly.

'I wouldn't mind.'

'Really?'

'I'd show those Germans a thing or two,' I say confidently.

'I'm not sure I'd be very good in a war,' Dimitri says quietly.

'Of course you wouldn't – you'd always be stopping to read your book.'

'No, I wouldn't!'

'Or looking for your glasses.' I giggle.

'Elèonore can't fight. She's a girl.'

'She'd still be more useful than you.'

Dimitri looks solemn again. 'She would, wouldn't she?'

I pat him on the back. 'That's not your fault, D. She'd be better than most people in the war – probably bore the enemy to death by showing them her dolls.' I roll my eyes. 'I'm starving, come on.'

Papa has been on the telephone nearly all morning to a man who works for him back in Paris. I can see the top of his head if I lean over the banisters. He is speaking in a low, serious voice, like the voice he used when he told us all the war had come to France, and the voice he used when he told us we would have to leave Paris. We move down the stairs as quietly as we can so as not to disturb him. He can be angry when we get in the way of work. We can hear Luc in his bedroom making aeroplane noises and bangs when he crashes them on the floor.

Papa is finally off the phone and I signal to Dimitri to follow me. I want to hear the news. I wonder if we will return to Paris. It seems like another world ago that we were there. We live here now.

We creep as silently as we can down the stairs, both trying to place our feet in places that might not give us away. We freeze when Elèonore walks right past us on the landing above – she is bound to give us away, but fortunately she's too busy running to check her hair in the little mirror in the corridor, so she doesn't see us.

I can hear the voices of all the adults in the kitchen. Madame Villiers is round here gossiping and slurping her favourite peppermint tea. I can picture her nodding furiously as they all swap news. There are gasps at something Papa has said which only makes Dimitri and me more determined to find a suitable spot for listening.

We move to either side of the kitchen door. I bend a knee to the floor and try and peer through the keyhole. All I can make out is the dusty black inside the lock and a tiny light beyond, but the voices are clearer and I remain still and listen.

Dimitri is sitting cross-legged, his back to the door, one ear up against the wood.

'He says people are eating their pets,' Papa says. 'Dogs are just roaming the city as no one can feed them. The prefect of Paris has had to issue health warnings against eating stewed cat.'

'Dreadful.'

Dimitri's eyes are out on stalks; I poke my tongue out in disgust.

'Hours apparently, just for bread, or milk, or whatever the women can get their hands on,' Papa continues.

'Terrible,' Maman says. 'A friend of a friend wrote and told me that she had heard that someone actually died in the queue.'

'You can't consider returning yet,' said Monsieur Villiers.

Dimitri and I look at each other.

'But the bank, the business…'

'Davide, there *is* no business in these times,' Monsieur Villiers says. 'It's enough that we all just keep our heads down. It will get better.'

'I blame the bloody *Maquis*, Communists and Jews bleeding us from the inside, slowing things up, making it impossible for a quick resolution.'

'I won't disagree with you there, my friend,' came Monsieur Villiers' voice.

'They're too soft – we need to pull together in these times. These people aren't with us, we need to act.'

'Enough talk of politics,' says Maman, her light, nervous laugh seeping under the door.

Madame Villiers doesn't sound like she is laughing. 'I agree. Enough.'

There is a long silence and I start to feel uncomfortable

from the cold of the stones underneath me. I gesture to Dimitri with my head and he nods.

'Well, things can't carry on too long in this way, that's all I'll say.'

'We're some of the lucky ones, Davide,' says Maman.

That is the last thing I hear her say before Dimitri and I turn to go back upstairs.

I explode into our bedroom. 'We've got to find a way.'

Dimitri has followed me in. 'What's a Communist?'

I don't know the answer so I ignore him.

'We've got to find a way to end the war,' I repeat.

Dimitri is nodding.

'But how?'

I walk back and forward in front of the window, my hands behind my back so that I look like Papa does when he is thinking in his study.

I stop, making Dimitri jump. 'The spies,' I say. 'We know where they are and if Papa knew, they'd be found out and then they'd stop telling the Germans everything and we'd win the war.'

It is decided. Tonight, after dinner, we will tell Papa about the house in the forest. He probably doesn't realize that's where they are hiding but we could lead him there, or he could call the police and then everything could go back to normal again and no one in Paris would have to eat their cat and Dimitri won't have to be a soldier because all the naughty people will be found out and the war will end.

I make Dimitri knock on the door and stand just behind him. He rubs his hands on his trousers before he does it and I nudge him in the back.

'Stop it,' he whispers quickly.

'Go on.'

'I am.'

'Now.'

He reaches out, hand in a tight fist, and knocks quickly on the door.

I hear Papa's voice inside saying, 'Come in.'

I nudge Dimitri again.

He turns the brass doorknob and pushes the door open. It's heavy and sticks a bit so he has to do it with two hands.

We shuffle inside the room.

Papa is sitting at the big desk that he had in Paris. It turned up on one of the carts a few weeks ago, after he told us that this was going to be our new home. It took four men to lift it. His study looks almost the same as in Paris: a lot of his books are here and he has the same armchair, which has leather arm rests and a back that comes up to over his head, with the same cushions too. The only real difference is there is no big mirror over the fireplace; instead, a painting of lots of swirls and drops of pinkish paint. Elèonore thinks it's very good but I think it wouldn't be hard to do, lots of twirling about with the paintbrush.

He's turned in his chair. 'What is it, boys?'

I think he's working as he has lots of papers out on his desk and even some in a semi-circle on the rug. He's wearing his glasses that look like they have been cut in half too, so I know he is probably busy.

I nudge Dimitri in the back again.

'We needed to talk to you,' he says.

I nod behind him.

'Well, then.' He doesn't get up.

I rub the back of my ankle with my shoe, focus on Dimitri's hair.

'We needed to tell you about the spies,' Dimitri says.

I breathe out like I have been holding all my breath in for ages.

Papa's face changes, he gets a couple of wrinkles between his eyebrows. He takes off his glasses and pushes himself up from his chair.

We both take a step back automatically.

'Don't be worried, boys. Sit down, sit down. What do you mean, spies?' he says, pointing to the sofa. We edge towards it and perch half-on as he stands by his desk. I can't make out his expression any more as the sun in the window behind him is shining all around him; he's just a big, man-shaped shadow.

'We know where they are,' I pipe up. 'They live in the forest. We've seen them,' I say, only stretching the truth a little, as we definitely saw something in the forest.

'*Seen* them?' Papa says, his voice sounding serious.

'Well, their house.'

'Where in the forest?'

'By the swing.'

'The tree with the swing,' Dimitri adds.

I nod.

Papa pauses and turns his back to us, shuffling papers on his desk before turning back around.

'Just there?' he asks.

I think it is a funny question.

We both nod.

He looks at us both for a long time.

'No other house?'

We shake our heads.

Papa puts two fingers to his lips, taps. 'I know.'

Dimitri and I look at each other.

'You must promise me not to go there again,' he says. 'These people are not friends of ours.'

We both nod at him, heads moving up and down at the same time.

'Good. They will be dealt with – they all will be.'

I wonder how many of them there are. I look at Dimitri.

'Now if that is all, I have work to do,' Papa says. He turns to sit back down.

'They need to be caught,' I blurt, sure that this is not how this should go. Papa doesn't seem to be taking it that seriously, and we need to end the war.

Papa looks at me. 'I agree. It is in hand. We have started already. Thank you for telling me, boys. Keep it to yourselves now, please, and don't go back there.'

He sits back down at his desk and I think we are meant to go. I look at Dimitri, who pushes his glasses up his nose and then shrugs. We get off the sofa and move back to the door.

It didn't feel quite like I thought it would, but Father seems to know what to do.

As I walk up the stairs I hear Father picking up the telephone to somebody. I think I hear him say, 'We need to drive them out of the forest!' but I can't be sure and then Dimitri wants to be pirates and I forget everything else.

SEBASTIAN

Peering in the last segment of the mirror still secured to the frame, I rinse the razor in the tub of water in front of me. Turning my face a little so I can see the targeted area I place the razor on my cheek, flinching as the blunt blade drags across my chin. After a few more failed attempts my face is red and pimply, like a piece of used sandpaper. None of this is helped by the last of the day's sun sinking with little warning from the sky, losing itself behind a layer of trees.

I wonder for the tenth time that day what the point of it all is, anyway.

I am living in a tumbledown building in the forest on the outskirts of the village. Isabelle told me that a local Jewish family have hidden in the forest safely for most of the war. They obviously don't run a bank. The villagers know but do nothing she says. She teaches the little boy. She tells me that I will be safe here. She says there might be more, she doesn't know – she doesn't meet my eye when she talks about it, knots her hands in worry.

It has taken no time at all to perfect the look of a man who might have been camping or held captive for a year or more: my clothes are filthy, streaked with grime, flecked with mud, my shirt collar has yellowed and I imagine the stench I give off, despite my pathetic attempts to stay clean. Even without the shadows of a night drawing in, the room is dark with dust.

I've swept the mud and stones into one corner and tried to make sure the little area of the room where I sit is relatively clean. There is an upturned bucket and a chair that has lost its seat. There are matches and scrunched-up newspapers and Isabelle has managed to get hold of an old stove her father used once for overnight fishing trips, to heat up the tins of food she brings. They appear, as if by magic, at unspecified times. I have missed her last two visits and I'm beginning to wonder whether these food parcels are from her at all. I am desperate to see her, but then I catch a glimpse of myself, flashes of my own bleak face in the corner of the mirror, and I am half-relieved. Restless in the day, alert at night, I cannot read when it is dark; mice scurry and I don't sleep. I think of my parents.

I have been back to Limoges on the tram to see Jean-Paul. He was at the bank, on the telephone trying to trace my parents. He has lost weight since we last met: no wobbling jowls, a strained look on his face as he tried to reassure me. He heard rumours; there were some people in the town perhaps who were working with the *gendarmerie*. He didn't want to alarm; nothing had been confirmed. He told me my note had not been touched, that my parents had not been back to the apartment. That other men had been.

Burning my fingers on the edge of the match I try to get as much life out of each flame as I can: I can't waste anything, nervous now as to when the next package might arrive. I can't rely on Isabelle. Apart from anything, it is humiliating having her wait on me in this way, forcing her to squirrel items from the shop. I pay her from father's money, glad to do that small thing at least. The transaction is awkward, me holding tins to my chest as she silently takes the money, brushes my arm. *I* should be protecting *her*, looking after her.

There are great holes in the thatched roof that allow dank puddles of rainwater to seep into the dust-lined boards. I can't search for my parents here; I know that I am useless to them if I stay. I wonder again where they are. Are they safe? Are they together? I imagine Father's soft expression when he turns to Mother, a hand automatically reaching out to hers, a soft chuckle of a laugh at something she says, now somewhere desperate to protect her, his delicate wife. A pianist. I picture her back in our apartment now, sitting on the leather stool, her hair twisted into a bun, her slender neck bent over the keys, a concentrated expression on her face as she follows the music, her feet pressing the pedals, playing softly in the corner of the living room as the sun pours through the windows. How can she not be there still, playing? Where has she gone?

I remove the slip of paper, my father's rushed handwriting scrawled across its surface, barely legible. The packet of money with my mother's ring is safe inside my pocket still. I read his note again, my finger tracing the lettering, slowly, slowly, following the loops and careful dots, over and over.

The logs scratch my forearms, tickling my flesh. Pushing open the door I move inside, depositing them down in the corner where they might dry out.

I nearly step on it. I can barely make it out in this light, but as my eyes adjust all the broken, dusty forms take form. I bend to pick it up. It's lying on the floor like a tiny doormat, one sheet folded. It's in an italic font, elegant, looping theatrically on thick, cream, embossed paper that seem at odds with the base words written there:

Leave now. You are not welcome here. Leave now or we will make you.

I release it so that it drifts down and rests on the wooden floorboards, the words still clear in the gloom, or perhaps burned into the insides of my eyes. My whole body slumps, beaten, as if the bearer of the note had come here and physically assaulted me. My head drops and I sink, back to the door, without knowing. In the semi-darkness, with the dank smell of soil and rain around me I hear a sob, and realize it is me. Reaching automatically for Father's envelope I pull it out of my pocket, remove the piece of paper carefully, wanting to replace the words, the ugly words with the comfort of Father's curved hand, as if he might be here to pull me back up to my feet.

You are not welcome here.

My whole body aches with the loss of them, with the loss of our life in France, with the realisation that it was never real, that they were all just waiting, that we are not welcome.

Leave now.

I reread Father's instructions, his list of contacts, my lifeline, his hope, and make up my mind.

ADELINE

1952, St Cecilia nunnery, south-west France

He is crying and I can't get to him. My hands bang against the wall in frustration. His wails grow louder, more desperate. She should appear, to hold him in her arms, bundled in his blanket, so that his little face peers out from a cloud of cotton. He should quieten, safe, nestled to her breast, hearing her heart beat in rhythm with his own. But now he is alone and screaming. No one is coming. She is not able to reach him. I can't reach him.

I am awake and it is nearly morning. The dream melts away gradually. It is simply me alone in this room, clutching the top of the bedclothes, feeling the cold sweat on my upper lip. His screams fade. Slices of shadow cut through the white wall of the room, across the crucifix, shapes hanging there, shifting subtly as I lie here, as another memory returns.

. . .

I am hanging out the washing to catch the afternoon sun. Isabelle silently helps me drape various items over the line, pegging towels and sheets, the effort turning her cheeks pink.

She is beautiful, an elegance to her movements, her skin glowing. Crickets sing. Birds swoop overhead back to the nests of their young. Hands on my hips, I breathe out slowly, feeling lighter. Isabelle reaches up to extract another peg from the line, and I see it.

So obvious. But how and when and... how... and who? *I continue to stare, looking her up and down, needing to sit down.*

Isabelle turns to look at me. She sees the understanding, her brow furrows and then she drops the shirt she is holding.

'I...' I gesture pointlessly, repeating, 'I... how... who have you...?' I can't form the words.

Isabelle walks towards me, arms outstretched, palms skyward. 'Maman, I—'

I stumble backwards, clinging to a sheet for support. 'How could you?' I whisper.

Isabelle looks as if I have punched her in the stomach: she stops, bends over herself slightly as tears form. A sheet, whipped up by a sudden breeze, hides her from me for a moment. Then she is back, standing there wordlessly, pale, frozen, meets my eye.

And then she turns on her heel and flees.

ISABELLE

Darling Paul,

I am shaking with the effort of writing these words to you, somehow it is worse than telling Father, not knowing what you will think of me, that I can't explain it to you face to face –

I am pregnant.

I promise I never meant to do it this way. Maman and Father are so cross, I have never seen Father so angry and with me, his darling. Didn't you always wonder whether he could ever be angry with me? Well, he can. Those permanently ruddy cheeks of his drained of colour when I told him. The napkin ring he'd been fiddling with moments before was forgotten. Maman kept repeating that people would talk, that I'd be the gossip of the village and you, Paul, would not come home to us, that the authorities would somehow stop it, how our family would be tainted and I have made it worse for you.

Have I? Is that possible? I never meant for that. Picture me here pleading with you to understand. You can't be angry too. I can't think of you somewhere loathing me. You are going to be an uncle to this child. He or she is going to be the most loved, cherished baby in the world. I can feel the little being moving around in my stomach, although I'm not sure if it is that likely this early in the pregnancy. Mother refuses to talk to me about it. She is always buttoned up on such matters and refuses to be drawn.

I haven't told him about the baby – it's not obvious yet, so I hide it under loose clothes. I know he has to leave France now, feel that I tie him here, and if he finds out he will stay and that cannot happen. Maman is so furious that I am unmarried and with no hope of a future now, but you know why this isn't possible. None of us has a future anymore, not a certain one anyway, and I know that this is right. God is watching over me, over us.

Come home to us. I need you.

Isabelle

SEBASTIAN

I left without a word to her.

She'd known I'd had to leave; I knew it was right, knew I was useless to everybody here. Yet I found myself finding another excuse to stay one more day, another moment to see her.

Sneaking about the countryside for days, my new life seems so far removed from what it was. Always moving at night, travelling to places I have only seen on a map before. I have become someone else. I pick up food where I can; I'm not proud of that, but I feel the dangers now snapping at my heels, and I can see Father and Mother somewhere out there urging me on, wanting me to get away.

I will find them, will track them down. For now though, I have to go somewhere safe, buy myself time to do this. I am not abandoning them, though the gnawing in my chest seems to contradict that thought. Swallowing the lump in my throat and hardening myself to the facts, I know I would never have stayed trespassing on Isabelle. If she too had been caught up in all this I would never have forgiven myself.

I said my own goodbye to her last night. She had wanted to hold me and I'd protested, embarrassed by my state. She'd taken my hand, looked to be on the edge of something, her mouth half-open, and then she had turned my hand over, stroked her thumb along the palm, pushing into my skin urgently, a film of tears across her eyes. We *will* be together again – that thought is a fierce little light burning in my chest, stubbornly refusing to go out, lighting my dreams with her face alone, and giving me hope to keep placing one foot in front of the other.

I reach Saint-Mathieu and here I know I am going to have to find food and a way of getting out of the country. My father's directions are clear but the journey seems an insurmountable task.

As if someone has heard my silent despair there is a noise behind me, the rattling sound of a cart. A man of no mean frame sits atop, a dirty straw hat obscures most of his face. I step out onto the road, holding up a hand to the farmer, whose goods are jiggling around in his cart as he navigates his way over the loose stones and uneven surface.

He eyes me warily as I move toward him. 'Where are you headed?' I ask.

'Market.' He nods his head south.

'Need help when you get there?'

'No.'

My shoulders sag.

'Get on,' he calls out to me, shunting himself a little further along the bench he is sitting on. He moves the reins into his left hand and holds out his right. 'Up.'

I take his hand gratefully and haul myself up onto the seat beside him; my leg twists and I grasp it as I sit down.

The farmer turns to look at me, then crinkles his nose a fraction. 'We'll try and find you a bath when we get there.' And with a roar of laugher he calls to the horse, and I bob along next to him, craning my neck only once to look around in what I think must be the direction of home. I send out a silent prayer that someone is watching over them and the people I love. We move further south as the day darkens.

We are climbing up a steep slope, the horse plodding so slowly we might be treading water, not moving forward. There is the sound of rolling apples slipping and sliding to the back of the cart as we gradually wind our way higher. The road turns slowly on a curve, like an oversized helter-skelter, the *chateau* of the village at the peak looking out, surveying the hills for miles, its enormous turrets forming impressive silhouettes against the cloud-streaked sky. The road starts to level out and a cacophony of noise – the chatter of shop goers, calls and cries from market sellers, the honking of horns, the shrill trill of bicycle bells – rends the air.

'Get yourself off and meet me back in the square in a bit.'

He tries to hand me some centimes, enough to get some breakfast, but I refuse to take them, touched by the gesture. I have my father's money.

'There's a well down that street' – he jerks his thumb over his shoulder – 'where you can clean yourself up.'

Shutters are being prised open to let in the daylight and someone has trained roses to climb the walls of their little terraced house. They snake round the window frames, the bold pink of their petals lifting the peeling paintwork and crumbling stone walls.

Two women are filling up buckets by the well as I approach, their grumbling complaints running the same course as ever: the shortages, the high prices, the extra work – the same chatter by every well in every village in France, I imagine. One woman, her hair tied up in a knot on her head, the scarf only just able to hold back loose strands of hair, moves aside for me.

Both fall silent as I join them, and I am well aware they will soon be grumbling about the smell of me. Strangely, the thought lifts my mouth as I haul up the bucket from the depths, gasping as I pour the whole lot over my head and bare arms, only just missing spattering the women. My skin bursts out into a thousand goosebumps as water streaks down my neck. The grime washes away in muddy rivulets towards the drain. I repeat the process, feeling better every time, flicking back my hair and rubbing my cheeks so that I feel as if I've dived head-first into a river.

A few hours later, we are sitting on upturned crates as our dwindling load is carried off in hessian sacks and bags by the locals. The farmer seems pleased with the day's work, and I have thrown myself into it with energy, bantering with the other sellers, charming the ladies who come to the stall, confident in my new guise. My suit and office patter are momentarily forgotten as I weigh out a load of onions, soil still clinging to their skins, hand over a bag and accept the money with a smile.

'I'll get you to Brantôme. You should be able to find some way of moving on from there,' he says.

'But I...' The town is a good twenty kilometres away and I know he had not been headed there.

'No arguing, that's what we'll be doing.'

I nod, acquiescing, 'Thank you.'

'Now there's a bit more room back there' – he jerks his

head to indicate the cart – 'get yourself under some rugs and I'll wake you when we're nearing.'

He hasn't asked me anything about my circumstances, or where I am headed, and I am grateful. Inside my trouser pocket the envelope, filthy and dog-eared, with my father's directions and addresses for people just inside the Pyrenees, contacts in Spain and England to help us get safely across the Channel. Father had planned it meticulously.

For all three of us.

As I lie my head down on some empty sacks, the smell of earth and vegetables still clinging to the itchy fabric, I think of my parents once more. Rubbing absent-mindedly at my knee – the day's work has made it ache – I push the pain away, concentrate fiercely on their faces – slipping – run through details: their wedding anniversary next month; the jewellery Mother wears; Father's favourite waistcoat, the spare buttons for it kept in his bureau; the vase they brought back for the hallway, streaked blues – my mother loved it.

Where are they now?

I close my eyes, and with the bump and slow grind of the cart we are off.

I don't know whether it is the motion of the cart that influences my dream but I am sitting on a bench in a station watching my parents board a train. They settle themselves behind a pane of glass in a carriage a little way down. The train is closed, the ticket inspector slamming the door.

I sink down deeper, my dream a comfort. They are together and heading somewhere: I don't know where.

TRISTAN

Samuel is nowhere to be seen. He doesn't turn up late and he isn't there at break and doesn't appear in any lessons all morning. At lunch, I ask André, who always plays with him, where he is, and he doesn't know.

We play football and one of the sides is short because he isn't here. I play on the side with only seven of us and we get beaten 0–2. I definitely think it would have helped having the eighth man. Samuel isn't exactly a great footballer, but it is better than having no one there at all.

We are covered in mud by the end of the lesson and we all wash in freezing cold water in the little building they call the wash house. It's been there for ever, with its barrels full to the brim with water that has little drowned insects floating on the surface. I make Hugues yelp by picking up one little bug by its wing and dangling it in front of his nose. He practically falls backwards into the barrel. He's such a little sniveller.

Mademoiselle Rochard is strange in our lesson today, looking at the empty chair where Samuel sits, and then out of the window. She sighs a lot. She doesn't get angry at all when

Michel spills his ink all over his book; in fact, I'm not sure she notices. She makes us read in silence for most of the lesson and I am so bored I can't concentrate, and anyway I don't understand a lot of the words I am reading and when I ask her to tell me what one means she seems to be cross with me for not knowing it. It's a long word though – *ineluctable* – which I don't think even Elèonore knows and she is in a class three years above me. Mademoiselle Rochard usually writes the new words on the board in her round writing with the i's with the big dots. She seems tired since the bump came.

She sets us a piece on what we have read and I work extra hard in the hope that she will snap out of her strange mood and notice.

At the end of the lesson I take my final piece up to her. 'Mademoiselle,' I say, pushing the paper towards her. 'I wrote over one side of the page in less than ten minutes.'

Normally she would be full of praise, but today she simply waves me away with one hand.

PAUL

Dear Isabelle,

Do you remember the day after Grandpoppy died and you screamed at me to cry? To cry for all the times he'd sit with us by the river, his trousers rolled to just below the knee, the scar on his shin, for his enormous reassuring hugs, his explosive laughter, his surreptitious passing of sweets beneath the table?

You were there sobbing your heart out for him, curled up and clutching the corner of his quilt that smelt of mothballs and peppermint, your face streaming, the pillowcase sodden and I patted you, pathetically, inadequate. And you reared up and shouted at me in broken words to cry for him, to show something.

I'd wondered it myself – was the stone that was lodged in my throat enough for a man who had taken me fishing for the first time, who had given me my first taste of wine, taught me to ride a bike? But, I thought, you cried over anything: a snatch of a song, a sunset bleeding over the tree line, a letter. You'd cry when you laughed too hard, snuffling, a hand to your mouth trying to cram both back in, but half-hearted, not caring to dab at your eyes.

'Cry!' you'd screamed.

They hung Rémi yesterday. In the courtyard. We were all watching. He pissed himself.

They hung him, Isabelle.

I cried then.

ADELINE

1952, St Cecilia nunnery, south-west France

All I see is Isabelle. My mind is suddenly full. Isabelle laughing, Isabelle turning in the doorway, bent over the vegetables, checking stock, cheeks flushed, grubby hands wiped on her apron, dancing in the aisles when she thinks I'm not watching. Laughing. Always laughing.

Isabelle pregnant, ankles barely swollen, a neat bump straining at her clothes. Puffing around the house, a hand always resting on her stomach, remaining tight-lipped as to the identity of the father. Her scarlet face when I asked whether she had been mistreated.

Her meeting the postman before he had a chance to step fully into the shop, squirrelling away letters to her room. Letters with a foreign postmark.

Isabelle ignoring the staring in the village, staying in the shop on the stool, no longer spending time with any other girls. Her gratitude to Monsieur Garande when he visited, her unexpected ally: wanting her back to teach at the school despite complaints from a ring of affronted mothers. Her face as it broke into a beam, her grateful thanks, her assurances she wouldn't disappoint, his gruff red-faced response.

Her silence as Madame Garande, not nearly as forgiving as her husband, eyes out on stalks, came to buy her weekly ration of butter, goggling as Isabelle reached up to the shelf behind the counter, her blouse lifting a little at the waist, the tell-tale sign of her shame on full display. Her pointed look at me. What kind of mother is she? What kind of girl has she raised?

Then Vicente – his open face, cheeks permanently brown. His anger forgotten as they made plans for the future. Him carrying the cradle down from the attic, washing and scrubbing it in the kitchen as I cooked, humming songs from his own childhood.

The cradle that first held my Paul, that tiny little bundle, lying on one side, underneath soft blankets, one hand thrown up by his face as I leant in to check he was breathing, so softly and silently I would lean in again.

Isabelle on the day her own baby came. Vicente banished from the house, Madame Martin summoned to take control of the room. Her orders, barked in a brisk voice, no-nonsense, five children of her own.

'Fetch more towels, madame,' she says, handing me a damp, soiled sheet.

The sweat forming on Isabelle's forehead as I stumble across the bedroom to the cupboard, reach down to collect more towels, Isabelle's cries fill the air, forced out of the little room on the second storey, into the street below. Terrible sounds, pain I couldn't alleviate, just watch helplessly.

Hours later, the sky darkens, candles throw snatches of light around the room, everything half in shadow, half out, fetching a warm saucepan of water. Vicente prowling the kitchen, starting at each cry.

'How is she, Adeline?' He rakes his fingers through his hair. I

reassure him, place a hand on his arm and look into his open face. Our baby. He pulls me towards him, holds me tightly, talks into my hair, 'My daughter, my poor baby.'

I soothe. I say it is going to be all right.

Madame Martin washing, tired, wearily smiling at us both as she wraps the baby – a boy – in a towel, handing him to Isabelle who reaches out to take him. He is cradled in her arms and she is cooing at him, her face full of love and tenderness, eyes not leaving his face even when Vicente rushes past, thanks Madame Martin, pulls up a chair at the side of the bed.

Our first grandchild: my grandchild.

'Hold him, Maman.' Isabelle holds out the little bundle.

A miniature face, darker hair and skin, different from the rest of our family.

I turn towards the door. 'I'll bring you a glass of water,' I say, leaving the room. Closing the door behind me I rest against it.

'Sebastian.' Isabelle's voice muffled, 'I want to call him Sebastian.'

I press my eyes closed with both hands.

The smile in Vicente's reply is unmistakable. 'Welcome to the world, little man.'

Sebastian.

His face when asleep. It is a narrower face than either Paul's or Isabelle's, and a shock of dark hair so startling to people when they look at his blonde mother and her family.

Isabelle's face as I ask questions, my confusion that Vicente is not concerned. Isabelle begging me to talk of something else.

I soothe. I say it is going to be all right.

A baby's cry makes my eyes snap open in the darkness. I lie there and listen to the muted sounds of Isabelle reaching for him, shushing him, rocking them both in the chair by her window as she nurses him. When they are asleep again I am still twitching, awake, alert, tense.

It is going to be all right.

Isabelle.

'The English doctor is coming. Will that change things?'

Marguerite still asks questions as if I will provide the answers.

She has brought me into the village. We are standing on a small triangle of grass, rough-edged and spattered with dandelions. In the middle there is a memorial to those soldiers who died in the wars – more names recently engraved. Its stone is pale and smooth even in this dull light; it is older now than some of the names etched into its surface, snaking around the base and across, some with the same surnames, again and again, around.

'Sister Constance says if he can't help you then you will be off to Toulouse next month. You must try.'

I continue to look at the memorial.

Sister Marguerite turns back to the memorial with a slight puff of frustration, then catches herself. 'So many,' she says, her hands clasped in front of her.

So many. I think then of all the other memorials in France, the other names that can barely fit onto the surfaces: so many names. I think of my father's name somewhere, he would be somewhere. I haven't thought of my father for an age. I feel tiny, a patch on a quilt, surrounded by other people's names and stories. For a second I feel the day sharpen, feel my limbs quicken for an instant with the feeling.

'It seems everyone has lost someone,' she says, a sideways glance at me.

As I look back at the names I feel my eyes sting with the truth of her words. And yet one name above all keeps running through my head. Her name.

Isabelle.

ISABELLE

Darling Paul,

You are an uncle. Will this news bring you home to us?

He is a tiny miracle, so small it frightens me sometimes. I can't imagine how his little body functions. I imagine those ghastly biology lessons at school, thinking of all the parts. Tiny. Pumping blood round his body, coursing through his veins, making his cheeks flush. I want to smother him to my chest, scratch the eyes from anyone who threatens him. It is a mad love: it hurts.

All the whispers and the words are meaningless when I look at his face. His father is out there. He doesn't know. I have done the right thing. This is the kind of love that would make a man cross an ocean. He is safe and will come home to us. As you will.

Isabelle

PAUL

Dear Isabelle,

I lie here sometimes and drag myself back with you all. I see the blues, greens and the hazy yellows of the village and I feel my heart beat slow. I hear the chatter in the high street, the gentle clink of cutlery from the round tables outside the Hotel Avril, Father's low laughter, the rustle of his newspaper. I feel my body slowly unclench, stretch my toes, roll my shoulders. I see me, the man you all remember, sitting languidly in the kitchen, a small glass of wine in my hand, teasing Mother as she cooks. The man whose concerns don't move beyond what she might be making for dinner. He smoothes the table with his palm. He has tanned hands. She is laughing, tickled by one of his stories.

I can't remember the stories any more.

It doesn't work. The noise is replaced – the lonely cough of my neighbour, distant talk from the guards in a language I don't understand, conspiratorial whisperings, the too-low whine of aircraft overhead, shouting, an explosion. I see only blacks and greys. My body is angular, bunched up, alert. My eyes move quickly to doorways, turned by the harsh clang of an order, my palms quickly dampen, my heart drills through my body.

I miss that man in the kitchen, the man you write your letters to.

Paul

ADELINE

1952, St Cecilia nunnery, south-west France

'And if you could remove your shoes and sit on the bed, that would be perfect.' The English doctor's accent is impeccable and he says the words with confidence. He hoists his bag onto the stool, unzips it and starts to pull out some of his instruments, placing them in a neat line on top of the woollen blanket at the foot of the bed. He must only be early thirties, mid-thirties perhaps. He has lost most of his hair, which always makes it a little harder to tell. He would be about Paul's age, I think.

'Our research has been focused on trying to help people with your affliction and we've had some successes both in England and across the Atlantic.' He straightens out a little stick with thin bristles around the top of it; a sort of toothbrush, although I have never seen one shaped that way. Another small box with wires emerges. The wires have pads attached. His things seem so at odds with the ancient stone rooms of the nunnery.

'I've brought some things with me and I don't want you to be in any way alarmed – I will explain each one to you before we proceed. But, of course' – he looks up at me – 'your other doctor tells me you have come across some of them before.'

I nod.

'Right, let's get cracking.' He looks at me. 'Oh, could you please remove your stockings? I want you to be able to really feel the effects.'

I get up from the bed and move behind a screen in the corner where I quickly roll down the offending stockings.

The doctor doesn't wait by the bed: hands crossed behind his back, bouncing on the balls of his feet, he walks across the room still talking. I emerge and pad across the wooden floorboards in bare feet. He is at the window, gesturing to the view outside, a little corner of the garden. 'Need it in this place, I expect. Place to grow vegetables. My wife would like it.'

I go to sit back on the bed, my back against the headboard, my legs now bare, my modesty protected by a rather ugly woollen skirt. A draught has triggered a spattering of goosebumps on my exposed legs but nothing is distracting the doctor.

He strides across the room. 'Shall we begin?'

The usual silence that greets any question directed at me does not throw him off course; in fact, he barely notices, perhaps relieved to be with a patient that isn't chattering away about their cold or their husband's chilblains.

'I must confess, madame, that I have been most curious to get over and see you.' A beat and he moves on. 'I'm going to try a range of methods to glean a vocal response from you. If at any moment you are uncomfortable and wish me to stop, please raise a hand and I will. Right.' He takes up the little stick with bristles and moves towards my feet. 'Doesn't last long on me – giggling like a schoolgirl after two seconds – but let's see how you get on.'

He tickles the soles of my feet and they jerk in response to the foreign feeling. The doctor glances up at my face, no doubt assuming I might break out into speech from the first touch. Not the least dejected, he spends a while running through different instruments on my feet: a rather shiny ball, cold to the touch; a sponge dipped in some kind of gel; a tiny needle which, he assures me, can penetrate only 1 millimetre.

At each surprise feeling I make little grunts, noises. They are new, I feel my eyes widening in surprise as another sound escapes.

The doctor seems to speed up the routine, switching back and forth between different instruments, trying various patterns, always checking my face for a response, encouraging any sound with a small nod.

Now he has set up the little box and wants to attach the pads to my left arm. 'It will administer a little shock to you in the hope of jump-starting . . . well, like all these things, prompting a response. I am hoping that one of these new-fangled tools might do the trick.'

I swallow, eye the box.

He presses a button and I start with surprise. Tiny vibrations course through my arms at the same time.

My passive response apparently troubles the English doctor, deflated now as he continues to manipulate and prod my limbs. He stops, a last little zing from a pad on my elbow making it twitch. 'This isn't working,' he says.

He removes the pads, slowly puts everything back into the bag and moves the bag off the stool.

Just when I expect him to make his goodbyes he drags the stool closer towards me and sits down. When he looks at me, his blue eyes seem enormous behind the thick lenses of his glasses. I shift a little under his gaze.

'I see you have a notebook there. I'd be most grateful to know a little more about you. Can you write some answers to my questions?'

I reach for the notebook and pencil on the side table and open up a page towards the back of the book in affirmation.

'What is your name?'

I write: *Adeline.*

'Surname?'

I don't remember.

Even as I write I feel a name nudging in my subconscious, just out of reach. Am I always doomed to repeat the same memories and not recall my own name?

'Can you remember when you last spoke?'

In my neat hand I respond.

Years ago.

'Can you be more precise?'

Before.

'Before? Before what, madame?'

I shake my head.

'Are you from the region?'

I shake my head from side to side, scrawling: *No.*

'Which region?'

Sister Marguerite has asked me this before.

I write *Limousin.*

'Ah! Famous for *la vache Limousine.*' He chuckles.

I nod.

He appears to have run out of questions.

'Madame, if I may – may I take a look at your throat?' He produces a torch from his shirt pocket. 'Open up.' He leans towards me and I duly obey. He inspects the insides of my mouth for a few moments, tilting his head this way and that, exploring every corner with the light and then, standing upright, he snaps off the torch, musing aloud: 'Had a roommate in the war from that area. Terribly nice chap.'

My pencil hovers.

'Whereabouts exactly are you from, madame, in the region?' He looks at my notebook, expecting me to write down the answer to his question.

My hand wavers.

He looks at me. 'When you lost your voice, was it after an accident, a fall perhaps? A knock to the head?'

I shake my head.

'But it came on suddenly, something triggered it?'

A pause as he holds my gaze. I nod slowly.

He persists. 'The nuns tell me you arrived late summer of '44. Where had you been up to then? Where was your home?'

I turn my face away from him, the pencil drops to the floor.

The doctor is still standing, waiting for my response. 'Madame,' he states. 'Madame, if you could help me to understand. May I?'

He reaches for my notebook.

I surrender it to him.

He reads snatches of the start, moments, dreams. He studies a sketch, lightly drawn. It is a girl's face.

He hands it back to me, searches my face. He has kind eyes. 'I hope very much, madame, to help you find your voice.'

He packs away his things, wrapping them carefully and placing them in his bag. I watch him as he shrugs on his coat, picks up his bag.

'I will see you tomorrow, madame.' He walks to the door,

one hand lifting the latch before he turns and looks at me still on the bed. 'Please let me help you.'

I lie back, staring ahead, hearing voices in the corridor just outside. The door finally thuds closed and the words are muffled.

I turn to the page in the notebook. She is smiling at me. Something in my chest flutters: a whisper. I remember more.

ISABELLE

There is a wedding today – Claudette's younger sister is marrying a boy in the village, about the only one left. As a farmer he might be left alone a while longer. They're both eighteen.

We are making our way to the church. Papa is pushing the big, old, navy-blue pram down the street. It bounces over the cobbles and makes Sebastian gurgle from inside. Grown women smile and coo before they have even peered over to see the baby inside. Papa reaches down now and again to tuck in a stray corner of blanket. A needless action, but one we all do: any excuse to fuss over him.

There are still a few stares, a few whispers behind gloved hands, but I link arms with Maman and pretend not to notice. I can feel her bristling as we walk. She looks soft today, wearing cream suede gloves Papa bought her years ago in Saint-Junien, and a floral dress that he loves. I'm wearing an old tea dress and finally feel my waist has returned. A tiny veiled hat is perched on top of my hair – which needs a trim –

and as I look through the netting, the whole street has been divided into tiny little squares.

The church has been decked out in flowers, in stands around the edge and on the end of pews in small bunches. The light grey walls are lifted and the sun blazes through the high, arched windows above the congregation. We side-step along a pew to take up our place towards the back. The scent of the flowers wafts around the church, finding every crevice, and my heart lifts when we all sing together. On the pew in front of us, pew cushions hang on bronze hooks – there is one that Maman made. She has just finished another one decorated with an image of a lily in white shot, outlined in yellow thread, a background of deep blue.

The church is full of faces, some familiar, others from neighbouring villages or further afield. In the front pew stands the proud mother, her eyes already glistening with unshed tears as she waits to see her daughter walk down the aisle. Beside her Claudette wears a steel-grey dress and a black wool cloche hat, as if she is attending a funeral.

The bride appears, faltering a little, her hair in a chignon laced with flowers. Then a smile behind her veil as she spots her equally nervous groom, standing waiting, wringing his hands, the small purple flower in his buttonhole already drooping in the heat. He is shorter than Sebastian, squat, broad in the shoulders, a tanned face suggesting that he is probably more at home baling hay than trussed up in his suit. For a moment I daydream of my own groom, the wedding we dreamed we would have. I glance down at Sebastian and almost whisper out loud, 'One day.' I think of his father's last words to me, his plan to get across to England. I haven't heard anything for weeks, pray he is safe somewhere, squeeze my eyes shut.

We emerge into the day and I take Maman's arm and

squeeze her elbow. She leans her body towards me, head almost resting on mine. I know she wants this for me, that she wants someone to come back and claim me.

We dance into the night in a marquee put up for the occasion; hay bales are scattered around for seating, rugs an attempt to soften the uneven ground. The evening is still and perfect, as if God had planned it all for the newlywed couple. As we step through the canvas, the smells and sounds pervade every pore. A local band are stamping their feet and playing old folk songs, while spinning girls and laughing children are squealing and stamping. Waiting girls tap their feet longingly, sitting perched like birds, heads darting one side to the other in search of a partner, looking longingly at a friend when an elusive hand is proffered.

Cider is being drunk, glasses overflowing from a barrel, so sickly sweet that it makes my head spin after the first few sips. Old men savour a last cigar; nearby, an enormous roasting pig rotates on a spit over the flames, its mouth wide open, screaming its last as it turns slowly, slowly, exuding the most delicious smells, its skin darkening at every turn. Tables are piled high with offerings from the women in the village, ration tickets pooled, other favours called in: *clafoutis*, bowls of lush peaches, meringues and every variety of cheese that this part of France can offer. I see Tristan, one of my most mischievous pupils, reaching up to stick his finger in the middle of the brie, earning himself a scolding from his mother. I hide a laugh in my hand as he catches my eye over her shoulder.

The portly Monsieur Lefevre, slumped in a corner, sinks lower and lower as I watch, until his body is almost flat on the ground, head crooked awkwardly at an angle. His wife steps over him to get some more dessert. Beyond them I catch the newlyweds in a quiet embrace, oblivious to jostling male friends making lewd jokes about things they know nothing about. They look at the groom in admiration and bewilderment: he has taken those first, tentative steps.

I feel removed from them all, carrying my own secrets.

Everyone glows in the evening light and the noise of talk and laughter and music merges so that I think that this is what happiness sounds like. I am exhausted, slouched on a hay bale, my son in my arms as I watch his grandmother move cautiously around the dance floor, one hand stiffly resting on the shoulder of Papa as he steers her around in the throng. Sebastian and I watch from our perch. He gurgles and my heart fills with love for him. I can feel his little frame, so small; he smiles and stretches his arms up as if dancing to the music. Papa comes over to take him home, takes him from me so carefully, kisses the top of my head.

Maman and I walk back down the high street. The moon is barely out tonight, muffled by cloud, and we stumble, giggling a little childishly, both full of cider and the mood of the evening.

'Maman,' I say, stopping in the street and looking at her. 'Sebastian's father is a Jew.'

I can see her confusion moving from one moment to the next, and then she repeats the words so slowly and quietly: 'A Jew.'

We walk in silence for a few minutes.

'He bought a tomato,' she announces.

I frown. 'Maman?' And then I remember the time he came to our shop, my surprise at seeing him there.

'Where is he now?'

'England.'

She nods.

'He doesn't know about the baby, Maman. I never told him. I couldn't – I knew he would have stayed and...'

She turns the key in the lock and lowers her voice. 'How many people know?'

'No one. I know what it can be like,' I say quietly.

She opens her mouth as if she is going to add something else but then pushes the door and steps inside.

Papa is in the kitchen, a tisane warming his hands. He looks at us both as we step into the little room. 'Isabelle?'

'I told Maman.'

'You knew?' she asks him in surprise, looking back at me, hurt.

'I met him, Adeline. He is a good boy.'

'You *met* him? Why did I not meet him?' Her voice rises.

The anger at our apparent collusion is obvious, her eyes filled with questions, the hurt of feeling left out. I can hear the words as if she has spoken them out loud. Do we not care that her son, my brother, is in prison, that having any kind of association like that might threaten his safe return? How many months have we hidden this from her?

'It wasn't like that,' Papa insists, moving across to her.

I don't know why I ruined things. Why I needed to say anything. She had stopped asking months ago. Yet tonight I'd wanted to tell her.

I feel my throat tighten as Maman stands there, looking so lost.

Sebastian starts screaming in his room above us and I hurry from the kitchen, leaving them both there.

Papa's voice, from the stairs, makes my eyes close. 'Darling. Adeline.'

'How dare you,' she breathes.

I lose his voice halfway through a sentence: 'We didn't want to worry you. But I regret it, I should have sa—' and then

I am shushing my baby, lifting him out of his cot, feeling his warm, soft cheek damp with his tears – or mine – as I rock and shush and try to ignore the voices under the floorboards: angry, snapping, as they wash around us, our making.

The anger doesn't fade and Maman stamps about the shop the next morning, jaw fixed, short with the customers, refusing to acknowledge me or Papa, leaving the kitchen before we eat breakfast so we are not all in the same room together. She doesn't look in on Sebastian either.

I sit behind the counter of the shop, shoulders slumped as she heaves and puffs in the storeroom in the back. But then a voice, a voice from the very depths of my mind, pipes up: 'What is there to be so serious about?'

And there, in the doorway, is Paul – our Paul. He stands in the entrance to the shop, his large frame blocking out the light as he towers there, dressed in dirty uniform, his face tired but a smile on his lips.

The storeroom falls silent and I feel my mother's presence in the shop. She is standing wordlessly in the doorway at the back, a bag of flour hanging forgotten in her hand as she stares at him from across the shop. The bag falls and before I can react she has walked across the floor to him, her hand reaching up to touch his face, then throwing herself into his arms that have flung out wide.

My stool scrapes back as I move to join them and, as I do, Sebastian can be heard crying upstairs.

Paul draws back. 'What is that?'

He looks towards the stairs leading up to the flat and at that moment I catch my mother's eye, a bubble bursts, and we both start to laugh.

SEBASTIAN

London, England

It is the porcelain figures standing resolutely in the window of a shop on the corner of my street in London that conjure up my mother's face: her hair drawn back in a low bun, a sliver of silk scarf around her throat, her eyes looking at my father as she dusts around the pieces in the display cabinet. She would hate the fact that no one will have dusted them. I imagine them now, standing in the shadows of the apartment; the shutters, no doubt left open in my haste, a thin line of sunlight highlighting the thin film of dust on their cocked arms, their fragile heads, as they wait for her to return.

I dream of them.

The dust has piled, layer upon layer on their delicate china forms so that they are drowning in it; particles in the air, heaped at their feet like a churned-up battleground... still they wait patiently, rigid, hopeful. The dust keeps coming, they are buried now, one delicate wrist protruding from the pile, the tips of the fingers manicured, the elegant arch of the hand pointing skyward until it, too, is lost underneath the dust that keeps coming.

I wake, snatching at the covers, looking around unseeing in the darkness, remembering France, Spain, London. Lying down again, I focus on my family, Isabelle, feel panic that I can't see their faces clearly any more – just lines and colours, parts of photographs, no distinct features, just a patchwork quilt that makes up something ugly. Their reality is slipping and now I can feel tears blurring their faces, melting them before me so that they lose their form completely, and become part of the rain, and then I am asleep again.

My arrival in England had seemed impossible for a time. There were months of travelling, waiting, sleeping nights in outhouses, barns – one awful week in the hold of a ship, arranged by a contact of my father in Spain, praying every moment it wouldn't be torpedoed. Bedraggled, confused, I was even more lost when I finally made it, realized there were no signs to anywhere and no one in the country spoke my language.

It seems to rain non-stop so my clothes never quite dry and have taken on the smell of London permanently: smoke and the press of bodies mingled with the musty smell of soggy cotton. In parts of the city the streets are a warren, narrow and never-ending, and the buzz of so many people in one place is more than I could have ever imagined. They emerge like ants, shoring up their colony.

I followed Father's instructions and stayed with a family he knew in North London for a few days, eating most of their larder in that time. They were leaving for the country, somewhere in the west, and wanted me to join them. But I needed to stay, was restless to feel useful, to be close to where I could get information. I looked around for another arrangement, a flat share. They left me, kisses on both cheeks, a shake of the hand; I promised them I would let them know when there is news.

I push the door to the flat closed, snapping off my little torch on entering the well-lit living room. Edward is hunched in front of the fire, a dusty bottle of red wine half-finished beside him. He looks up as I shake the rain from my coat in the doorway. 'Sit down, my friend, sit down.' He struggles with the s's a little.

Cab Calloway is singing in the background. Edward fell in love with his music after seeing *Stormy Weather* at the pictures with a girl he was sweet on. I can't decide whether it's the jazz or the girl that has him drumming his fingers on the armrest of his chair, a sleepy look to his eyes. The newspaper is open beside him. He has a melancholic habit of reading the lists of men who have died or who are missing when the jazz singers play on the turntable.

He holds the bottle out to me and in stilted French asks if I want a glass. In fact, the line he slurs roughly translates as: 'Glass, drink, me,' and I can't help but grin at him before accepting it, making a silent toast to him. I don't ask where he got it from, this rare treat.

The grey bags under his eyes seem more pronounced in the light from the flames, showing up the thick lines underneath. He is a special constable in the city, a fire warden, while all his spare time is spent furiously cramming revision for his medical exams. Edward Taylor is a wiry chap, all limbs and angles, who'd been turned down in 1940 on account of his terrible eyesight. A pair of glasses, one lens nearly as thick as my little finger, is testament to his affliction. When he doesn't have them to hand he screws up his eyes and holds his arms out, patting nearby tables for them, his thighs must be spattered with bruises from his various clashes with furniture.

He, too, understands what it's like to be largely impotent in a war.

I pull up the card table in front of the fire and we start to play a convoluted version of gin rummy. He taught me the rules, slowly and patiently, but I still stare stupidly at the collection of diamonds in my hand. We don't talk – we already know each other's sorry stories after swapping them in both broken languages after getting wonderfully drunk the evening I moved in. Edward now knows every detail of my life so far, and nearly every detail of my romance with Isabelle. That is the effect of a bottle of brandy.

Sirens wail. We stagger down flights of stairs to the cellar, pushing open the door to see our neighbours already sitting in huddles on flattened cushions. Light comes from lamps on occasional tables. It's a strangely comfortable scene, only marred by the woman on the ground floor: a mother of four, whose face is always pale despite the warm glow of the room; her children sleep, oblivious, around her. One man is eating a late dinner off a plate on his lap, joking with Edward in a quiet undertone. My stomach rumble, the reconstituted eggs and powdered milk I had for dinner in no way adequate.

We carry on playing gin rummy, frozen like deer in the moment when the floor vibrates – something a little too close for comfort, no one wanting to be trapped here. I focus on my hands as I start to feel the room close around me, the shadows on the walls dancing. Picking at a nail I breathe out slowly; Edward catches my eye, understands, gives me a weak smile. We rest against the walls, shut our eyes.

Father's burble of a laugh, tickled by something I've said; Mother's easy presence, her piano pieces fluttering around the apartment like they are tripping on a breeze, and then…

Isabelle. A halo of sunshine around golden hair, green eyes that flash in my dreams, waking me with a start like she's been watching me sleep.

In the morning, we stumble out and survey the streets around us, staring at the blown-out upper half of a nearby house, bed and belongings dripping out of the exposed wall, spewing its contents into the street below: the bath, balanced precariously at a slant, tiles, bricks, books, china, fragments. Two figures standing wordlessly hand in hand staring at it, the woman's neat grey curls under a burgundy felt hat, the man in a large overcoat, as if they are about to take their daily constitutional.

There is no word. Jean-Paul and I are in regular correspondence – without his wires of money I would have never made it this far – but he has heard nothing from my parents. The local *gendarmes* are being wholly unhelpful, and a lot of their mutual friends either can't help or refuse to do so. Never once in the letters do either of us hint at the reasons behind the silence, neither of us ready to admit the rumours we have heard. I beg Jean-Paul to keep up the search, desperately guilty not to be back in France helping him.

'I am so pleased you got out,' he often repeats. 'And your parents would be too.'

He continues to run the bank in both mine and Father's absence, for us to return to after the war. I cling to his optimism: I devour newspapers for news of them, not knowing how much of what I am reading is simply propaganda served up by the Allies, but shocked anyway by the talk of camps, of men, women and children being shot, sent away.

How can everyone stand by? Is it really all true?

I try to picture my mother in these appalling circumstances but can never fully convince myself that the delicate woman who loves her figurines, delicately embroidered patterns, the pianoforte, can have found her way to one of these places. Nor can I conceive of my father being treated as some faceless nobody; I see him grumbling about the heat on a summer's day, noticing a speck of dust on his coat and removing it with a quick flick of his wrist. Any fool can see that my parents are simple, pleasant, well-mannered people.

I hold on to this hope as I continue to enquire. I write dozens of letters, haunt the gates of various embassies, read every newspaper, beg Edward to make his parents use their contacts, their friends' contacts. No one has heard anything.

It's as if nothing extraordinary has happened at all.

Edward helps me find work with an ambulance crew. I learn how to check the tyres, battery and radiator, how to keep the levels topped up before every outing. They need help, physical strength, and I feel useful, enjoying the ache in my limbs at the end of a day as I weave back through the darkening streets of London, in amongst the bustle of other commuters, or uniformed men and women on leave, hastening to whichever social event might drown out their war-weary thoughts for a moment.

For me, in my head, I am stuck in France. I see Isabelle everywhere: in every laugh, a glimpse of blue dress, a red suede shoe, blonde hair. It is never her – a flash of her, but always smaller and disappointing: the shoes belong to a stout brunette, the laugh jars, the blonde hair is too short. For a second though, a second of possibility, I ache for it to really be her. I crave her reassuring gaze, steady on my face; to see myself as she sees me, somebody strong. I try to conjure up the feel of her touch on my arms, the small of my back; I try to recall her laugh captured in a glove, a sputter. The ghost of her kisses remain on my cheeks and, as I wipe my face in the mirror, I imagine I am wiping them away. I am scared that we will stay apart for years and I realize that, in many ways, I need the agony, need the sharp jolt when I realize it is not her, because then I'm reminded what I feel is real and if she feels a fraction of it, she will wait for me.

I write letters to her in a neat scrawl, fold them up carefully, buy envelopes for them. They speak of nothing and everything: the smeared grin of a toddler on a bus; the sound of the anti-aircraft guns over the city at night; the sky, almost free from stars above my head; my introduction to whale meat. My parents. The war. Then a series of questions enquiring as to the minutiae of her day, her life, questions so humdrum that they force me there, across the Channel, back in front of her, listening to the details first-hand.

Every time a letter arrives in barely legible, slanting blue ink – she has always had terrible handwriting, she admits – I feel I am at home again in my bedroom in Limoges, my mother downstairs singing a little aria as she plays, Father reading in his favourite chair. I sit, head resting against the whitewashed wall of the single bedroom, a threadbare rug, scrubbed-pine chest of drawers, washbowl and faded photograph of Westminster Bridge the only accessories to the blank space, and close my eyes.

ISABELLE

My darling,

Please don't despair, I can't bear the idea that you are giving up on them. Someone is bound to know something and will help. It's all the chaos of war, everything is so slow. Do have faith, they will be so happy you are in London. It sounds as messy and loud as I imagine Paris to be and you caught up in it all. You really mustn't doubt the decision. It is safer this way.

Can I share our news with you? Paul has returned. He walked straight into the shop as if it were four years ago and nothing much had changed. It was so strange I can't tell you. The whole camp was released because the Germans were going east. I think he's still in shock. He looks impossibly old, I almost didn't recognize him and he has a full beard and his eyes seem darker now than before. We are all so pleased to have him back with us. I know he doesn't want to talk too much about things but the village will heal him. Maman is so happy she could burst, she hums snatches of songs in the shop, our customers don't know how to take it. It is wonderful.

Please let me know if I can do anything to help you. The rumours are that it will be over soon, the British are on their way, the Americans too, it really can't be long now. I will pray for that day and keep writing to you in the meantime.

There are things I want to share with you, so desperately, but I want to see you in person, to be able to see the look in your eyes and feel your arms around me when you learn them. Please don't blame me for concealing them.

Don't give up hope,

Isabelle

ADELINE

1952, St Cecilia nunnery, south-west France

Frost coats the windowpane and the windows are cloudy with steamy cold. I dress quickly, staring at the grille on the door, freezing at a distant noise, a sneeze, some steps. They disappear off and I push my feet into my shoes, brush at my skirt as I catch my eye in the square of mirror above the washing bowl and jug. My eyes are red-rimmed, the deep lines around them made more prominent by lack of sleep. My thin lips have been chewed.

I put a hand to my throat. The woman in the mirror copies me. We pause, staring at each other.

Blinking once, I know I can't procrastinate any more. I place a hand on the top of the chest of drawers, the smooth wood grounding me in the moment. I walk towards the door, pausing by it to listen. The hint of coffee and croissant wafts through the grille.

I open the door, looking to the left where, at the end of the corridor before it turns, another door awaits me. I don't want to be seen, could not bear the look on Sister Marguerite's face: hopeful.

It will be empty. I know there is no service at this time – the nuns are eating, having finished Prime a few minutes ago. I heard them leave in a long line, the gentle swish of their habits, cloth brushing stone, whispers from some, a small cough. Then the sounds of benches being scraped back in the distance, cutlery clinking.

I know I must leave now, have been building towards this moment, promising myself it would be today.

Stepping into the corridor I feel myself wobble. Swallowing the fear I move in a straight line, eyes not leaving the door cut into the stone. I pass arched windows, the stained glass dulled by the weather beyond; in an alcove to my left, I can feel the chipped marble figure of Saint Bernadette watching me walk past. I wipe my hands on my skirt, my throat feeling like sand.

There were times when I wanted to attend services, when the church had been a sanctuary, lying watchful at the top of the village, when I would feel relief as I pushed open the heavy door, feel the coolness wash over me, slide into a pew, rub the rosary beads, familiar as they ran through my fingers.

Standing in front of the door now I swallow again and place a hand on the door. The iron handle is bolted into the wood, the deep oak panels weathered with age, rough to the touch. Gripping it, I pull and open the door. It swings into the corridor, a faint creak as the heavy hinges move.

Stepping over the threshold and ducking through it, I have made my choice.

The room is darker, smells closer and thicker than in the corridor. I turn and pull the door back; it thuds shut and I shiver with the sound. Tentatively approaching the bottom of the aisle, the chapel seems to be holding its breath, observing me, this small figure.

No one sits in the rows of wooden pews; the stained-glass windows turn the light into streaks of red and orange that split the air like a rainbow. Behind the altar Jesus breaks bread with his disciples; the scene of the tableau is a relief carved out of wooden panels on the back wall. Sister Marguerite has read the familiar story to me many times. Candles stand ready to be lit in brackets on the wall, a lingering smell of smoke suggesting they were used that morning. In the lectern, the gilt-edged Bible lies open at the middle, awaiting a reader.

Sister Constance wants me to attend the services, but I can't sit there and join them: so many other bodies around me, crammed into the pews on either side, filing in and down the aisle, their breath warming the air, the candles lit, their shadows quivering on the walls, the tightness in my chest as I sit trapped on either side by the black habits of the nuns, pale hands clasped in laps, a hundred rosary beads and mouths speaking familiar words. I can't do it. Even alone in the chapel I feel the darkness of the corners inching towards me as I stand here, head now clogged with thoughts; my chest rising and falling to a quicker pace, I lose the sense of calm as my preparations melt away into the cracks of the dusty flagstones.

I am walking up the aisle with my family. Vicente is carrying Isabelle, her bony legs like matchsticks compared to his forearms, Paul scowling as I smooth his hair down once more, looking awkward in his shirt and tie, tugging on his collar, looking at the window high above the altar, clearly longing to be outside.

The first hymn rouses the building and Isabelle stands on the pew to my side, trying to follow the words in the book. The sermon is ponderous and the prayers come as a relief. Paul scuffs the floor with the toe of his shoe, practically shouting the 'Amen' a second too late. I look at him, my mouth set in a line, and he reaches for my hand.

We go to file out. I whisper a prayer, make the sign of the cross at the crucifix and place a hand on Paul's shoulder to lead him out. Vicente follows, Isabelle resting on a shoulder, her eyes fluttering closed. We move down the aisle as a four, past the plaque, the names of the soldiers who died in the First World War listed on its surface. I walk past it without a thought.

I am walking up the aisle with my uncle. I am clutching his arm, staring at the wide figure at the end, feeling a hundred eyes on me. Overwhelmed I look away, past the faces. A cream ribbon on the end of one of the pews has come loose. The church is crammed with flowers and the air is warm with the scent of lavender and roses. My breath is thick beneath the veil, which gives everything a creamy wash. Vicente turns then, his eyes searching for me, and then I see his teeth as he breaks into a smile and I can't help but giggle, nerves fluttering in my stomach as I approach him. The veil is lifted over my face and my uncle kisses me on both cheeks but all I am aware of is the reassuring shape on my other side as Vicente waits for me to turn to him.

Looking around at the chapel it is the now, the present, which seems to have become blurred – the images of the church in the village seem clearer, the faces that have often been in the background, faceless, now step forward, features sharper: her eyes no longer indistinct but green, there is a spot in an iris, a ringlet of blonde snaking over a shoulder; his enormous muddied hands rest on my arm, he is wearing a familiar checked work shirt; and then my boy, sandy hair sticking up, younger than I normally recall him.

My family.

They have found me in this place.

The room becomes darker around me as I focus on them: the walls blend with the floor, the smell of burning softens the edges. Then they are fading, and the corners of the room seem darker than night. I can feel my breath catch in my throat, try to control myself.

I close my eyes, refuse to be dragged under, picture the corridor beyond the chapel door, light flooding through the windows, the worn patches in the middle of the stones where so many nuns have made their way down the halls.

As I slow my breathing and open my eyes again, the room returns to normal: the candles wait to be lit, the wooden pews a rich brown, the stained glass glowing in the space. Things have righted and I allow myself a small smile. Turning to the crucifix ahead of me, I incline my head a fraction and leave.

Leaning back against the door in the corridor, my eyes adjusting to the brighter light – more pale blue and grey now that I am out – a sudden breeze forces me to wrap my arms around my body and I hurry back to my room, wondering if things have changed for me.

Wondering if I am ready now.

PAUL

Some nights I forget and I wait in the darkness to hear the ragged breathing, a distant cough, of another man. Then there is nothing but the quiet hum of insects in the night air, the gentle wafting breeze that lifts the bottoms of the curtains and for a moment makes my heart stop as a shadow crosses the opposite wall. I sit up quickly, a quick breath out, before I realize.

Father and I speak of his own war experiences and I feel like I have been given a key to a different man's past. Men he fought alongside, men he rested up against, mud, rainwater filling their boots, the shudder of shells all around them, smeared photographs of girls with mild smiles, earnest eyes, passed around. Promises made. So many men.

I tell him of the others. The work, enforced monotony, our reckless attempts at sabotage, our utter helplessness, kept for months, then years. Some escapes. Mostly failed. I tell him about Rémi.

When we talk it is dark and I just hear the steady rumble of his replies, talk to the space, able to spill our secrets to the night without having to meet each other's eyes and recognize our own fear there. I know that next door my nephew lies sleeping in this other world, untouched by the ugliness.

His brand-newness makes me think of the old me, the boy who left, so full of excitement, so naïve. He gives me hope that I can find that boy again, that this gentle village life can be mine again. I don't want to venture further; I feel like I am truly home now.

Some nights I sleep, fully, no dreams, wrapped in the warmth of our small house, my family around me.

TRISTAN

Christmas is absolutely my favourite time of the year. Every Christmas Eve, Maman lays out a glass of sherry and a couple of macaroons and a carrot for the reindeer and we get into our pyjamas, say our prayers, and hop into bed. I pray for an extra-large present in the morning, but don't admit that to anyone as I know Maman would be angry with me. 'Un-Christian,' she would say.

I can never sleep for the excitement, and I am always convinced that I hear Père Noël tiptoeing around the house leaving goodies for everyone at the foot of their beds. Dimitri says it's impossible that I could ever see him as he has to visit so many children in one evening and he worked out that Père Noël can stay for only 3.2 milliseconds in each house and that isn't even as long as a blink. He has to visit around a million billion thousand children in one night. Approximately. And he doesn't even just visit the children in France – he goes all over the world. He probably won't go to Germany this year though, because the children there have been really naughty.

Anyway, I'm not sure Dimitri has factored in the time-zone difference. We have been learning about this in Geography. Apparently in Australia it is daytime when it is night and summer when it is winter – most peculiar. I'm sure that Père Noël does stay a while, as the sherry and the macaroons have always been drunk and eaten, and he is magical so can probably stop time, or something like that.

I'm nervous that he might not come at all because there is a war on and a lot of things have stopped because of it. No one drives cars anymore, although I know Père Noël has a sleigh with reindeer, so a lack of petrol won't stop him. Maman has told me that he will still visit but might bring different types of things this Christmas because of these 'trying times'. Hitler must be trying to win a war in Lapland too. And what with the fact that we've moved house twice, I'm really not sure Père Noël will be able to keep up – it makes *my* head spin and I am a part of this family. He has remembered for the last two years, so I sincerely hope he will this year too.

Papa has been reading to us by the fire, stories about an English king called Arthur and his Knights of the Round Table. My favourite is Sir Gawain and the opening part of the story where he beheads the Green Knight who then picks up his head from the floor and walks out! Elèonore only seems to like the sissy bits where they all fall in love and squeals every time Papa mentions a duel. I imagine she sees herself shut up in a tower, waiting for a prince to come. I wouldn't mind so much if she was but I can't really imagine who would want to travel all that far to free her. Oh dear, I think that was another 'un-Christian' thought. I hope Père Noël can't listen to my thoughts like Jesus can.

Luc and I are playing snap. Elèonore has asked to join us and I have said yes – it is Christmas after all. It is a lively game and only hard when Elèonore or I have the matching cards as Luc is so slow, and often yells 'SNAP!' when he has turned over a different suit or number. Elèonore patiently explains the rules to him one more time and he looks at me over her shoulder and rolls his eyes. It makes me giggle and Elèonore gets in a strop and refuses to play with us anymore and goes back to her book but that is fine by me. I win quickly after that, and Luc still continues to shout 'SNAP!' at all the wrong moments.

All this is interrupted by Papa dragging in the most enormous Christmas tree. Instantly the room smells of Christmas. I jump up to run and get the little men that I have made out of pinecones. Maman asks Claudette to help her. One special decoration is wrapped in a box with lining to stop it breaking, and I recognize it from Paris when Claudette pulls it out.

'Careful. Tristan darling this one is made of glass and my own mother watched the man making it,' Maman says, motioning for Claudette to pass it to me to hang. It is beautiful, all gold, like there are little lights dancing inside it.

We spend ages decorating the tree so it looks as if it is dripping in diamonds, like a film star. As Papa removes the final piece, the star for the top, from the box, we all gasp in unison. He reaches up to the top of the tree and places the star over the twig sticking up at the top. The six-pointed star completes the tree and we all stand back and admire our work.

I suddenly think of Samuel, the boy who never returned to my school. I wonder where he is this Christmas. The star twinkles in the light of the room. I beam at it and at my family as Papa sits down and plays carols in the soft light.

ADELINE

1952, St Cecilia nunnery, south-west France

I scribble frantically now, sitting on a chair by the greenhouse as the nuns bend and sow various seeds. The memories are bursting out and I can barely keep up as I scrawl the words. I am remembering that delicious feeling: my son returned. Never had the house been happier.

He talks in garbled language to his nephew, bouncing him on his knee and chattering on as if he can understand him.

Resting in Vicente's armchair, his eyes closed, two lines furrowed in his brow, reliving memories in his sleep.

He starts and wakes. A shout. He snaps at Isabelle, makes her drop her glass. His eyes are elsewhere: not with us. They are a deeper shade of green.

He is in his pyjamas jabbering about the drone of aircraft overhead but there is nothing but crickets to be heard in the still air of the sleeping high street.

My hand, palm flat, on a wall, the bricks cold under my

hand. I am listening. Paul and Vicente are talking about the factory, about where Paul was held.

My eyes on the ceiling, pulling the blanket up under my chin. Paul is home with us at last.

Paul at the sink, staring at the chickens out of the window. My tisane is cold but I can't look away. Still amazed he is standing, real, in the kitchen. He looks older than the boy that left, much older. His cheekbones are more prominent, he has unfamiliar, muscular arms. He turns around and there is a new expression on his face. He asks something and my response makes him laugh. His laugh, his low, gravelly laugh, that so echoes Vicente's, is him, and I relax back into my chair.

Paul leaving the shop, kissing me on the cheek and gently pinching Sebastian's nose to make him gurgle. He passes the window, a man with purpose, a renewed energy in his stride, his chin up. Off to see a man from Paris who is rumoured to be hiring. He greets the barrelled, humourless Monsieur Lefevre with a tip of his hat, turns back to make a face at me through the shop window. I muffle a laugh in my hand.

I remember feeling blessed, that we deserved it; we deserved to have him back.

ISABELLE

Paul has returned to us. I still catch myself in the mornings, surprised to see him bustling into the kitchen, holding his arms out for his nephew. He is slowly returning to us piece by piece: his laugh has returned, slow at first, as if it were unsure. His face creases in new ways now.

We take Sebastian down to the river, talk about life before the war and what Sebastian's childhood will be like in the village that seems in so many ways not to be unchanged. He is incredibly gentle with him, holding him to him like he is the most fragile thing on this earth, dropping kisses on his wispy hair without thought. He doesn't sleep well and when I am feeding Sebastian he will lie quietly at the foot of the bed, staring at the ceiling as we talk into the early hours.

I'm so thankful he is back but sometimes... I feel it is as if I've bargained one for the other – like I can't have them both. Too much happiness.

Sebastian. What do I miss about him? The feeling I get when he looks at me, that plunge in my insides like I've just swallowed something heavy that makes me full so that I don't want food. The sound of his low laugh, bubbling up, unashamed, the way he nods in quiet agreement when I'm telling a story. The feeling of his hand as it takes mine.

The missing gets worse, and some days I want to write and tell him, tell him about his son, tell him we will find a way, that it is safe, that he should come back. His son is sitting, turning over. He looks like him: the same dark hair, guileless expression. I write half-letters, abandon them in the middle of words, rub them out, go over them again. Then, when I realise I can't explain, ball them up and push them into the fire so that I'm not tempted to start them again.

And the fear, gnawing, fear that we will never have those days again, that it is lost to the war, that I will grow old, lined, and he will still be gone. That he will miss these things, that I will stop noticing, that the war will have killed it, if not us.

That the absence will be all that I'll ever know.

TRISTAN

Papa is more relaxed these days – kissing Mother on the head after mealtimes, which I think means he is happy. He said something about the place being safe but I think it has always been safe, as in Paris there were a lot more dangers, like cars.

I look for André in our corner of the schoolyard. He towers over everyone else and his hair looks like one of Clarisse's mops but he's not here today. André is my best friend now. He has moved to the desk next to me. He used to sit with Samuel but since Samuel left he sits there. He is brilliant at throwing and catching and has taught me and Dimitri how to fish. He has only really been my best friend for a few weeks and Michel is now my second-best friend. André's been in the village since the start of the war but he came from a place in the east, near the border, and his family fled the Hun and his dad has been sent away somewhere in the north. He likes our house because the garden is huge. Also we can stand and press our faces up against the gate and watch as the tram passes down below. When we press our faces into the railings our cheeks sort of buzz and hum against the metal when it goes past.

I want to tell him about the strange dream I had last night about giant pigeons. André knows all sorts of funny things about the war and he was telling me that the Allies use carrier pigeons when they advance on enemy lines and then send all the details back in little pouches tied to their legs. He told me that the pigeons can fly to England, or other places far away, with all this information and the Nazis can't stop them because pigeons are so small so most of the aircraft can't hit them. He says some of them have been awarded medals for bravery. That made Papa laugh and ruffle my hair. It sounds so clever to me, and now I am going to look out for pigeons flying over the village, as you never know – they might be carrying secret information about the enemy that will end this war.

André told me that earlier in the war some men in Germany tried to kill Adolf Hitler by blowing him up but they didn't succeed and when I asked what happened to them André said he didn't know. I imagine, much like the pigeons, Hitler would want to shoot them down too. I think about the spies in the forest then. Everything seems all right since we told Papa about the spies so I think we helped. I think the war will probably end soon, what with the spies being caught, and all the pigeons.

It has been so cold this winter and it has dragged on and on. I swear I have icicles hanging from my nose when we are in school. My knees are practically blue with cold by lunch and I pull up my socks to try and keep out the worst of it. My writing has got all squiggly as my hands are so numb. Most of the teachers tend to leave us to it in the cobbled yard we have to run around in at break. There is a stone wall at one end and André and I invented another game the other day, to try and stop from freezing, but it is already banned because stupid Hugues nearly broke his nose. The rule is you must close your eyes and run at the wall and then stop when you think you are just about to hit it. The closest to the wall wins. But of course Hugues went and ran into the wall and got a nosebleed and his mother yelled at him in front of everyone as she had to leave the hotel where she worked, to come and take him home.

Today, however, I'm too cold to play ball games and André isn't here. He had a sore throat yesterday so he is probably at home, his mother bringing him warm soup. I suddenly wish I had been taken ill. I scuff my shoe on the ground and wait for the bell so I can go back inside. I blow out, my breath making a little puff of smoke in front of me, like the clouds of smoke that hang around the tables in the café opposite, from the men's pipes. I amuse myself for a few moments pretending I too am smoking and enjoy making the little swirls in the air.

'Very impressive.' Mademoiselle Rochard laughs.

I jump and blush a little when I realize who it is. I don't normally talk to her at break times and now she's caught me doing something so silly, but her face is kind. She looks a little different, not how I think of her in my head. She still has her long blonde hair, although she has it in a big plait thing around her head. Her cheeks are pink from the cold. She rubs her hands together; she is wearing leather gloves, a faded red colour, they look soft. She hasn't been my teacher for ages. She teaches the younger ones now, but since the bump went away and the baby came she doesn't come into school every day.

'You look older,' she says.

I don't know what to say.

'You too.'

She laughs.

'How are your family getting on?'

'Very well, thank you.'

'Your mother visits our shop and talks about you all.' She waves in the direction of the high street. I wonder what Mother talks about and hopes she puts me in a good light. 'I'm sorry if I seem nosey... A bad habit.' She laughs again.

I smile at her – you sort of can't help it; she has one of those faces. It is at that moment that a bird flies over and I watch it carefully, wondering if it is a pigeon – it's about the right size. And suddenly I am telling her all about what André had told me and she laughs too, the way Papa had.

'England, really?' she says. 'How wonderful.'

'Some have won medals for bravery,' I add.

The bell goes for the next lesson.

'I wouldn't mind being able to fly to England,' she says, as I turn to go inside. She watches the pigeon fly right overhead and away.

My heart sinks, but I don't tell her that I was wrong: it is a blackbird. Blackbirds don't fly anywhere with little messages on their feet for spying or win medals. In fact, mostly I think they go in pies.

SEBASTIAN

London, England

Some weeks I hear nothing from her. I try to blame the war, the delays, the censor, the unpredictable crossings, but when the letters arrive, I find I don't know how to read them, filling in the silences, what isn't said, with worry. I can't pinpoint what it is at times – she seems to be holding something back, not wanting to disappoint me, perhaps? A cold grips my heart.

I imagine her head has been turned by another man; I lie on my bed trying to picture her with someone else. He is tall and faceless and she is laughing up at him, touching his arm, tickled by a joke. He draws her to him, one hand on her neck, covering the round mole, feeling her soft skin. I sometimes wonder whether I will send myself mad with these imaginings; I hate myself for my lack of faith in her. She tells me her heart is mine and she is waiting for my return, fervently hoping it will be soon. She signs off two letters in this way; it twists my gut.

I see myself growing old as this war rages on, a lost, rambling soul in a foreign country, utterly alone. I try not to dwell on these thoughts often but it strikes me, standing at a bus stop, or catching sight of a hat my mother might have worn, a man of my father's stature, a blonde girl. Everyone is moving forward and I am stuck in a dank country with nothing and nobody to call my own.

Huddled under a thin blanket staring out at stubborn rain that appears to have settled in, unending and persistent, I try to think myself out of this mood. Edward is at the hospital, has been all night, will appear soon, eyes red-rimmed, heading straight to bed. A half-finished book rests by my side: he keeps lending me crime novels. This one is set in Egypt but I lost the story pages back.

I drag myself out of bed to boil the milk, something we do daily to stop it going sour, and stare listlessly out of the scratched pane of glass above the kitchen sink: grey skies, the rooftops of the houses opposite, a tiny glimpse of the barrage balloons hovering in the low rain clouds over London.

I have exhausted all sources for my parents, have stood in lines with a hundred other immigrants, and have written endless letters to a dozen or so relatives and friends. Some have replied, and all have been polite but hopeless.

Until today. A letter arrives, news Jean-Paul announces in the first sentence. I walk unseeing to the sitting room, lower myself into the chair by the fire, the page a smudge of letters as I want to read on, don't want to read on. I get up, leave the letter open on the side-table, move to the door of the kitchen, look back, his writing a meaningless scrawl from here. I consider leaving the flat, running down the stairs, bursting out into the street and walking away, not looking back.

He has news.

Slowly, my feet return me to the spot by the fire; I stay

standing, pick up the letter. It is shaking in my hand as I reread the first sentence. Then the words come, the words I knew would come, didn't know would come, didn't want to know.

My parents were taken by members of the local *gendarmerie,* and some members of the *Milice,* that night. They were arrested after a tip-off from an unnamed source. Someone had accused the bank of funding resistance efforts. Jean-Paul says the claims are false. He urges me to remain hopeful. The track has gone cold at Drancy, where they were sent.

The track has gone cold, he is still looking. Will keep looking.

I see a man in a café. I see a pencil-thin moustache. Then the kind faces of my parents.

I blink once, the letter creasing as my hand tightens on it. I look listlessly about the grim little room, the sparse colourless furniture, someone else's possessions, and know I have another day stretching ahead.

ISABELLE

My darling,

I am so desperately sorry for you. I have never wanted to be in England with you more than when I heard your news. It is cruel that we are apart and that I can't hold you, cling on so tight to you so that you can't possibly feel alone. We will be together again: you must hold on to that one true thought.

When this war is over, people will have to answer for the horrific things they have done, but you are right to be sad, not angry. We will find them, remain hopeful. Your parents love you fervently and are the most generous people. They want you to be safe and they would be so heartened to know where you are now, that you will get through this awful war even if it has meant being apart from them.

The seasons are changing, the air is warmer, the wind no longer carrying that sting that makes your cheeks red and your ears ache with the cold. This war will be over soon, everyone is saying so, it is not far away now. The moment it is, we will be together again. There are so many new memories we can make and you must look forward, to the horizon, because it will come. You must never give up on that, you must never give up on me. I am waiting for you; I will spend the rest of my days with you. Hold that tight to your chest at night, feel the warmth of that thought blocking out all the ugliness and the cold and dark.

Don't give up now Sebastian when we are so close.

I love you,

Isabelle

ADELINE

1952, St Cecilia nunnery, south-west France

I have already removed my socks and stockings and position myself on top of the bedclothes, back propped once more against the cushions, ready for the doctor's treatment.

The doctor doesn't waste a moment, placing his bag down on the stool as the fire crackles and warms one side of his face. 'Madame, I mentioned a few new pieces of equipment a company has been developing in America and I am pleased to say that they have sent me a prototype to assist me with my research. I wondered if you would permit me to use this instrument on you.'

He holds up a long line of fabric, like a man's belt, made of a thick black material, with long, thin wires protruding from it at regular intervals, little grips on their ends.

'We tighten it with this new-fangled Velcro, you see – we simply attach this to a limb and it can administer a short, sharp, small charge. The voltage is very low, so there is no danger of it doing any damage or causing you too much pain.'

I'm not bothered by pain.

'I would first like to try it on your thigh, as this area has the most padding, so to speak' – he glances at me apologetically – 'and you shouldn't find it too onerous on a small charge.'

He coughs lightly after this announcement, trying to act the professional, but I imagine in this setting that he is feeling a little out of his depth. Perhaps in his treatment room on a sterile table but here, in a house of God, it must feel bizarre.

I begin to lift up my skirt so that he can manoeuvre the belt around my leg, and he moves towards me with it.

He notices the scar immediately, his hand wavering over the gouged-out hole where once my flesh had been above the knee. He says nothing and I relax back on the bed, relieved.

He wraps the belt around my other leg and attaches the wires to my skin. They are like little metal pincers, the flesh pulled together in their cold grip. Without any warning, my leg spasms and I feel a short, sharp pain that runs through my body, making me gasp.

Doctor Taylor looks up quickly, hearing this new noise – a cry. He waits a few seconds. When I don't speak, he simply apologizes to me and another surge runs through my body. This is more painful, and before he lets me pause for breath, another surge rips through me.

My heart is pulsing, sweat has formed on my top lip. I am clutching at the bedclothes and I am making noises, not words, but a jumble of sounds, and the doctor looks momentarily encouraged.

It continues on my thighs, my lower legs, around my arms but, as the charges fire through me, this brutal treatment seems to prompt nothing further. I repeat the same noises, almost used to the pain; I feel, as the electricity runs through me, like I am being switched on, shocked into something new.

I don't know how many moments have passed, I have slumped further down in the bedclothes and can feel the dampness in the roots of my hair. I am breathing heavily and then, finally, it is over. A sigh and a satisfying rip, and the Velcro comes away and he loosens the belt from my left arm.

Doctor Taylor deflates, dropping onto the stool by the bed, his mouth turned down at the corners. I am used to seeing the same expression on the face of his French counterpart – nothing has worked, once more.

He tries to make amends: instructs me to wash my face and cool myself down, pointing at the oak chest of drawers in the corner where a porcelain bowl of water stands.

I get up, a little wobbly, the red marks on my skin unsightly reminders of what has gone on. I deserve the marks and the pain. He can't do it: I am a lost cause. I hobble over to sponge my face.

'I'm returning to England tomorrow,' Doctor Taylor says, as he packs away the belt. He looks about the room, eyes not lighting on anything in particular. 'Somehow I thought, well...' He peters out, and I feel sorry for this man who has travelled so many miles to be this disappointed. 'I will make my recommendations. The sisters here believe you will be better served in Toulouse, but...'

He slowly and carefully packs away the rest of his equipment into zipped compartments inside his bag, wiping many of them with a clean, white handkerchief, like a mother cleaning the grime from the faces of her babies.

'What happened to your leg? Were you shot, madame?' he asks.

I shift uncomfortably under his gaze and then give him a small nod of the head, down, to the side: a yes, a no. I don't remember, although something is breathing close, threatening.

He doesn't look surprised. 'It looks like a… but who would shoot you?' he asks himself.

I close my eyes, suddenly nauseous.

He rests a hand on my shoulder. 'I can help,' he says, fresh urgency in his voice, 'I want to help.'

Unpleasant images push at the edge of my mind. The doctor's question, the red marks on my skin that smell of burning, skin singed, that cloying smell.

It is in the room with me now, my breathing quickens, my stomach lurches, breaths coming faster.

The doctor is looking at me and makes me start as he asks, 'May I?' He is perched again on the stool by my bedside and reaches forward, gesturing at my notebook.

I look at him with wide eyes, returning myself to my body and this moment and then acquiesce, turning to pick it up and then place it in his hands.

I can still smell the burning and I will myself to focus on the doctor's movements.

He examines the book, then flicks through the notes, past the answers I gave him before, to the rest of the book. He turns the pages quickly, and then back again, examining my strings of nonsensical words. Paragraphs that start and then end in a nothing. Names I know and moments that have flooded back to me. A jumble.

The little book must seem as mute as me, as much of a mess.

On the back pages I have scrawled, doodled, thoughtless shapes and words, an old habit I had in the shop when waiting for customers to decide what they wanted. The doctor notices, holds each page up to his face, studying them as if they are ancient paintings inside an Egyptian pyramid, trying to decipher a meaning.

I draw bells, silhouettes of a face – a woman – over and over, branches of trees in winter, a myriad images. The doctor pauses, looking intently at the top right corner of the book, leaning towards it to scrutinize it from only an inch or so away, turning it, mouthing the letters of a name I have written so many times before as he does so.

He looks up at me, his mouth open, and then almost to himself he states, 'Isabelle.'

I start, as does he; we both meet in the same moment.

'Isabelle,' he says again. He abruptly stands up as he does so.

He is leaving, he is deep in thought but he is walking towards the door to leave me to myself and my thoughts and this small cell.

'The chap,' he says, quietly, as he turns at the door, 'the chap that I lived with during the war. His name was Sebastian. He loved an Isabelle. An Isabelle from Oradour.'

I watch his lips form more words but can't hear them. He is muffled, speaking from a distance as if he has already left the room.

An impossible statement.

He searches my face for a response and, as he looks at me, a hundred other faces seem to flash before my eyes. They are flooding into the tiny room with us, crowding us, the doctor almost lost in their noise. Faces of villagers and customers and refugees and Vicente, Paul, Isabelle. They are swarming into the room and they are all looking at me, waiting on me.

The doctor turns his back to me once more, lifts the latch on the door, his bag over one shoulder. As he pulls open the door my unfamiliar voice stops him. My voice. One word.

'Wait.'

SEBASTIAN

London, England

The water slops over my feet but I barely register it. We only have a butler's sink in the flat so lumbering up the stairs, splashing water, is not uncommon.

Edward calls to me as I slam the door behind me with a foot: a letter has arrived. I rest the bucket down slowly, breathe out. Edward is holding it out to me from the doorway of the sitting room. I take it from him. He nods.

I recognize Jean-Paul's distinctive handwriting on the envelope and tear open the letter with my thumb. He talks of the recent landings in France, the excitement as it seems the Allies are making headway. My eyes scan the details. He talks of sand testing, of floating harbours, the scale of this war. He doesn't mention my parents. Hasn't mentioned them for months.

In the last paragraph one word stands out. Oradour. It's just an aside, a brief comment about atrocities in the

Limousin region carried out by the Germans on their way north: a hundred men killed in Tulle, and then in his careful round hand I read: 'and a nearby village of Oradour has been wiped out.'

My eyes hover uncertainly over the sentence, as if I have imagined it, created the word *Oradour* because I'd been thinking so much about her.

Edward is there, watching me read, his eyes enormous behind the thick lenses, a questioning look on his face: too polite to interrupt, already assuming the worst. Everyone does now.

I gabble in French, he is shaking his head, doesn't understand. I fall into a chair. 'Oradour, it's... Wait, I...'

How could we not have heard if something had happened?

I get up, the letter still clutched in my hand and race to where we keep the heap of daily newspapers, the *Mirror*, the *Herald*, all there in a pile by the fireplace, ash lightly coating the surface of the first one as I move down the pile checking the dates: 6 July, 3 July, 27 June... Nothing before then, and no mention in them, I'm sure.

I open one at random, as if the words might jump out. What does Jean-Paul mean by 'wiped out'? I trawl through the papers as Edward stands there in silence, watching me, not sure what to do or say.

Finally, he joins me and picks up a paper. 'What are we looking for, Seb?'

Was it really as Jean-Paul said? How? By bombs? A whole village? It seems an exaggeration, a typical war-time rumour, spread around and growing despite an absence of facts: like the sighting of German parachutists dressed as nuns; German soap made of human fat; every American soldier getting a free Ford when the war is won. Wars are rife with rumour and no one ever seems to know the truth. I remember seeing a newspaper headline back in 1940, on the eve of the defeat of France, which claimed our boys had never been doing so well.

I send a telegram to Jean-Paul: *Send more news Oradour. Have friend there.* I return to our flat, at a loss with what to do with myself, spending the evening scanning the pages of the newspapers, my eyes aching from the effort as the sky darkens. I draw the blackout curtains, still reading by the single paraffin lamp in our living room.

I pace the flat, and then, when Edward returns, practically leap on him to find out what he has learnt. He has asked around but no one has heard of Oradour. He has a journalist friend though, he assures me, a woman he met at a dance whom he could ask. He repeats my own hopes that it is an exaggeration, a wide-of-the-mark comment made without realising the consequences.

I soak in his words like a man parched of all hope, feeling the empty hole inside me gnawing, gnawing at me as the faces of my parents are joined by another face, a dash of olive coat.

Edward's hand hovers over my arm, pats me once. I don't remember much of the rest.

In the days that follow, Edward helps me discover as much as I can. Unlike my parents, we get somewhere and fast.

The journalist rings her contact in the government who confirms that a small village called Oradour in France appears to have been targeted by a Nazi division on their way north. It is assumed the attack is in some way connected to Resistance work in the village, but I struggle to imagine the sleepy village of Oradour housing renegades.

Where is she? I can't picture her face any more. I squeeze my eyes tight and try to focus on a single image but my brain is panicking, can't settle, can only see her looking frightened; and she has never looked that way before.

I wait to hear Jean-Paul's reply, impatient, short, prowling the flat unable to be still, to concentrate on anything. And when it comes, finally, I am waiting. I meet the post boy at the door, reach for the letter, say nothing and take it up to my single room, my palms already damp.

Edward is out and I have the house to myself. Sitting on the end of the bed I take the envelope in my hand, feeling the bulk of a letter inside.

I tear slowly along the top edge, careful not to rip the paper inside. One sentence leaps off the page: 'They found bodies down a well, in an oven; it was a massacre.'

He expresses his sadness at me knowing someone there. He is clear on one thing: there are barely any survivors. A few injured men, a couple of boys.

The letter flutters to the floor at my feet and I sit, staring at the crumbing whitewash, in the full knowledge that the emptiness inside me is real; that Isabelle will never send me another letter. That it is all over.

PAUL

The afternoon sun is high in the sky, a few small clouds breaking up the blue. I think of Sebastian, awake now after an afternoon snooze and feel a lurch, want to bounce him on my knee, be rewarded with a smile, a giggle, a gabble of nonsensical words. I roll up the sleeves of my shirt; my arms are already turning brown.

'When I talked about the village to the other men I used to tell them about the days we spent down here as children, skimming stones across the surface of the river. We stopped talking about things like that after a while.'

Father nodded, briefly laying a hand on my shoulder.

We are at the south end where the fields slope away to the river and all you can see when you look back at the village is the tops of houses, small and insignificant from our vantage point. There were moments where the world I had known became a foggy memory in my mind and my reality was the stark stone of the factory, the long lines of the machines, the stench. Now I am back here it is as if that was the dream and this the certainty. The village: same faces, new details perhaps.

My family: the enormous hands of my father, his scuffed trousers, worn leather boots. The shop: sparser than I remember, Maman still perched on the stool by the till, leaning over marking the ledger with a pencil as if she had not moved in three years.

The banks of the river are dried out, cracks appearing in the mud, lost in the long grass of the verge. I haven't seen the water this low in years. Insects hover over the surface hopefully, and the leaves in the trees are perfectly still.

'I used to walk here a great deal and think about you when we hadn't heard in a while.'

I feel touched by my father's admission, not knowing quite how to respond, looking across the fields beyond, catching a scattering of men working the land in the distance.

I go to speak, am distracted by a low, unfamiliar rumble that stops Father and me in our tracks. I turn to him at the same moment that he wrinkles his brow and looks towards the noise. In the distance, we can make out a convoy of vehicles throwing up dust into the air.

'What the—?'

The doctor's motorcar is about the only one still serviceable in the village, the rest under dustsheets in garages or disused barns, waiting like so many people for the war to be over. I am about to say just this when I see them: the unmistakable shape of a convoy of German trucks. My stomach clenches and I turn to Father.

'We've got to get back.'

He nods.

'I thought you said the Germans didn't come into the village?' I say.

'They don't – well, they haven't.'

Questions hammer through my mind. I speed up, walking quickly, nearly a jog. 'Come on, Papa.'

I feel a flood of shame as, for a fleeting moment, I think of persuading Father to stop, to turn and run and hide. I won't be sent back – I've heard of them co-opting other men to fight on the Eastern Front and I know I can't go back there: the endless waiting for an end, the constant panic as planes drone overhead, searching out targets in their path.

I am running now, my breath coming in short gasps. We hurry on in silence, craning our necks to see the last of the vehicles enter the village. There must be a dozen or more.

When we reach the high street, we see that a couple of the trucks have stopped. Soldiers jump out of the vehicles, rounding up passers-by and calling for an identity check. We are all to go to the village green.

Sweat has formed in pools under my arms as we turn down the street, our little shop up ahead in the distance, Isabelle and Maman unaware of the commotion.

A knot of tension releases as I hear the repeated instructions of the soldiers: an identity check. I avoid their eyes, look strong for Father as we walk side by side.

'We'll see if they're there first,' Father says. We both automatically cross the road to avoid an armed soldier. Father is unable to resist looking back at the man, younger than me – the unusual sight of armed soldiers in his tiny village.

Madame Garande, carrying two bags, is rolling her eyes as she is swept up in a sea of teenagers who have all been herded from a football game, up beyond the telephone exchange. A few of the boys, flushed from the sun, have rolled their shirt sleeves up, their faces coated in a film of sweat and dust, eyes narrowed into slits behind the backs of the soldiers calling out their orders. One boy holds the football in the crook of his arm, jiggling it.

In the distance I see a man arriving in the village on his bicycle, a soldier barring his way. He is clearly asked to abandon the bicycle and so it is left, propped against the wall of a shop. He is unable to put up a fight, doesn't look back at the soldier who requested it of him. I feel humiliation for the village and our people, a loathing towards these men who can sweep into another man's country and lay down these arbitrary rules: announce identity checks, disrupt the tranquillity of a village that has remained largely untouched by war.

'Don't,' says my father wearily. My face relaxes as he says it.

The soldiers are still driving through the village as people emerge from the other end of the high street, winding around the sides of the church to flood into the fairground, so that as I get closer, the sound of a hubbub of people all whispering conspiratorially hits me. Eyes search out family members and then flick constantly to the stationed soldiers lining the streets and edges of the green. Jaws are clenched, women clutch children to their sides, soothe and shush and look to their husbands for direction.

I am searching for Maman, and Isabelle with the pram. The green is already bustling with people, the whole village and more congregating in the same place. I see the mayor with one of his sons, their faces relaxed in amongst the growing unease, and feel better. Father has seen them too and smiles in acknowledgment, moving across to greet them both, asks if they know what's going on.

My eyes light upon Isabelle in the distance and I call to Father. He nods and we both move off to catch up with them, check Maman has our papers. Monsieur Renard falls into step beside me; I haven't seen him since I left all those years ago. His face has got new lines, thinner creases have appeared around his mouth as he talks, and talks: '... so young, that one over there can't be more than seventeen if he's a day...'

I let his voice wash over me. So many soldiers. Isabelle's blonde hair lit up by the sunlight, a beacon in the greens and greys. I focus on her, wanting Renard to shush, not able to focus any more, starting to feel my breath shorten. *An identity check,* I think, *but surely they could send me back? I could be back there.*

Why didn't I run?

'... never thought I'd see the day...'

I reach Maman and Isabelle, who is holding Sebastian, resting him against her so that his sleeping face is nuzzled on her shoulder, blissfully unaware of the action around him. I can't stop myself reaching out to stroke his smooth forehead. Isabelle smiles in relief at seeing us; questions rend the air from every direction. Maman is holding her papers in a fist. Now we wait.

People are still arriving on the green. A truck appears and five or six men dressed to work in the fields, soil swiped on their faces, mud underneath their fingernails, jump down. I notice Monsieur Lefevre, a nasty, piggy man, crude and fearsome, watch them. My heart is in my mouth as I see his eyes widen: he's sweating. He jumps when one of the soldiers barks an order at him.

Time passes and people begin to sit down. I have too much energy and pace uselessly. I try to look relaxed, knowing Maman's eyes will be trained on me and Father, that Isabelle will want to feel reassured. I bite down on the inside of my cheek. Father is smoking a cigarette with Renard. They are both silent, waiting. We are all waiting.

Some soldiers are talking to the mayor, he leaves with them. The town crier translates what another soldier is telling him: 'We believe there are weapons in the village, we are going to search for arms and ammunition...' He continues, but I can only hear the roar in my ears as everything shifts.

This is no identity check.

My mind gallops through the possibilities. The little

German I know is useless – they are speaking too quickly and I strain to make sense of any of it. I wonder whether any of the villagers are hiding weapons and, if they are, will there be reprisals? Isabelle is hugging Sebastian close to her. He has woken now and will soon need feeding.

A machine gun on a tripod.

The weapon is being manned by a young soldier with sandy hair and freckles. He is chatting, carefree, throws back his head to laugh at something his companion says. The mayor returns. I watch his group, a frown on his face as he talks again with the soldiers, indicates one of his sons. A few of us jump as a shot is heard in the distance, and another. A woman nearby whimpers.

'The women and children will wait in the church as the village is searched.'

At this announcement, chaos ensues. Families cling to each other, soldiers parting the ways, pointing to the men, directing them away. We are going to be separated, and I instinctively huddle close to Isabelle, reach for Sebastian.

The order is repeated, and we are all being swept along. Father and I are pushed back as people move between groups; a soldier appears at my elbow; indicates I should follow. Father pauses momentarily, torn, then joins me. I twist my head around, turn: I can't see them. I don't see them. I see the heads of others. They are somewhere. I think I hear Isabelle's voice calling to me.

We are ordered to sit facing the houses. We can see the women and children move away; they form an enormous line, a snake winding down the high street, punctuated by the soldiers. Two girls, twins, freckled and wide-eyed, hold hands. We can hear the clatter of the children's wooden shoes, the crying, the shouts to loved ones intermingled with the harsh orders in a foreign tongue, in our village. The day takes on a dream-like quality, as if at any moment I will be awake in my bed in the barrack hut with the others, that we will pass round the illicit cigarettes, swap our nightmares.

A farmer has come forward, tells a soldier quickly that he owns a 6mm rifle, has a permit, describes where it is, asks whether he needs to fetch it. He is gabbling, droplets forming on his brow; we all sink into ourselves. The soldier dismisses him, starts to divide us all into groups. I am glued to my father's side, reach out for his arm when it looks like we will be split.

We are told to stand up. There must be fifty or so men in our group when we do. We are led off, down the high street, in the opposite direction to the church. I see the spire in the distance, a comfort.

They make us clear the barn of machinery, so that we can all fit inside; they want us there while they search. We move rapidly, eyes meeting. I recognize some of the other men, not all. We are all moving in a terrified silence.

As we work, two soldiers share a cigarette and another sets up a machine gun on a tripod in the entrance. My back beads with sweat. There are a couple of tiny squares of window in the back, covered in thick, yellowing cobwebs; a door that is padlocked. We are hemmed in and I feel nauseous, trapped.

A man to my right whispers to his neighbour: 'They are going to kill us.' My hand slips and I drop the crate I am carrying. I can feel eyes on me, pitying; my own father is close to tears.

We are shoved into lines and there is a moment of waiting, of silence. I see a soldier sitting on a step outside the barn. He cradles his head in both hands, and it is then that I know it is true.

We are going to be killed.

An explosion. Shouts. A relentless noise as they let off

rounds of the machine gun. I look across to see my father falling at the same moment as I feel a spattering of pain in my legs and chest and I too am off my feet, flung backwards into the filth, landing on top of another.

My head turns, I can't see my father. As I lift my head to search I hear a sentence spat in German, see the figure of a soldier stepping around bodies, heading towards me, young, focused, his uniform starched, the light from the window reflecting off a watch polished to a gleaming shine.

He is pointing a pistol at my head.

He throws a comment to the man behind him, and then his eyes meet mine.

TRISTAN

They arrive in the village at just after lunch.

Papa has been away in Paris 'tying up loose ends', which I think is some kind of business talk. Mother has been getting rather tired of just us for company – you can tell because she has snapped at Luc twice today, and she never snaps at Luc, really. Dimitri and I have been keeping out of harm's way by playing hide-and-seek around the house.

We both know Maman is in the front room and we won't hide or look there but we haven't told Luc as it is quite funny when he gets snapped at. Elèonore is off at some girl's birthday party. I imagine it will be deadly dull, but Dimitri does point out they will probably have goodies there and we are both secretly hoping Elèonore will bring us back some treats. *I bet she won't,* I think, scowling. I would for her.

I hear the call from the attic. I was about to hide in the trunk – Luc never finds me up in the attic. He's too much of a baby to come up here, ever since I told him about the ghost who haunted it – an old farmer who had shot himself a hundred years ago. Dimitri wasn't scared when he heard my story: he doesn't believe in ghosts and ghouls. 'I am a scientist,' he announced, puffing out his chest importantly and sniggering as Luc wailed at my words. He told him it was all nonsense but Luc just looked between both of us with worried eyes, unsure which older brother might be lying. Best not to test, best to simply stay away from the attic.

I lean out of the top window to hear what's going on, pushing on the window and cringing at a row of shrivelled flies, their little corpses all lying still on the windowsill, their tiny legs sticking up. The town crier is calling the whole village out onto the green; he's ringing his bell in the high street.

I hear Maman call us all from downstairs. Luc calls back to her and Dimitri must have appeared from his hiding place in another part of the house, as I can hear footsteps running down the stairs.

I climb down the old wooden ladder that hangs from the attic space and quickly brush the dust from my trousers away – Maman doesn't like us playing in the attic. I race downstairs.

'Not so fast, my darling,' Maman says, handing me my coat. She is carrying Luc, his arms round her neck. Dimitri is standing by the door.

We leave the house in a huddle, Maman shooing me to hurry up. I have my arm stuck in my jacket though, and I nearly trip over the edge of the pavement trying to keep up and get my arm in.

It's strange seeing this many people in the village at the same time. Even when we go to church there doesn't seem to be this many people hurrying along. Through a group of people nearby comes André. He looks odd, all wide-eyed. His mother is nowhere to be seen. I stop, wiggle my hand through my sleeve and wait for him to catch up.

'Pssst, Tristan!' He beckons, running into a little side street off the pavement. I don't want to lose Maman, but André is signalling to me. I can see Maman making her way to the edge of the village green – she has stopped to talk to that bore, Monsieur Renard. Mademoiselle Rochard is standing near them. She is holding her baby in her arms, whispering to him as he rests against her. His name is Sebastian; she told me once at school in the playground.

I make my way over to André.

'Come with me,' he urges.

'I can't,' I reply.

'I'm not going up there,' he says, nodding his head at the village green.

'What? Don't be silly! Everyone's going.'

'I won't. It's the Nazis – I'm not going. Don't go,' he says, pleading with me.

'I've got to.'

'I'm not going,' he repeats. 'It feels like in Alsace the last time. I'm not.'

There's an awkward pause. I don't know about Alsace and I don't know what to say. André is still looking at me. I peer down at my shoes mumbling, 'I should go to Maman.'

He doesn't say anything back.

'Well...'

Still André doesn't say anything. 'I'll... see you at school,' I say, turning.

I leave him in the shadow of the side street and find my way through the people, back to my mother.

'Thank God,' she says, wrapping an arm around my shoulders, drawing me to her side.

I look back at the side street but André has already gone.

There are so many soldiers. They are standing in their uniforms, the sunlight glinting off the buttons on their coats.

Their boots are gleaming. Papa said that they are so clean they must eat off them. I think he must have been joking although when he said it he didn't smile. Dimitri is staring at them too. We haven't seen many soldiers in the village before now – just one or two outside the hotel, with drinks. They seem very tall close up.

Maman is looking at the crowds of people for Elèonore. I see the girls before I see Elèonore – two of them are still wearing party hats, and I am sure one of them is holding an apple tart in her hand. Elèonore's eyes find Maman and she comes running over, hugs her.

'What's going on, Maman?'

'It's an identity check, my darling.'

I wonder what that is. It's busy and confusing as we wait. Everyone is looking for someone. One of the officers is giving orders to his men in German and signalling to the various groups of people. One soldier is speaking into the town crier's ear. 'Will the men and women please separate,' the crier translates. 'Children are to go with their mothers.'

There is movement and I am glad Maman has a good hold of me. A woman nearby starts making a high-pitched sort of noise. I squeeze my eyes shut, hope the sound goes away. The crier repeats the command: 'Will the men and women please separate. Children are to go with their mothers.'

People are getting out their identity papers and kissing each other on the cheeks, like we're all preparing to get on a train.

Maman is herding us over to a group of women and children. I scan the crowd for my friends. Michel is too far away – he is looking solemnly at his father, who has kneeled down to talk to him. They hug each other. I want my papa but he is in Paris, and we are being bustled about and Maman is talking in a low voice to Luc. Elèonore looks a little pale and I have a sudden urge to hold her hand.

The soldiers have surrounded our group and we are walking in lines to the church. The men are left on the green. I see the old postman, who Maman always invites in for a morning *café au lait,* half kneeling on the ground. A couple of the younger men in the village are surrounding him, looking concerned. A soldier nearby is shouting something in German at them. I can't hear. The postman is clutching his chest.

Mother pulls me towards her. 'Come on, Tristan.' Some of the children are singing as we walk. 'Come on.'

The heavy wooden doors of the church are open and we are pushed inside. There is noise everywhere now. The soldiers shout things to each other and a couple of the women are clutching at them. Wives are crying for the husbands they have left on the green, asking to be with them. Michel's mother is sobbing, Michel pulling her away from the soldiers.

I think of André and wish I had run down that side street with him.

Maman sits us all down in the corner; the stone floor is cold and uncomfortable. I want to be outside. Luc is whining and Maman tries to soothe him. I stand up, trying to see what people have started pointing at.

A black box, a strange thing with long wires coming out of it, has been placed in the middle of the church. People are pressing themselves into corners, staring at it. It starts smoking and there are screams and cries.

I cry out as well, take two steps back, bump into a woman I don't know. She's staring at it, too. Women run around the pews, finding their children, calling out for grandparents, friends. The soldiers are leaving, and the big doors are being pulled shut. Women start flinging themselves at them. We are being locked in.

Maman turns to us. 'Tristan, Dimitri, Elèonore. Sit down.'

We look at her blankly. We are all looking at the box in the middle of the church.

'Tristan,' she beckons, pulling me onto her lap and drawing Luc closer. 'Stay with me here.' She is calling to Dimitri and Elèonore too. 'Come on, my darlings.' We are like tiny ducklings, all keen to get close to her.

Her voice is a familiar sound – that voice has told me tales of knights in shining armour, soldiers going into battles, great wizards who have done amazing spells.

'Listen to me, darlings,' she says.

In the distance I hear cracks, like a string of loud pops. Maman makes a strangled sound. We clutch her. Moans go up from the women. Another round of popping, and the shouts in the church grow louder. The black box is still smoking and everything is hot and blurry. Yet another round of pops and people fall silent. Where are the men? What is happening outside?

The black box starts to pump out thick, black smoke and I cough, watching people race to escape, my eyes stinging. Fists bang on the doors. People claw the stone walls. Mother wraps her arms around us. 'Elèonore, keep your brother safe.' Elèonore looks like she is in a dream, but her arm reaches round my shoulders. I lean into her.

We all move closer to each other, Maman still speaking, still asking us to listen to her. I can hear Elèonore's heart beating, so quickly, drumming, and her skin is all hot. We look desperately at Maman.

A girl drags herself up to a narrow window behind us. Other people are trying to climb out of other windows by the altar. We follow the girl's every movement. Maman stops talking. The girl, about Elèonore's age, is nearly out – she's dangling through the window, then she pushes her way through the gap. She is going to make it; she is leaving this place.

A burst of popping and her body slumps forward.

'Elèonore, look at me,' Maman says firmly. 'Tristan, Luc, Dimitri… boys, please listen.'

Luc has stopped whining and is looking at her, his eyes huge.

'Tristan,' Maman repeats.

My eyes are still on the girl in the window. Her foot is twitching.

'Tristan, please,' Maman says.

I curl into her arms and she speaks to us all in a low voice.

'Close your eyes, all of you,' she says. 'Come on, all of you – eyes closed, no cheating.' She laughs a little, as if we are back in our bedroom, as if she is about to tell us another fairy tale.

I close my eyes. It is a relief from the stinging of the smoke.

Maman's voice continues. 'Imagine you are sitting on the bridge over the stream,' she says. 'Can you see yourselves there, my darlings? Luc, can you see yourself with your big brothers? Dimitri, can you see yourself? You are reading, mouthing the words the way you always do, and Elèonore, you are bathing in the sun. Luc, Tristan, you are both sitting on the bridge, dangling your feet in the river,' she explains. 'Can you see yourself there?' she repeats.

I open my eyes, looking up at Maman.

'Darling, close your eyes,' she pleads gently.

I obey.

'I'm there on the bank, sitting on our old blanket, eating the first strawberries.'

A scream pierces through our daydream and she hugs us tighter.

'Can you see me?' she whispers. 'Try, darlings. Can you see me there?'

'Yes, Mama,' we croak, almost at the same time. Elèonore whispers it; I think only I hear.

'Luc, Tristan, you are both there on the stream with your rods and your little pot of bait and you are watching the silvery fishes darting just below the surface.'

The noises in the distance seem to dim, seem to join with the sound of crickets in the long grass, the gentle plop as we toss the end of the line into the water.

'Father is there, looking so handsome in his suit, and you all run over to him and he sweeps each of you up into his arms, and twirls you around.'

A woman is crying nearby and I open one eye, but Maman is focused on our faces, looking at us as she says, 'He holds you close, and he hugs you tightly and tells you he loves you and that you are good children.'

There is an explosion from the corner of the church, and Maman rocks Luc gently, an arm around Dimitri. It is getting hotter.

'Darlings, can you see it? Can you see us all by the river?'

I squeeze my eyes shut and I focus on the scene, picture Papa's laughing face, my mother smiling at us. We are all there. It's summer.

'I can, Maman,' I say. 'We're by the river.' I can smell the freshly cut grass, I can taste the strawberries, I can see Papa and Maman on the blanket. They are laughing.

A massive noise, a burst of hot.

I am sitting with Dimitri on the bridge over the stream, holding our rods and looking at the silvery fishes that are darting just below the surface. I turn and see Maman, Papa, Luc and Elèonore. They're on the blanket and they are laughing.

ADELINE

1952, St Cecilia nunnery, south-west France

I remember. I remember it all.

The town crier, who doubles as the smith of the village, a man who always looks as if he has missed his last meal, is beating his drum in the high street. I can hear the muffled sound through the walls. I move across the landing to my bedroom, pushing open the little window by my dresser to peer out. I hear the call the moment the window is open. He is calling everyone to leave their homes and bring their papers to the fairground.

At the same moment, Isabelle is calling the same message up the stairs from the shop.

I look down to see the tops of people's heads moving towards the green. There are soldiers in the distance and I feel a sudden coldness clutch my chest. Paul is out somewhere with Vicente – a walk after lunch – and I move quickly down to Vicente's study to collect our papers and make my way down to the shop.

Isabelle and I shut the shop quickly. Sebastian is sleeping in the back room and Isabelle decides to carry him rather than take the pram. The whole village seems to be moving in a swell towards the green, and I am looking around for my husband and my son.

There are a huge number of soldiers on the road and, as we reach the green, we can see dozens of them in different groups: some on the edge of the green; some in the high street, ushering people out of their homes. Everywhere they are telling people to get their papers for an identity check.

A few vehicles arrive with people they must have picked up from outside the village. I recognize Madame Thomas as she steps down, a bright ray of colour in a lilac sundress, sunglasses perched on the top of her head. She has a book in her hand, as if she forgot to leave it when they told her to come.

The soldiers are wearing camouflage uniform, many of them are young, Paul's age, and look bored, hot in the sunshine in their uniforms. A few moments later the doctor, about the only man in the village to still drive a car, is directed to park on the edge by the main thoroughfare. He gets out and his identity is checked; I can see him talking to the soldier who is scanning the papers he is handed.

I can see Vicente looking for us and put up my arm in a half-wave, calling to him at the same time as other voices do the same to their loved ones. Vicente's eyes light on us and he starts to make his way over, Paul in his wake, talking to the elderly Monsieur Renard, or being talked at – you can never be absolutely sure. I feel instantly lifted that they will be with us, waiting, and kiss both of them on the cheeks when they appear with the same questions on their lips as everybody else.

Paul is nervous, quiet, as he reaches out to stroke the sleeping Sebastian. I imagine the proximity of the soldiers is unsettling for him and I see a glimpse of the man he must have been these last few years – his eyes have momentarily lost their light as he wraps one arm protectively around his little sister. I smile at him and he returns it.

Vicente is a little more relaxed, looking over at a few of his friends who are standing in a group, puffing on cigarettes as if they are still sitting around a table in the bar, about to challenge one another to a game of backgammon. Many look untroubled by the noise and chaos around them and, looking at them, as I imagine Vicente feels too, quells the unease a little.

The baker approaches a group of soldiers as we wait, many eyes swivelling towards him as he asks if he can go and check on the loaves he has put in the oven – he doesn't want them to spoil. A nearby soldier answers, 'We will see to it,' and I frown as he moves back to his family, a slight shake of his head at his wife who rolls her eyes.

'What did he say?' Isabelle whispers.

My answer is cut off by the arrival of a parade of children, who have all come from a party of some sort. They're in high spirits. Their voices – curious whispers and squeals on seeing their parents – add to the noise. Families reuniting, complaints from those waiting, questions on everyone's lips. Some worried looks, others soothing. We are all gathered, waiting for the check.

A gaggle of girls – four Lauder sisters – dressed in neat, matching clothes, are whispering to each other nearby. The eldest daughter holds the hand of Renée, who turned six only the week before. She announced it proudly in the shop, showing off a new yellow ribbon that her mother gave her as a present. The two middle daughters are talking quietly to each other as they stare with a mixture of curiosity and alarm at a group of nearby soldiers. Their mother prowls their little circle, looking warily at the foreign men.

We have been on the green for nearly an hour. Paul is holding Sebastian, circling his back with his hand. Isabelle is talking to Monsieur Renard, who came into the village this afternoon to pick up his tobacco ration. I assure him I will be back in the shop serving him when the identity check has been completed.

The soldiers eventually begin to separate us into men and women and children. We have never had an identity check before and I allow myself to be herded. Paul and Vicente are blocked from view as others come between us and soldiers move through the crowds directing everyone. I briefly see a look on Paul's face that makes my breathing quicken and then remind myself to stay calm. I don't want to upset Isabelle.

The whole process takes a while and I watch as Paul and Vicente move to one side of the green and Isabelle and I move nearer the high street. I am glad they are together. I can see them talking as they are asked to sit and wait on the edge of the green.

As we are instructed to join another group, my heart freezes as I hear, in accented French, a soldier say, 'We believe there is ammunition and weapons in the village...'

Some people swap looks and my stomach plummets again.

'... we will be searching the village...'

More whispers.

'... it would be better if the woman and children wait in the church while this goes on.'

We are swept along in a tide towards the church at the bottom end of the high street. Madame Garande is still carrying her bags and the two Dubois girls are arm in arm – Claudette seems so thin compared to her sister, who is about to give birth any day now. I am craning to look back over my shoulder at Paul and Vicente but the crowds are in the way and I can't see them. Isabelle calls to me, Sebastian woozily awake in her arms, and I hurry along to be by her side once more; my hand reaches out to rest on her arm. My own growing fear shows on her face and I swallow.

Some of the soldiers up ahead have encouraged the children to sing and as we make our slow progress to the church, leaving the men behind as the soldiers search the village, their sweet voices unite, lifting everyone as we step into the church, out of the day's heat and the light.

We make our way through the clusters of groups in the church as more and more people file in. It is crowded and whispers fly around the echoing space. The singing has stopped, some people are crying and one woman is pleading with a nearby soldier. She wants to be with her husband – he has been ill, she explains, she is worried about him. She is pushed roughly and I watch the expression of the soldier who has done it harden as he looks at her.

The look sweeps through my body as if he has looked at me in the same way: uncaring, cold. I start to take big breaths.

More and more people flood in and Isabelle and I are pushed further into the body of the church; we are near the choir stalls when I hear people call out. Soldiers stand at the entrance, stopping us leaving, even though some women are begging to be let go.

There is smoke. It's in the air, making me cough. I move with Isabelle towards the altar, Sebastian in her arms, a sea of other woman and children around us both. There are hundreds of us. I try to peer around at what is going on. People are moving against the walls, behind the altar, anywhere, filling every hole. The window above me throws light down on the crowd, I can see the blue sky through the panes of glass. We are bustled and shunted beyond the pews, crammed to the sides as still more come. There are shouts now, the soldiers angrily swapping exchanges with the women who are beseeching them in a language they can't understand.

Some soldiers drag a box further into the nave – it's this that is letting off the smoke. They move back down the aisle and then, with no warning, there is a loud bang. Everyone screams in unison. Sebastian is crying, growing red in the face.

Smoke, heat billows, panic. The noise. Where are the men? Where is my boy? Shots from outside. Even in this madness, in the church people fall silent.

More shots. Closer now. Fired into the church. Women start fall-

ing, others curve over their children. I move Isabelle towards the back of the altar, against the wall. The smoke keeps coming, worse now, we are crouching on the floor, the sides, anywhere to breathe the air. I keep shouting to Isabelle to get out, we have to get out. The doors are shut, they have locked us in. Isabelle's eyes are huge; through the smoke, I can see her clutching Sebastian closer to her chest.

'Hush, hush, hush.'

We must get out. *It's my only thought.* We must get out.

I start to look around us, at others clawing at the thick stone walls, clambering over the wooden pews, calling out familiar names. Isabelle stands fixed to the spot as I look about, see a small ladder, picture the ankles of the chaplain as he stretches to light a candle. I blink, start to drag the ladder towards a window at the back of the altar. It's within reach. Children are crying so hard their faces have turned bright red, as if their lungs are bursting with their cries.

This is hell. This is what hell will be like.

I clamber onto the stool, call for Isabelle, beckon her to me. 'I can reach the window,' I insist, hitching my skirt up, forgetting any decency. Isabelle stares at me, already lost to another place, her arms wrapped around her baby. Sebastian's cries now blend with the rest.

I can't think.

The glass of the window is smashed and I can feel the hopeful hint of a breeze on my face as I heave my body up to the gap. There are blasts from the centre of the church, and great belches of black smoke make my eyes sting as I turn to help Isabelle up. I see people everywhere, a room of women and children half-obscured in the smoke. Some have picked up a long pew, trying to ram the doors open. Flames have begun to lick the opposite wall. A young girl tries to get out of another window.

She is shot.

The shots in the village continue to ring out beyond. Fists pounds on every surface of the church. Endless faces below me, distorted with wailing. Children clinging to their mother's legs, women I have known and schooled with, women I have worked with, dined with, served in the shop.

And my own daughter standing below me.

'Isabelle!' I call, one leg now half out of the window. 'Climb up,' I urge.

I have manoeuvred my whole body onto the edge of the window frame and can make out the ground below. I will surely break a leg jumping.

'Isabelle, come on,' I repeat, preparing myself for the leap.

Isabelle looks up at me as another blast explodes, puts a foot on the first rung. My face burns.

'Isabelle,' I cry. Everything has slowed down, sounds far away.

Isabelle is holding Sebastian up to me.

'Take him,' she says.

I look at her, at the baby just out of my grasp. The smoke, their faces, my tears, the screaming in my head.

'Maman, quickly, take him!' she screams, lifting the little body an inch higher. He is so close me. I am half dangling out of the window. The gentle air of our French summer is wafting around my legs, my upper body is still in hell.

'Take him.' She is trying to scramble up the rungs; others have noticed this exit. The ladder sways.

I stare at her face, and then I turn to the ground below. I look back one last time. It is so hot in there, she must follow, we have to get out now. Our eyes meet. A look.

I jump. I jump and while I am falling, all I see is that look.

As I land awkwardly outside the church something bites into my leg. That look.

The smooth walls of the church loom before me as I stare up at the window I have escaped from. I hold one hand out to the cool stone. The window is high above me. I can't get back up. There is another explosion from inside, bigger this time, and smoke pours out of the gap. The screams and the wails are dying down on the other side of the stones.

Her face. That look. The next blast throws me away from the wall, the stones crumble in front of me. I stagger, move quickly, there is mud and bushes and I am fumbling, covering myself with dirt, burying myself in the darkness.

That look.

ISABELLE

Pushed, shoved by other mothers and daughters. Children swarming around my legs. I am clutching Sebastian so hard I momentarily worry that I will smother him.

Soldiers walk by, marching us up the wide stone steps and into the church. It is decorated with flowers for tomorrow's First Communion. The air is sweet with their scent. I whisper nothing and everything in Sebastian's ear. He is stirring again, blinking at me in recognition.

My heart is hammering and Sebastian is crying now, hungry, can feel his mother's frightened breathing. Maman is here, backed into a corner by others. What is happening to the men outside? People are screaming for their husbands, fathers, and I can see Maman pale with the absence of Paul and Father, her face etched with questions. There are so many of us in here.

They are dragging something inside; Maman is looking at it, she returns to my side, her head looking left and right for an exit. There is a window just out of reach. There is smoke now and we are moving without thinking.

An explosion, a noise, heat.

'Isabelle, come on, come on.' She urges me forward somewhere. I am coughing, unseeing, feeling only Sebastian's little body in my arms.

Maman has dragged a ladder from somewhere, she is pulling it towards the window. She is clambering up it.

I go to follow, put a foot onto the first rung. She has made it to the sill, looks down at me, her eyes rolling, almost unseeing, one foot already in the outside. I push Sebastian up to her.

'Take him, Maman.'

She reaches an arm forward, struggles to reach him, looks behind her. It is so hot, I can barely make her out in this smoke. I clutch with one hand on another rung, feeling for the next.

I see her face one more time, reach Sebastian up so that he is nearly at her fingertips.

She slips away from me, through the window, her upper body slowly falling backwards. When I see her face for an instant, our eyes lock. The last time I will see her, the whites of her eyes, a blink. And she is gone.

Shouts, smoke, fiery heat and then a rattle of gunfire. I am falling, my head hits stone, sliding slowly down, down, down, Sebastian still in my arms. It is so hot. Sebastian cries, his face red, we are all burning, slowly, quickly, it rages.

ADELINE

1952, St Cecilia nunnery, south-west France

I wait for him in the orchard.

Doctor Taylor listened as I told him my story, the part meant for him at least. I spoke in short waves, taking sips of water, my tongue swollen in my mouth, weighty, some words slurred or lost, and then another sip.

My jaw aches at the end of the day. I open my mouth in the darkness, purse my lips, practise the movement, want it back.

He returned one final time. A phone call was made to Sebastian in England.

I knew this moment would come. Sister Marguerite found me this morning in the chapel. I lit candles for them. The flames quivered as I cupped each one, whispered words to them all. She drew me out here gently, precious, guiding.

I smooth my skirt down, tuck a strand of hair behind my ear, glance at the book I am holding and wait: every fibre of my being waits. The breeze is gentle and the subtle noises of summer seem in stark contrast to my drumming heart. My eyes flick to the road; little hints of shingle can be spotted between clusters of trees, any movement makes my chest constrict, a breath sucks in. A passing cart, a bicycle, will appear fleetingly before diving back into the trees, and I will wait once more for the rare sound of an automobile on the road.

I hear him before he arrives – the bumping of the tyres as he makes his way off the road and navigates around the potholes on the dusty track to the nunnery.

The engine is switched off, the crunch of his footsteps – just his – on the gravel. A knock, a bell, some words in the distance, a question and answer.

My palms are damp – perhaps it isn't him, perhaps he won't come? It sounds like one person, it must be him, it is time. They will direct him here; the sisters know where I am waiting. Perhaps they will offer him a drink. Perhaps I should greet him inside?

And then like a visitor from another life, another world, he appears beneath the crumbling stone arch. He is looking around and then, as his eyes focus on the figure underneath the apple tree, he freezes, just for an instant. Our eyes meet and, after a little hesitation, he makes his way across the lawn towards me.

I go to stand, pause in mid-air, bottom only centimetres from the bench, waver, sit back down and start pleating and smoothing my skirt once more. I look anywhere but at his face. I can't help it, though; I'm drawn to it, want to see if I recognize the boy he was.

His hair is shorter than I remember, he has a slight limp, was that from the war? Had he always walked in that way? I don't know, have never known.

He gives me a sort of smile as he approaches, as if we are meeting by accident, two near-strangers in a park, and then he points awkwardly to the other side of the bench and I nod as he goes to sit.

A man. Tall, well-dressed, dark hair, the ends slightly curling. A stranger in a park.

The bench creaks, gives in to the new weight as he sits. I swivel my body round to face him. Neither of us speak, and my head fills with shadowy faces.

'Thank you for meeting me,' he says.

He has thanked me.

I half open my mouth to respond in some way. *Thank you.* I blink, feeling hot tears building at the back of my eyes. *Thank you.*

I wave my hand towards the trees behind me and say, 'Paul used to love orchards, the mottled shadows on the grass, the fallen fruit – and the promise of apple pie for dinner, no doubt.' The smallest laugh. Someone else. I hear my words, said in a voice that still sounds too scratchy to be mine, and wonder at the memory. Paul crouching low over a half-chewed apple, staring in childlike wonder at the maggoty inside.

'My boy has to be force-fed any fruit,' Sebastian replies, with a small, proud chuckle.

'Your son,' I repeat quietly.

'I have a son,' he says, looking at me. 'And a wife, and a baby daughter,' he states, searching my face. In a whisper: 'We called her Isabelle.'

'That is, that... wonderful, I think, I, perhaps... where are they now?' I ask, needlessly looking around, feeling my chest tighten.

'They're in England. At home.'

I nod.

He has the faintest hint of an English accent.

Home.

A silence descends. There is movement outside the abbey: a nun holding a pair of secateurs, rhythmic clicks as she moves around the building. Perhaps it is the presence of another being, perhaps he realizes we can't skirt around the issue forever, but Sebastian asks, 'Can you talk about it?'

I know to what he is referring. For months, years, people have asked me to talk, have asked me to tell them my story, and I haven't.

Perhaps the right people never asked because, as I take a deep breath, I am convinced I need to speak. This is what I have been waiting for.

He listens without interrupting as I tell him about that day. I do not spare him the details.

I fall silent after I recount the noise of the black box going off, the shattering of glass and the sudden feeling of being outside, not in... outside, not with them... outside.

He clears his throat. 'What happened to Isabelle?'

I look up at him. 'She was there, inside, we were together but the noise and the smoke and...' My confession now. He understands. I look away as I continue. 'I was by the window.' I close my eyes, replaying those moments. 'I didn't wait, or think, or... I didn't *know*, it was so hot and I didn't stop to think and...' I must stop – I am gulping, forcing out the words and I am back in the darkness, fumbling to get out, without my daughter, without my grandson.

Guilt threatens to choke me as I try to carry on.

'I escaped,' I state, looking down at my hands – those of an old lady now. 'I got out.'

'And the baby,' he asks, so quietly. 'Edward told me there was a baby. What happened to him?'

My words are so soft they might have been lost to a stronger wind, but he hears every syllable as I say, 'They were both in there.'

The weight of my words has forced us inside ourselves and it is a while before I hear his next question. His voice is shakier, slower. He loved her.

'What did she call him?' he asks.

I look at his face fully for the first time: kind eyes, grey flecks at the roots of his dark hair, a straight nose. Would my grandson have looked like this?

'Sebastian.'

Tears edge at the rims of his eyes so that he has to look up to the heavens and blink them back.

'Sebastian,' he repeats, a flicker of a smile and then gone.

As he says his name, my grandson's name, something cracks within me, and I huddle over myself – the story told but not answered – gripping my body, back outside the church, there again. 'They burned the women and children. They burned them. I left them there. I covered myself in dirt and I hid, I *hid*. I'm sorry,' I whisper. 'I am so sorry.'

He makes no move to comfort me.

We sit side by side on the bench as my breathing slows and I start to hear the subtle sounds of the garden alive around me once more. I look beyond Sebastian to the nunnery, see the outline of Marguerite inside. One hand rests on the glass as she watches us. What does she see from there? We are simply two figures beneath a tree in an orchard, surrounded by dappled shadows and juicy apples.

I look back at him. 'I left them there…' I say, pausing over every word. 'I left them and I can see them always there, where I abandoned them and… I… I can't…'

I am for ever outside, and they are inside, and I made my choice and I am living and they are not. I am in an orchard and the sun is shining and I am with him and they are not.

TRISTAN

There is something on top of me. It's heavy and I take a breath.

There is only a tiny bit of air, like I'm buried underground, like in a shallow grave. Dimitri told me about a murderer who buried his victims – smashed them around the head and put them in a wooden box, and threw earth on the top until they were stuck with the ground on top of them, the holes leaking mud and dirt and their cries being lost in the wind.

I'm underground, in a shallow grave and it is hot and heavy and I can't breathe and I'm going to die, and no one will hear me.

I gasp, eyes opening, but it is dark and smoky and my eyes sting. There are noises too, around me, groaning, murmuring: smells, smells so terrible that when they are in my nostrils I can't get rid of them.

I try to move, it is so heavy; I push and I wiggle and I push and suddenly the weight is slipping away, he is falling to the side, he is off me. It is my brother. It is Dimitri. He isn't looking at me, he isn't looking anywhere anymore. I tell him to come, I reach out to him. His glasses have fallen off. He doesn't follow me.

There are so many bodies everywhere and they are all blurred and there is such heat, I can see barely centimetres in front of my face. I drag myself along the stone floor that seems warm, like the heat is coming from below, like hell is underneath the floor, warming it from the bottom. I'm dragging myself and I can see a patch, as if it is the outside and I try to crawl to it. I am tripping over things in the way and I feel a shoe with a foot in it but they don't pull it back or tell me off for clambering over it. I don't want to look at them but I can't help it. The skirt has hitched up a little so below the knee I can make out a sliver of cotton shift like Maman wears.

That patch is still there, it is bigger and I can make out green. I have to get to it, I have to get to the patch of green as I think if I don't I will have to stay here in this, for ever. I am so close to it now, it's so small, little stones are all crumbled up around it, I reach out a hand and as I do I can hear something, a wail. A baby's cry.

I look to my side, the smoke is still thick, swirling just above the floor like fog on the fields in winter that you can't see beyond. But then there is the wail again and I have to move towards it. I can hear my name now, whispered – is Maman calling me? Am I going to find her through the patch? Is she there?

There are more people here, lying down, curled into balls and I stumble in a half-crawl, slipping as I put my hand down on someone's hand. It's still so hot and I don't want to move away from the patch but it might be Maman calling me.

'Tristan.' It isn't her voice. I think my arm hurts but it could be my head; I hear the wail again.

I cough and, I can see an outline. Mademoiselle Rochard is slumped in the corner, her head funny, resting on the wall.

She is calling my name, quietly though, so quietly, and in her arms is her baby. He is the one wailing at me and as I approach her she is holding him out to me, this bundle who has gone quiet now. Her eyes are half-closed and she is mumbling, 'Tristan, please, please, I can't. Please.'

She is repeating that and I know what she means, that she can see the tiny patch, a sliver from here, where the stones have come away, so small, and then she coughs and I have the baby and it is so hot I sink my face into the bundle and the air is closing in on both of us but when I look up again I don't find it any easier to breathe. I can't see in front of me and for a moment I have no idea where I am, where is the patch? The green?

I crawl to the left, feel with one hand for the wall. The heat drives me on so that I start to feel my skin blistering as if I have suddenly come out in terrible sunburn, like when Luc had a patch on his back that went red raw and then all the skin fell off a few days later. I haven't seen Luc. Where is he?

I have to get out and the patch is so close now I can see the hint of green beyond and know it will be cooler there, anything to get out. I'm hurting now, I can smell so many things like rubber and smells when the saucepan catches. I'm at the hole and I can just reach and so I push the bundle through.

He is out there on the green, in the safe patch, and then I wiggle and I squirm and the heat is roasting behind me and I think I won't make it out of there, that I'll be stuck half in hell and half out and I don't know whether I want to leave. Isn't Maman in there? Dimitri, Elèonore, Luc – I can't see them in this new green world, I can't leave. I shouldn't leave them. But it's so hot and I have to take the baby and then I am free and I'm crawling along grass, knowing I have to stay out of sight in case they are still there, and I can see a shed and I try and get to my feet.

If we can just get there. I take the baby, he's making noise again, little noises, and I say 'Ssh' to him.

A girl is lying nearby, there is blood and some of her insides are beside her. I am sick. I keep moving. There are noises and shouts in the village, vehicles moving, we have to get there, we have to get to the shed. The baby is still now. I don't want to be in the shed by myself but I can't go back and I can't get help.

Pushing open the doors I climb behind a barrel full of filthy water, moss growing on the side as I squeeze us down into a gap and wait.

The baby is calmer, his heart beating a rhythm next to mine.

It is quiet, and there is dark all around me.

ADELINE

1953, France

My legs feel shaky as I lower myself onto the smooth leather: there is no way back. Sebastian closes the door behind me, revs the engine and I try to nod, to convince, as he swivels slightly in his seat to look at me.

In a too-bright voice, he asks, 'Ready?'

We are not.

It is the anniversary of the day it happened and there is to be a service in the village. He wants me to go with him. I can't believe I am going back there.

The day is clear and the fields around the nunnery are a patchwork of yellows, browns and greens. Cows stand in the shade of the trees as we pass, a flock of startled birds soars quickly up ahead. We speak little over the rattle of the engine. Villages turn into towns and I stare in disbelief at the people walking by on their daily business. A woman, skirt skimming her knees, reaches down to talk to her daughter who has stopped to stare into the window of a bakery crammed full of pastries. An elderly couple sit and drink coffee on the edge of the pavement, both chairs turned towards the street so that they can observe the comings and goings.

It seems that the world has kept on turning. There were days when I felt it was just me in my room, in the stone corridors of the nunnery, as if France stopped at the edges of the garden.

I look over at Sebastian, at his profile. A straight nose, his hair even darker in the car, curling up over his shirt collar. Hands, resting on the steering wheel, clipped nails. I see a small scar on his left hand and comment on it.

'First time my father allowed me out on a bicycle by myself. I had cuts all over both hands,' he explains.

'Where do your parents live?' I ask.

He glances over at me. 'They died during the war.'

I hadn't expected it. 'I'm sorry.'

'Belsen. 1943. Within weeks of each other.'

I haven't heard of Belsen.

He explains. I hear the details of the couple I will never meet, an ordinary couple who were going about their lives in Limoges, a few kilometres away: another world.

The scenery grows familiar and I shift in my seat, clasp both hands together, twist my ring around and around. We are turning off the road and the sign points us to Oradour – a different direction, a newly built village of Oradour. It's further up the hill.

Sebastian parks facing away from the village and I want to urge him to keep driving.

He sits there, turns the engine off and then gets out of the front seat and helps me out. He offers me his arm. I take it, breathing slowly, not able to look up yet.

'We've arrived,' he says softly.

We turn towards the old village and start walking. As we walk down the slope, my head is spinning with flurries of memories: the tram as it approached the arch; the signs to Limoges, Saint-Junien; the first building, low stone wall intact, grass mown neatly. For a moment nothing has altered. Then my head turns to gaze across the road at the shells of former buildings: the old town, the real town. We enter the high street, down past familiar buildings, their inhabitants all gone, their walls crumbling, weeds creeping unchecked through cracks in brickwork, through broken flagstones.

Sebastian has told me the details. The truth is everywhere. We move wordlessly past the tram stop, the post office, the old schoolyard. Its roof is coming away. As we walk towards the green my feet slip on the cobbles. I hear the rusty sign of Monsieur Renard's garage as it swings lightly in the breeze, the owner dead, the bodies of his two sons never identified – shot in their garage with nine others, the place torched.

I have to stop in the road. Catch my breath. Up ahead of us, people are clustered on the green. More are arriving.

I stand looking at the façade of the shop. The walls have crumbled in, the back part of the shop is totally exposed, you can see beyond our old yard to the view of the hills beyond. It is as if there was never a second storey. It is as if no one ever lived there.

Everything I owned, loved, everything I held, sold, sat on, slept in, everything. It has disappeared; there is no evidence it ever existed, as if I am mistaken.

Sebastian takes hold of my arm and I am grateful as he urges me to keep moving. With one last look I allow myself to be led past the house.

There are more than a hundred people meeting by a simple stone memorial to the village. The mood is sombre and from my vantage point I can just make out the space where the spire of the church used to be. There is a flat line now, where it collapsed from the fire; it is no longer a sentry to the village, but another empty ruin.

I step a little closer to Sebastian.

The service passes quietly. Boys and men are holding their hats in front of them in respect, a couple of younger girls, faces I don't recognize, are holding hands side by side. I see one blonde boy, in his late teens, standing in front of me, earnestly mouthing the Lord's Prayer, his hand resting protectively on the shoulder of his younger sibling. The younger brother, with brown hair curling up at the ends, reaches to tug distractedly on the lapel of his coat.

Paul always resented dressing up in fusty attire for formal occasions, too.

The sun peeks from behind the cloud, and as its rays light up the group I can hear the voices of my own family. I close my eyes. They are saying goodbye to me, they are moving through the village and beyond to the hills and the forest and the Glane as it makes its steady path below us all; unstoppable, always forging a course through the landscape. I remember Vicente telling me once that water will always find a way through. I feel him by my side now, repeating this simple fact, my mouth lifting at his memory.

We lay flowers at the foot of the memorial and I move away to a shady corner of the green. Sebastian falls into step beside me. A younger woman holding a handkerchief to her face is comforted quietly, and a large group of women pass us with gentle nods.

As we turn to leave, the two brothers walk past us, the younger one turning to take his brother's hand: 'Tristan, wait...'

Something nudges at me. A faint laugh, tripping past us in the high street.

She is here.

HISTORICAL NOTE

I teach History at a secondary school in Berkshire and was looking for something to teach Year 9. A colleague of mine told me about this tragedy and I started to do some research. On discovering that there had been one survivor from the church that day, I started to build a story around her. The book grew from there. All the characters are entirely fictional.

On 10 June 1944, a small village near Limoges, Oradour-sur-Glane, was targeted by a small division of Nazi soldiers. It was a sunny Saturday and the village was bustling. Men were out collecting their tobacco ration, the hotels and restaurants were busy with inhabitants and weekend visitors, and the children were in school that day (although I have not adhered to this).

The SS arrived in the village at 2.15 p.m. in eight trucks, two heavy-tracked vehicles and a motorcycle. People were aware of some troops moving through the region but it was assumed by most that they were headed north to Normandy and the new front opening up due to the recent Allied invasion there a few days earlier.

Most of the soldiers were aged between seventeen and twenty-five. They drove through the village to ensure both ends were blocked off. Soldiers stood on guard at the entrances and questioned anyone coming in or out of the village. The mayor and all the villagers were told they were there to carry out an identity check. The town crier, accompanied by two soldiers, was sent to bang his drum and order the villagers to the green, with their identity papers.

The villagers had no real reason to question this and while many were surprised, they were not afraid. The mayor seemed calm and this helped some who might have panicked. People were brought in from the surrounding houses, fields and farms on trucks.

The children evacuated from the school were largely unfazed: it was a break from their Saturday lessons and they had no reason to fear soldiers, having not seen them before in the village. This was not the case with the children from a smaller school, refugees from Alsace-Lorraine, who instantly started screaming when they saw the soldiers. The teachers had a much harder time getting them to the green. One boy, eight-year-old Roger Godfrin, escaped through the schoolyard and through a hedge. He was shot at by a soldier and fell down, pretending to be dead. Roger survived but the rest of his family, his parents and four siblings, did not.

Evidence suggests that when the women and children were separated from the men, and sent to the church, the mood changed. People were forcibly separated. Women were seen weeping, some barely able to stand, as they were led away. They were told they would be there while a search of the village was carried out. The men were divided into six uneven groups, and made to sit in rows of three facing the houses. They were then led in their groups to different locations in the village. The biggest group was led to Laudy barn.

At an appointed time, 3.30 p.m., it seems an explosion or burst of machine-gun fire was heard, which acted as a signal. The men were fired upon simultaneously in their various locations. Machine guns had been set up in the barns and garages where the men were being held (in some cases, the men had had to move carts, farm equipment and other items outside to ensure everyone could fit). Some survivors claimed that when the machine guns were being set up in the entrance to the barns, the soldiers were laughing and joking. One report talks of seeing one German soldier crying softly on some stairs. Many of the men were tense, some terrified, their only consolation being that the women and children were safe in the church.

The soldiers shot low and those who were not killed were hit in the legs which stopped them escaping. The soldiers then piled straw and wood onto the bodies, some of whom would still have been alive, and set them alight. Five men did manage to survive the shooting in Laudy barn and escaped the village when it became dark.

A 'box with wires' was dragged into the centre of the church. It appears to have been the source of the explosion but perhaps did not go off as had been planned. Hand grenades and machine guns ensured that any women or children fleeing were stopped. There was only one survivor from the church, a woman called Madame Rouffanche, who managed to climb up a ladder used to light candles and get out through a window about ten feet above the ground. She was shot during her escape and was wounded, but managed to cover herself in earth in a pea garden nearby until people found her the next day. The rest of her family were all killed. A woman holding her baby attempted to follow but both were seen by the soldiers and killed.

The soldiers searched the rest of the village and shot

anyone found hiding where they were discovered: one old, invalid man was burned in his bed; other bodies were found dropped down a well; and the remains of a baby were found in the baker's oven. After this the soldiers set the whole village on fire and left after a few hours, with looted valuables.

In total, 642 men, women and children were killed on that afternoon in a small village in France, which had been barely touched by the war up to that point. Whole families were wiped out: there were eighteen Bardets and twelve Thomases on the list of the dead.

You can still visit the village today, which remains as a memorial to this event.

No one is sure why the attack happened, and this is why I have left it as a question in the novel. There did not appear to be any weapons found in the soldiers' search and there is no evidence that there was any Resistance activity in the village up to that point. There had been no attacks on the SS in Oradour or in the surrounding area. The SS themselves never gave a reason for the attack, even when on trial for their crimes in 1953.

Some people believe the attack was, in fact, aimed at the wrong Oradour. A Waffen SS officer, Helmut Kampfe, had been captured and was being held in a village called Oradour-sur-Vayres, not far away.

One thing is certain: the attack came as a shock to many. The unoccupied zone of France had been largely unaffected by war, and there did not appear to be an explanation for this massacre of an innocent people.

. . .

In January 2013, it was announced that there was be a new German inquiry into this event, after investigators uncovered reports in archived files of the East German Stasi secret police. Two SS officers, now eighty-seven and eighty-eight years old, are alive today, and the German prosecutor said he hoped a new legal process would begin in Germany.

On 8 January 2014, one of the men was charged with his involvement in the murder of twenty-five people, and with aiding and abetting the murder of several hundred others. He was nineteen at the time.

Printed in Great Britain
by Amazon

85431990R00200